THE SESSION

A Fiction Novel

BILLIE J. GILLIAM

authorHOUSE®

AuthorHouse™
1663 Liberty Drive
Bloomington, IN 47403
www.authorhouse.com
Phone: 1 (800) 839-8640

Published by AuthorHouse 08/29/2018

ISBN: 978-1-5462-5770-7 (sc)
ISBN: 978-1-5462-5768-4 (hc)
ISBN: 978-1-5462-5769-1 (e)

Print information available on the last page.

Cover Art by Fresh Fox Design Studio

This book is printed on acid-free paper.

To those who want their hearts to beat a little faster

CONTENTS

PROLOGUE

She closes her eyes, feeling the warmth of the afternoon sun radiate across her face. She hears his voice in the distance as he comes near to her. A tingling feeling rushes through her body as his fingers slightly twirl her hair; she exhales with a deep sigh. She is so content as she lies on the lilac blanket with her head resting on his thigh.

She used to come to this park alone—now she comes with him. Smiling, she remembers the road traveled to discover the love of her life. Chuckling softly to herself, she cannot believe this moment is real. Accidental encounters? A story like this only happens in the movies, right? No, it happens right here in *The Session*.

SESSION 1: THE ENCOUNTER

Belle and Joe have been married for three years after having dated for seven. They are having a tough time getting along. I first see them in my lobby as they sit at opposite ends of the room. He sits on the couch facing the television, and she is in the plush chair, flipping through some papers in her hand. I laugh to myself, as I already know it will be tough pulling these two back together. Watching them closer, I notice that they barely acknowledge knowing each other.

"Mr. and Mrs. Riley-Button," I call out to them. As a marriage therapist, my job is to pay attention to body language, also known as nonverbal communication. A body can communicate an unspoken message the individual may not be aware of. Such communication acknowledges the true nature of the message. These messages fill the spaces between the individuals involved in the session.

Joe Riley-Button rises first. His eyes never meet his wife's eyes. He looks almost through her to me. "That's us," he says and begins walking toward me.

Belle Riley-Button gathers her books and phone and the papers she was completing for my secretary. She looks like a tornado just blew over her. With wild eyes, rushed movements, and full arms, walks behind Joe toward my office. I wonder if they are at least friends. I quickly discard the thought, because I will find out soon enough.

I pride myself on my office. I love the warmth and the energy it

1

provides. It's designed not only to comfort the body but also soothe the mind. The room quietly calls your heart to parole the pain you have locked in your spirit. If trapped pain is all you've ever known it becomes a self-inflicted prison where depression can become institutionalized. Knowing this, I've purposely designed my office to disarm negative feelings or memories and provide a haven for hurt to expose itself. It is where one can become acquainted with one's pain, evicting it as a houseguest in the rooms of one's heart.

Belle and Joe enter the room, with Joe first. He's wearing basketball shorts, a backwards cap, a dirty tee shirt, and work boots. He walks in with a slightly arrogant stride, which is a poor attempt to improve his physical appearance. His brilliant copper skin is dimmed by his obvious "I just got off the jobsite" apparel. Bypassing the love seat, he decides to sit in a chair in the corner of the room. He chooses the greater distance despite the love seat's whispers of unity and oneness. I wonder if that is how he feels in this union: distant.

Belle's haphazard black ponytail swings back and forth with each step she takes. She is dressed and ready to go to work after the session. Her run-over Mary Beth heels are a telltale sign of a lack of a party life. Her bronze skin is highlighted by the contrast of her white dress, and together they reflect like precious metals.

Belle sits on the love seat. However, she places all her belongings on the empty seat beside her and fills up the cushion so no one can sit next to her.

I sit in the understated gray wingback chair. It is the gray of a sky preparing to scold the earth with its rage of a storm. Yet, if you look close enough, there are pink flecks that seem to have gently drifted on the fabric, almost the shape of tears. Honestly, the chair would look somber, melancholy even, if it were not for the specks of hope embedded in the sea of gray. It sends a message of masculine power that has been harnessed by a feminine presence.

I allow for a moment of silence to overcome the atmosphere—not the kind that calls one to remember the lost but to acknowledge a genesis.

I begin with discussing the rules, which include taking turns, respecting one another, and honoring each other, the values of counseling—blah, blah, blah. It's pretty much the same ole, same ole I provide for every couple.

Belle cuts me off. "Dammit, his ass forgot to pay the bill again," she screams across the room. "Yet again, I will have to pay it to keep the lights on.

Joe is consistently inconsistent with responsibility. After ten years, one would think he would get it together. We have been married for three years after dating for seven, and he still does not get it! He also never comes home at a decent hour," she whispers, throwing the disconnection notice on the floor.

Belle is obviously tired. Her eyes hold the weight of purgatory as she lives the cycle of despondency with Joe. Not once does Joe even look up.

Oh, boy. *This is normal.*

I acknowledge Belle's frustration but remind her that this is a process. I also remind her that with time and collaboration, we can work together to get her marriage on track.

Joe sighs. He states, "This was my decision to come to counseling, and I no longer know what to do to make Belle happy."

I ask the miracle question: "What do you want? What do you both want?"

"I want to be happy," they both say at the same time. My face falls flat. Wow. Thank you for that unique answer. Of course they do. Everyone wants to be happy. Unfortunately, not many people know exactly what that looks like. They have difficulty understanding that life is a series of moments. We must decide how to spend those moments. We must know that true happiness is finding evidence of light in the darkest of dark.

Sitting back, I remind the troubled couple that happiness is not some abstract concept. It is a series of choices to either witness or embrace life in all its glory and destruction.

"Belle, do you want your marriage with Joe?"

Belle cuts her eyes at me. "Do you plan on asking him?" She throws her thumb in Joe's general direction and inhales deeply.

I remind Belle, "I plan on asking both parties, and I am on the side of the union. I am only on the side of the marriage, and I will question any behavior that is not conducive to the success of the union."

"Well then, we have a child. I really am only here for her." She offers this short, snappy reply with her head twisted to the side and her nose turned straight up in the air.

It's interesting how people avoid direct responses. I wonder if it softens the blow of reality for both parties. The weight of "No, I don't want the marriage" is heavier than "I am here for the children." The first sounds like resolve; the latter means obligation.

I make it simpler for her—you know, let her off the hook. "Belle, do you want the marriage, yes or no? Do not qualify your answer; just provide it. It is imperative that we are honest with each other here."

Belle says nothing. Her body collapses into the love seat. All the tension from earlier is expelled from her body. It is like watching an out-of-body experience. Her soul leaves the marriage before her body. Here it comes. She is going to break his heart and tell him it is over. Well, this was quick. One session. This will be over after today.

She runs her hand through her hair. With her eyes closed, she says, "Yes, sure I do."

Joe sits up and brightens. His eyes are beaming as though he's gained five years of light.

I am careful not to show my surprise at either of their expressions. Her body tells me this marriage is over. She is coming to terms with herself and will be honest with Joe. Many times the body speaks the truth, and it can take a while for the conscious mind to verbally say what the unconscious has been screaming for years.

"Me too, me too," Joe chimes in from the other side of the room like a little kid with an ice cream cone in his hand. He seems to have more energy now that Belle has spoken.

I switch my attention to Joe. "Joe, why do you want this marriage?"

As Joe is talking, I glance over to Belle. Joe is speaking highly of his wife. He adorns her with the highest accolades and attributes. Usually a person is honored to hear someone speak so highly of him or her to others. There is body language that demonstrates connection to reverence.

Belle shows none of this. Not only does she not seem to be listening, she looks mentally preoccupied. She glances at her watch. She has a slight smile across her face, her pinky finger in her mouth, staring almost into nothing as if in another room and perhaps another space in time.

Hmmm. I am curious. But I leave it for now.

2

SESSION 2: BELLE AND JOE: THE BEGINNING

I peek around the corner to the lobby. The Riley-Buttons are here. *Riley-Button.* What a weird name. It makes me laugh a little. It sounds almost like a mechanic's shop. *Hey, welcome to Riley-Button's Auto!* I smile at the thought. Still, it sounds a little dumb.

Belle has her back to me, but I can see that haphazard ponytail a-swinging, and she appears to be reading something. Joe pulls out his phone and appears to be engrossed in some meaningless swiping.

This couple piques my interest. I am not sure why exactly. There is nothing magical about them or any real demonstration of love. I am just curious about their process. I want to know and understand how they came to be.

I realize I haven't called them yet. Geez! Sometimes I get lost in my own process of other's processes. "Mr. and Mrs. Riley-Button."

"That's us!" Joe gets up. Is he informing me or just saying words to fill the space? Of course it is they. I smile and beckon to him to come in.

Belle follows close behind, her head still down, reading a magazine. I hope it is not from the lobby. I haven't read all of those yet.

They sit.

They sit in the same places they sat the last time—very interesting.

"So, last time I got a glimpse into some issues that you guys are experiencing—just a glimpse. Like looking at a peephole into someone's apartment, I have not seen enough to grasp the lay of the land. But I've seen enough to know it's messy."

They nod simultaneously.

"Today, I'd like to know how you guys met. Tell me the story. Tell me what drew you to each other. Not just how you met. What drew you together?"

Silence.

I look over at Joe, who happens to be biting his lip and looking out of the window at the sky. He has the look of a memory collecting itself in his mind. I glance at Belle and find her in a different mood. She is rubbing her fingers over each other, head back and eyes closed. She has a frustrated look on her face.

Joe speaks.

"Well, it was ten years ago. We met on a blind date. Belle was single with a five-year-old little girl, Jasmine. Belle was going to a family reunion and did not want to go alone. She had been dateless for about five years, and her family was questioning her."

He looks over at Belle with a questioning look on his face, waiting for approval of his rendition and permission to continue with his story.

Sensing his silence, she opens her eyes and rolls them over at Joe. She raises her eyebrows and opens her left hand, swaying it over to me. That must mean *go on*.

Joe continues.

"Anyway, we have mutual friends. They felt sorry for her, I guess," he says and then laughs out loud. Belle shoots him a hard look, but Joe is in his own little world, telling the story, and does not see her quick look of death.

"So, they tell me about her. I ask for a picture, and of course they don't have one. They say she is pretty, smart, witty, and oh yeah, she has a daughter."

Joe has drifted off into his world. Clearly, he is really into the story of his first encounter with Belle. He is not even looking at her.

"I think to myself, *Well, hell, if she is all of these things, why is she single? She must be a total bitch!*"

Another look shoots from Belle. Yikes! I feel the ice from her eyes. The dead look on her face gives the appearance of a soulless shark.

Joe is not aware that he has been mentally murdered twice already. Poor guy. He has to get in the car with her.

"They give me her number, and I call her. I was seeing multiple women at the time. So, I figure, I'll do this lil' honey a favor," he says, laughing at his own wit while rubbing his chin with his fingers.

Alone. He laughs.

I look over at Belle. She checks her watch, and again she drifts off, a sly smile approaching her face. Her index finger embraces her hair slowly, winding it around, and I watch her again disconnect from the experience we are all currently having. Her eyes are lost in some distant place.

Where is she? I do not ask, but I am intrigued.

"She has this voice, this very sweet voice," I hear Joe say and turn to Belle. "Her voice is sweet; I can hear the mother in her voice—the voice of someone who has a good heart. So we talk for hours about nothing, really—cereal, movies, dreams, and her hate for small talk."

"Is that what attracted you to her? The ability to just talk for hours about nothing?" I ask.

"No." He pauses. He is visibly trying to find the words. He closes his eyes to tap into the internal vision located in his heart. He continues: "It was more like she was dreaming as she spoke. It's hard for me to really explain. I could tell that I was entering her world, never to return to mine." He sighed. "I was disturbed and happy about it at the same time; does that make sense?"

I nod. I fight the urge to explain why I understand. I settle for saying, "Yes, continue."

"Anyhow, she had to go to a family function, and she dreaded going alone. Our friends hooked us up, and I showed up." Joe looks down at his clothes. "I showed up just like this, actually," he laughs.

I allow for a moment of silence as I watch Belle slowly return to the room. Her once-fixated eyes that had been boring the depth of something invisible suddenly return to the present.

She looks at me. "Is it my turn?"

"Sure," I say.

"Well, he is right. I did not want to go to the function alone. I had been single for a couple of years, and my family was beginning to rag me about it. My daughter's father's family was coming, and I needed to not look like I was pathetic." Belle's nose crinkles as if she smells something foul, and she continues with her side of the story.

"Lord knows I do not want to be pathetic! I have spent years being pathetic. As a thirty-five-year-old woman, I never again want my every breath of life to be dependent on the existence of a relationship with someone else."

Wow. What a statement. There's a story there. I really do not have the time for this battle, but I am very interested in it. Maybe it's the influence of my own life, but the problems that Riley-Buttons are experiencing are causing me to have such a need to understand their relationship. I must disconnect my personal stuff from them so I can focus. Oh, I know, I'll laugh at them. Riley-Button: still a stupid name. The thought makes me smile little. Good, now I am focused again.

"Belle, I am interested in understanding a bit more background on the statement you just made. That was such a powerful statement."

Belle obviously is not ready to have this discussion. Her face falls, and she takes a deep breath. Joe looks at her in a way that shows his concern and that communicates he will be there when she falls apart.

He will be there even if they are falling apart.

"Well, Ms., Miss, or Mrs.? I noticed I never addressed you formally," Belle says, arms folded.

This is interesting. She wants to know if I am single or married. I'll keep her guessing a bit more.

"Well, Dr. Meadows or River is what I usually go by, but Ms. River Meadows will do if you want to be formal," I state.

Belle looks dissatisfied with that statement, but she continues, "Ms. Meadows, I am sure once or twice in your life you have been hurt by someone you love?"

I nod.

"Well, I was not just hurt, Mzzzzz. Meadows." I raise an eyebrow.

"I was broken. Do you know what that is like?" She does not wait for a response. I suspect she was not really seeking a response so much as permission to go to the deep end of her pain.

"I no longer existed when my ex left me. I was a shell. Imagine being gutted while still breathing. That was me ..." Her voice trails to a whisper. She suddenly appears smaller than when she came in.

It is fascinating how suffering can extract one's life force. I work to teach my clients that pain is inevitable, that it is even useful. However, suffering is never necessary or should even be an option.

Joe gets up and walks to her. He sits by her, and she continues, her voice barely audible. "Well, I dated him when I was very young. I was so in love with him. He was the reason for my every breath." She pauses. She is entering the depths of her pain. I can tell this was is pleasant for her, but I need her to be here for a moment.

"I supported him; I wanted to water his dreams. I dropped out of school and took care of him and our daughter. Whatever he wanted, I became, until I no longer knew who I was. When he left ... my life grew pale. I could no longer see in color. I became the silent partner in my destruction.I was depressed for a long time. Time no longer existed for me; I was at sea, like a purposeless buoy."

She sits straight up, and her eyes widen. Her face lights up. She holds her index finger in the air.

"But!" she exclaims in a deeply emotional and animated voice. "My daughter Jasmine brought me back like Lazarus. She could see I was dying, and she poured life into me. I was sitting on the floor, welcoming the death that no one notices—the one that happen by the millisecond."

Wow: the millisecond. She is quite in touch with her pain. I accompany her to the dark place—the place we all have, but bury under years of denial.

"Jasmine," she continues, "with her sweet little three-year-old hands, comes up behind me. She places her warm cheek next to mine. She says in the most angelic little voice, 'Mom, everything will be okay. I know it."

Tears stream down Belle's face, and her voice begins to crack. "That. Little. Girl." Belle pauses. "She has no idea what she did for me that day.

My heart began to beat again. I knew I was alive and had something to live for."

Belle looks intensely at me and very declaratively states, "It was then I woke up, River."

River? Okay. Maybe her voyage to such a painful place with me alongside her gives her the permission and safety to use my first name.

Joe is holding her hand, and she begins to shudder. "Phew, now that I have officially made a cameo appearance in hell, I can return," Belle says as she sits up. "I began to search for help. I found it in a small church, and the budding of my life began all over again." A knowing smile accompanies her recalled resolution. For a moment, I can tell she has evaluated the outcome and is pleased. In her pause, she takes a deep breath and exhales, releasing the bondage she has visited on my account.

"Anyhow, my family was having a function. I was dating, but as Joe said, I really had no one to take with me. Most of what he said was true regarding talking on the phone to me."

All the emotions Belle manifested in the ripping of her emotional soul have changed now that she is back to discussing the present day. She is cooler. Her retelling of the discussions she and Joe shared is robotic. It is as if she is naming off the capitals of the United States from a list. She does not seem as nostalgic Joe had seemed when recalling the events.

She removes her hand from Joe's grasp. He sighs, gets up, and returns to his original seat. Belle does not even flinch when Joe returns to his original chair.

3

SESSION 3: THE PROBLEM

It's Thursday, and it is raining outside. Thank goodness it is warm enough today. Early spring in the Midwest definitely has it's share of snow. I truly enjoy the calming effect of the rain. It brings to mind the idea that life is constantly immersed in the grips of near death. The gift of Adam's Ale arrives and like a phoenix, the earth fervors with life again.

As I sit in the wingback, I look out the window. The Riley-Buttons will be arriving soon. It's half past two o'clock in the afternoon, and their appointment is at three. I wonder if Belle will check her watch and show her secret smile. Her smile is a poor attempt to hide that her mind has left us alone in the session while her body occupies the chair, her spirit evicted by the knowledge she holds within. Her eyes have changed space and time. A trained clinician can see when people are physically in the space but not mentally.

I wonder what type of car they drive. Why am I so curious about these people? They are clients, just like any of my other clients. However, something draws me to want to know more about them. I have to keep processing their verbal and nonverbal language to see what's connecting me to them. Maybe it's the secret Belle seems to have.

They pull up. I close the curtain and peer from the side. It looks like they drive a Jeep Wrangler; the top indicates it's a newer model. Joe jumps out first and walks toward the door. Belle seems to be rustling around the truck, looking for stuff. Joe never looks back at her and looks slightly aggravated. Belle climbs out of the truck with a mess of papers, just as she did the first day they arrived to their session.

In the lobby, Joe is mumbling something to himself. He looks awfully irritated. This time they sit on the same couch. Well, that's an improvement.

Belle fumbles through the papers on her lap. Her eyeglasses hang on the edge of her elongated nose. This looks really annoying to me. I am not sure how she could possibly tolerate the weight of the glasses on the tip of her nose like that! She is immersed in her papers and doesn't even notice that Joe is having a full-blown discussion with himself.

Well, it is three o'clock. I suppose I should call them in now.

As Joe adjusts his bootstraps, I call their name. Belle gets up first and swiftly walks toward my office. She does not even look back at Joe. The papers are still in her hand. She looks angry and a bit distracted.

Joe slowly stands, takes a deep breath, pulls his cap backwards, and walks toward the office too.

They sit in their usual spots.

"So, Belle, you seem a bit upset," I say.

"Umm, yes I am. We were talking about our history on our way here. I am just not over it. He does not understand that the history is also the present!"

"What does that mean, Belle?" I ask. I think I understand, but I need Joe to understand what she means.

"It means he says that he has learned from his mistakes, but what he fails to realize is that he constantly repeats his mistakes over and over again."

"What does he repeat?" Now, here we go. We are getting to the nitty-gritty of the issue in this relationship.

"I cannot depend on him. Financially, he devastates me. Also, he seems to enjoy the company of other women. He tells me, 'She don't mean shit to me. You are the woman that I love.' He has all types of relationships with other women. He must think I'm stupid or something. He tells me that he is not cheating if he is not having sex with them."

Joe's head is tilted back, and his eyes are looking up at the ceiling. He draws out slowly, "I am not sleeping with those women! I told you that." He takes a short pause. "Yes, I did sleep with *some* for about six years, but she needs to get over that."

I see Belle suddenly reach for her purse when he says *some*. God, please don't let this lady shoot this man in my session—not today. She pulls out another ink pen, because the first one must have stopped writing, and I am relieved.

He continues. "The women I know now are just friends! Why can't she get that? Also, I am trying to help with the bills. I buy gas for the car, and I pay the cable bill. She cannot see that I am trying? Jesus!" He throws his arms in the air and never looks down or at Belle during his tirade.

Belle is quietly chuckling to herself, as if to discharge the ridiculousness of his statement. So, on the surface they have issues with finances and relationships with other women. There are probably deeper issues too, but they have not given me access to them yet.

Many times couples arrive in counseling only wanting to understand their surface issues. They do not seek to understand their core value differences, differences that should be understood *before* they either get together, move in together, or get married.

Each couple engages in their self-made rules, and many are largely unspoken. These rules are unspoken because couples typically do not take time to discuss their beliefs and rules. If each person understood what the other's personal rules were, they could then make relationship decisions based on these rules.

Can Joe have friendships with other women? In his world, he probably believes he can. He probably thinks, because he is not sleeping with them, he is in the clear from cheating on his wife.

In his eyes and probable value system, he thinks having sex outside of his marriage is cheating. However, Joe is failing to realize that Belle has a different set of values than he does. In her eyes, relationships she doesn't approve of with other women outside of their marriage are not okay. She views his relationships with these women as cheating. In order to make this marriage work, they will need to discuss and reconcile their core understanding of outside friendships and relationship values and then decide how to proceed with fixing the mess they have made.

They need to define what types of relationships are acceptable outside of their marriage and which are appropriate for each one of them to engage in.

Finances tend to break many couples up as well. Joe is looking at what he *does* do and not at what he *does not* do. I am hearing a lot from Belle about what she believes their biggest problems are. Now, I need to hear from Joe.

"Joe, from your perspective, what problems do you see in the relationship?"

"She is not connected to me. No affection, no attention—nothing," he abruptly states. Then he goes on and on about the lack of intimacy in the marriage.

I glance at the clock on the wall. It is half past three o'clock. I turn my attention to Belle, and like clockwork she glances at her watch, smiles for a while, slightly bites her lower lip, pulls her fingers through her hair, and closes her eyes. She is gone. I find this series of movements very interesting. I almost want to interrupt her moment. I mean, *really*: she is supposed to be in the session with Joe and me! Fortunately, I am more curious about where she is going in her mind than aggravated by her mental disappearance.

I pop a glance at Joe, and he is still talking. I feel a little guilty, because I want to watch Belle to see how long her mind event lasts. Belle is lost in thought for a full two minutes. I can see when she returns to earth. Her face falls flat, and her eyes deaden. She is surprised to see me watching her, and she silently gasps.

I smile at her, communicating that I know a secret—not her specific secret, of course—is present.

She looks slightly uncomfortable.

I turn from her and face Joe, who is currently explaining, " … and she does not seem to ever want to let it go. She won't even kiss me anymore."

To look fully engaged, I ask Joe, "How do you feel about that?"

"I feel like there is a brick wall between us. I feel lost, River. It hurts. It really hurts me." His voice cracks and pains with isolation and desperation.

Joe begins to tear, and years of hopelessness seem to stream down his cheeks.

He asks me for a tissue.

I take a deep breath, as I am about to explain a concept to him that he may not understand cognitively, but his heart will understand immediately.

"I don't keep tissues in my office, Joe. Usually when we cry, we are quick to try to 'get it together.' We wipe away tears and try to self-soothe, but we do not allow ourselves to fully experience the moment. Sometimes we really need to understand our pain, be one with it, so we can integrate it into our beings. The goal is to learn and grow from pain, not to whisk it away so it can plant a seed and grow the tree of suffering."

Joe looks confused. His eyes are heavy with newfound truth. He looks at Belle, who has been studying him. She still does not come to him in his moment. I see the look of concern in her eyes, but it has a boundary around it—a boundary that has been born from walking this path with him far too many times.

Joe is dramatic as he surrenders to his pain. He is crying, almost sobbing. I allow the sound of his heart to enter the room, and the deafening sound fills the room. I close my eyes and enter the outburst of his emotions with him.

I let this go on for about ninety seconds. Then I ask, "Joe, what are you mourning?"

Belle quickly gazes at me. I suspect that she has already mourned the death of her marriage. He has only just now acknowledged its terminal status.

"River, River, I … I … I don't know. I can see we are at a place I do not think we can return from," he says through the tears.

"The real question, Joe and Belle, is do you *want* to return from it?" I flatly ask.

Many times people feel the need to hold on to relationships. They neglect the counselor that lives within themselves. If life is an ocean, they live on the surface, having no appreciation for the depth of their lives. So, they live life dogpaddling through, barely holding oxygen in their lungs as they struggle for coexistence. The testament of life is trusting your inner voice, and allowing yourself to descend into its bosom is to truly live the life you deserve.

This descending means that we have to let go of the things we believe are keeping us alive but are actually killing us inside.

They both sit in silence. Neither is willing to be first to risk allowing his or her inner truth to rise to the surface, breaking the illusion they both have created through obligation and familiarity.

I redirect. "Let's come back to that question," I offer. Their truth may change, I figure. "Let's save it for another time. I want you guys to think on the question more deeply, to marinate a bit on the idea of what you both want. I am going to give you both homework."

Their eyes speak volumes, wide and surprised, demonstrating the ridiculousness of my words. They laugh simultaneously like two college students questioning their professor. "Homework?" they ask in unison.

"Yes, homework. I want you both to go on two dates this week. We'll go over the details of your experiences next week. This week your dates will have no rules, but you must do as I ask you."

Belle gets up to leave, but not before she locks eyes with me for a moment. She has a look of concern on her face. Surely this must be about her secret. She drops her gaze and walks out the door. Joe collects himself, shakes my hand, and rushes out the door.

4

SESSION 4: THE DATE

I cannot believe I am late to my session with the Riley-Buttons! I was at home having another discussion with my husband about the importance of allowing me to be me—the importance of my being able to express my feelings without being cut off by him.

I might as well be having a discussion with myself. Jude, my husband, was only there in body; his mind was elsewhere. His spirit was not in the same space with my desperation as I sought to be understood by him, which a place where I continually reside. I have no idea where his mind was during our conversation. He gave me answers and comments that did not welcome further discussion. He was polite enough, but I could tell he was not in the same mental space as I was.

I decided to stop talking to him, because I would be spinning my wheels trying to figure out what planet he had landed on mentally, and unfortunately had him drop me off so he could use the car. I said we could revisit our discussion at another time. Because I educate him on the importance of fair fighting and proper communication skills, I keep being told that it is hard to be married to a therapist. Well, he will just have to deal with it!

Jesus, I really hate being late for my clients. It does not show them respect for their time. I jump out of the car without even looking his way. However, I can see that he is purposely trying to look distracted. It is okay. I just need to get out of there, and fast!

The Riley-Buttons are already in the lobby when I hurriedly walk in. I offer them an array of apologizes for being fifteen minutes late and beckon them to my office.

Joe sits in his usual seat, as if it were labeled "Joe Riley-Button." Belle takes the loveseat, also as usual. This time she looks a little dressed up. She is wearing jeans, heels, a leather blazer, and sequined tank. Her hair is loose, with bangs covering one eye. Her makeup is heavier too—her lips red and plumped and her eyes dark with a dark-blue mascara that brings to mind summer nights. She is wearing a noticeably sweet perfume.

She piques my interest. Why is Belle so dressed up, while Joe is practically in uniform with his tattered shorts, steel-toed boots, dirty tee shirt, and misshapen hat?

I decide to ask Belle what is going on with her appearance today. I notice that since I arrived late, we only have ten more minutes before the soul evaporation that arrives around half past three.

I turn my attention to Joe instead. I am interested in how their dates went over the past week.

Joe responds, "Well, they were polite."

"Polite?" I ask.

"Yes, polite. We were nice to each other the entire time, but you can tell Belle was really somewhere else," Joe states, not looking up while cleaning out his fingernails with a toothpick.

"So, take me through it, Joe. Where did you guys go, or what did you do?"

"We went to dinner and a movie. I took her to her favorite restaurant for Italian food. She ordered the same thing she orders on a regular basis. She was talking, and then all of a sudden she seemed to no longer even be there with me. It was almost as if she had a seizure or something." Joe, amused by his own statement, chuckled out loud.

Belle shot a look at me. It is 3:25 p.m.—almost time.

"Well, what time did you guys go to dinner?" I ask.

"We actually went early, because Italian is so heavy I knew she would be full later on. It had to be about three o'clock," he responded. "Anyhow, for the rest of the dinner, not only was she no longer polite, she was downright not there. I asked her if something was wrong, and I had to ask her three times before she heard me."

It's half past three. I look over at Belle, and I honestly cannot believe Joe does not notice this more often. Belle is obviously trying to control her facial expression, and she is fidgety in her seat. She is staring at the wall but not blankly, as usual. It seems like she's doing this on purpose.

Wait a minute. *She's trying to avoid eye contact with me,* and she is trying really hard to control a smile. How odd. I want to ask her a question, but something tells me not to do it yet, and especially not in front of Joe.

"So, Joe, how about the second date?" I ask.

"Oh. We did not get to the second date. I had to work late most of the week and even the weekend this week," he quickly responded.

Belle is back. "Uh, yeah. Work. That's it. Let's go with that," she says with a snicker.

"I am going to come back to that statement, Belle, but first I would like to know how the date went from your perspective?"

"It was okay. I mean we watched a movie at home, even though I wanted to go to a play. He stated he did not feel like being around people. Then we went to Luciano's for an early dinner." She throws her hand up. "Like he said, it was polite. So, I guess it was okay.

Polite. Polite.

That word does not stop whirling around in my head. It feels as if we are talking about an encounter with a grocery-store cashier. Polite.

In a relationship there is an inherent risk of pain, which is a quite beautiful concept, actually. We have to acknowledge the vulnerability of letting go and exposing oneself to another person. You are exposing all of yourself. Trust dipped in passion is required for love to be fruitful. Unfortunately, that passion can result in moments of discontentment. Passion usually exists within healthy relationships, yet it can become riddled in conflict, resulting in instability. We need to learn how to navigate conflicting waters when they create storms in our relationships.

But polite? Polite? Wow. Save *polite* for passing the salt at the dinner table. Save *polite* for holding the door open for the little old lady. Polite is saying please and thank you or allowing someone to get in front of you on the road as you are driving. Polite is offering your food but secretly hoping the person declines because you really do not want to share.

Love. There is nothing polite about it. It is all consuming and beautiful. It can be scary, because it is without reservation. The safety net is removed, and you walk the tightrope, knowing full well that this could be it. It could end, and you could be in *a lot* of pain. Yet, the beloved is worth taking that risk for. Love is awesome if you really stop to think about it.

I bring myself back to the room. I almost have to shake my head to come back. *Polite*, they say.

"Belle, how do you see love? What does it mean to you?"

A crooked smile appears on her face, and her eyes grow brighter.

"Well, you didn't ask me," an irritated Joe states as he is adjusting his clothes.

"I will, I promise." Promises mean everything to me, so I must remember to get back to Joe.

"Loooovvve." Belle drags out the word and kicks her feet out. I see her sparkly heels more clearly. They are nice. I realize that I forgot to ask her why she is so dressed up today.

She puts her hands on her thigh, bites down on her bottom lip, takes a really deep breath, and begins as if she has been waiting for this question her entire life.

"Love is God. God is love. Therefore, when you truly love, you are experiencing God at that very moment. When you love, and I mean love without concern for yourself or protecting yourself, you not only receive God, but you also give God away." She smiles, quite pleased with her response.

What the hell? What an answer! Usually I am not surprised by what people say. I have been doing this work for fifteen years, and people are usually predictable.

However, "receive God" and "give God away": wow! I want her to continue. I have to hide the shock on my face. I look over to Joe, and I can tell he has never heard her say anything like this before.

He had been playing with his phone when she began talking and dropped it when she finished. He now has a look on his face that shows that her idea of love is a room he has never entered with her. It is painful to see.

Joe's face drains of color. He appears to have aged twenty years in just a few moments. It is almost as if his soul has been ripped from his body.

He winces. Wow. *He winces.* The internal pain from acknowledging that he has been sitting with a stranger he thought he knew all too well must be overwhelming for him.

"Continue," I state nonchalantly, hoping she has more to say.

"Well, there is no more than that," she says, looking up to the ceiling and then returning her gaze directly to me. Her eyes burn though mine, communicating that the secret has returned to this space. Right now. It is here in this moment with me. She gives a half smile.

Belle is in love.

Just not with Joe.

It is fascinating how we can communicate without words. Humans can experience spirit-to-spirit communication, because words can place limits on the soul. The soul needs to be free, and the eyes can free what words have placed in bondage.

I redirect my attention to Joe. "Joe, what is love to you?"

It takes time for Joe to collect himself. He has just entered a space with Belle that he has never seen before. He has peeked into a part of her heart that she has probably never exposed to him.

Joe clears his throat and sits up. "Well, I do not think it is much different than what Belle stated. She had a great explanation." He shoots her a look that says, *We'll talk about this later,* and then continues. "I mean people who care for one another, who make one another feel special. That is what I think. Someone who wants you and you want them. A person you want to spend time with, hang out with, and talk to."

Belle sighs, rolls her eyes, and raises an eyebrow. Her face seems to say, *You are about as deep as a puddle on the sidewalk after a toddler has jumped in it.*

Joe senses her frustration. "Belle, I love you. I care about you."

Belle cocks her head to the side and crosses her arms, "Joe, you have never been able to love me the way I need to be loved. You only want to own me. That is all."

"Own you? We own each other!"

"No, Joe. We do not own each other. We choose each other. The goal is that we should be choosing each other every day."

Joe sits back, the white flag of surrender on his face.

I almost forget that Belle is dressed up a bit, and I am a bit curious—or just say nosy. Curious sounds better.

"So Belle, you look a bit different today. You are usually dressed in work clothes; any plans?"

A smirk arrives on Belle's face, almost telling me to mind my business. However, I am a therapist, so I can ask! Turning her attention to her purse, she pulls out a pretty pink compact. "I am going out with friends," she says, as she checks her lipstick in the mirror.

After the Riley-Buttons leave, the rest of the day is fairly quiet. There are appointments with the usual clients, the ones who are either depressed or anxious. For some reason, I feel bored after the Riley-Button session.

I look outside and see clouds forming. I feel my stirring soul begin to quiet itself in anticipation of a storm.

It begins to rain. I like the sound of the rain. It pitter-patters against the window as I sit in the lobby and wait for Jude.

He is late, which is so aggravating. However, this is not new for him. I decide to fiddle through the magazines as if I were waiting for my own appointment.

I cannot stop thinking about Belle's statement on love and the aroma of love that surrounds her—an aroma that Joe cannot seem to smell.

Joe must be very self-absorbed at times not to notice Belle.

If you are that full of yourself, you will have a hard time receiving and giving love to anyone else. Now, there is nothing wrong with loving and liking oneself. People used to think that the Earth was the center of the solar system. A concept called geocentrism. Either we were then limited in our scientific understanding or incredibly narcissistic. However, if your self-concept is geocentric, then you will lose love every time. You will not be able to relate to the concept that Belle discussed about the importance of transferring God's love. You cannot transfer love when you cannot see anything beyond yourself. You can only extract the energy from others, draining them of their vital life force.

This is why God's love is so perfect. If you practiced it you will feel compelled to give it away. Love is something that cannot be possessed by the ego. It is so hard to explain in plain words sometimes.

5

INTRODUCTION OF HIM

I look back outside, distracted by the pitter-patter of the rain.

I have an odd need to go outside. I go out without my umbrella and just stand there. At first, the sensation of water against my face is jarring.

I lift my face and close my eyes and begin to no longer feel wet but just feel the rain. I lift my hands, running them through my hair.

Yes, this is it. God's love is like water. It bends and shapes. It is the source of life. We cannot live without it. It can be muddied by our treacherous ways, disguising its power or, better put, perverting it.

Yet, when we are willing to stand naked before it, we can feel it and become alive. The alternative is the fear of being wet, which is translated into the fear of having to sacrifice. However, when you feel the rain, you seek to share the experience of the source of life with others.

"What the hell are you doing?" A voice yanks me back to the surface of everyday life.

Jude has pulled up, but I never noticed. It takes a moment for me to respond.

"What the hell are you doing?" he repeats.

"Nothing," I say. "Nothing at all." I get into the car. I lean my head against the cool glass of the window. I look to the sky and watch the clouds spill their drops of life on the earth below.

Once home, we decide to go out for dinner. I am tired of cooking, so I look forward to this. Now that my children are grown, we cook sporadically, and we rarely eat together.

One would never know that a therapist who loves working with couples cannot fix her own relationship.

It is almost a cruel joke. However, as stated before, marriage is the consummation of God's love. Two souls become one.

If one of those souls decides to destroy what God has brought together, nothing but God can repair it—if that is God's will.

At times the pain of loneliness in the presence of the one who joined your soul can be overwhelming. It makes one feel much more alone than being truly alone could ever do.

We decide on Spanish. We arrive at A Prima Vista's about to seven o'clock. I have heard a lot about this place. I once overheard a client talking about how romantic this restaurant is. Maybe this will provide a surge into a relationship that is currently in a coma—a relationship that probably needs to be taken off of life support.

For the entire course of this marriage, I have been responsible for its emotional development. This means that I have had to pour into Jude, but I never realized that I was becoming empty. This time, I did am not offering conversation. I want to see what will happen. It is not pleasant; for the entire ride, the sound of silence drowns out the space meant for possibility. The mere possibility of a romantic connection with my husband has been murdered by apathy. The drive is about an hour, and it is torture.

I am so happy to be able to jump out of the car to get connected, even just for a moment, with other breathing human beings. This will remind me that I am alive, that I matter.

As Jude parks the car, I am trying to get our names on the list. I ask for the wait: forty-five minutes! I'd asked Jude to call before we left; had he done so, we would almost be ready to be seated.

"Do you want me to put your name down or not?" the waiter asks impatiently.

"Yes. Yes, please," I surrender.

I look around the foyer. It is bathed in oranges and reds. The restaurant is reminiscent of Romanesque architecture, an architectural style of medieval Europe characterized by semicircular arches, large towers, and decorative arcading.

Its stately and masculine outward appearance is only softened by the soft kisses of Isabella I, Queen of Castile portrait. Her soft and beautiful feminine appearance is a decoy for her political savvy. The dining room is dressed in candles. The light is romantic enough to trick the mind into believing one is alone with one's date. Tables are dotted with single candles and single red long-stemmed roses, as reminders of the richness of the moment.

I navigate myself to the waiting area. It is crowded with individuals seeking to share intimacy with one another.

Jude runs in, out of breath and soaking wet from the rain. I inform him that it is going to be almost an hour. He becomes agitated, sighing heavily, and sits across from me.

He is back to his phone, probably playing a game. I just cannot seem to enter his world anymore. I watch him for a moment and then decide to check out who's around me.

I am sitting next to a pretty good-looking guy and his friends. I listen to their conversation for entertainment.

He is a tall baritone man with skin as smooth as rich caramel. He is telling his friends how he was trying to put his name on the list to be seated right before me. The waitress, according to him, was having a hard time understanding how to say his first name.

"I spelled it for her and everything and said it real slow. It is E O G H A N, pronounced Yo-wen, but she was still trying to pronounce the E!"

I giggle a bit too loudly. Oops. I have real problems being stealthy sometimes. He looks in my direction and then directly in my face, with hard eyes apparently agitated by an unwelcome intruder. As his eyes meet mine, they suddenly soften, and a micro expression of confusion flashes across his face. He smiles and turns back to his friends.

I love what I do. Micro expressions are brief facial expressions that last fractions of seconds. They are usually beyond our awareness. I watch for them constantly with clients and people I connect with. His look of confusion confused me. I was instantly intrigued. I wanted to find a reason to talk to him. Something pierced me when his eyes softened and smiled. It was a knowing smile—a smile of déjà vu.

I turn my attention to Jude, whose positive energy seems to have returned.

"Hey, sweets, I gotta make a run. I'll be right back. You know these car sales! The dealership is only five minutes from here. We have another thirty-five minutes to wait anyway. You don't mind, do you?" And with that, he leaves. I do not get a chance to protest. I was going to say that I would rather he not run off. Oh well, this is nothing new. He has been running off a lot more since he was promoted to finance manager at the dealership. Everything is an emergency, and he is off just like that.

I turn my attention to the object of my curiosity, Mr. Eoghan. He is talking about other things, yet occasionally he glances my way as if he does not understand a word coming out of my mouth. This makes no sense, considering I am not talking. His glances become more frequent and longer in duration.

I am also a bit uneasy about this piercing feeling I am experiencing. It is almost as if something I have known forever has returned. It flusters me, so I decide to go to the washroom and put some cold water on my face.

"Get yourself together, girl!" I say to myself as I sprinkle some cold water on my face. "You are an attractive, not-so-young lady. It does not matter if your husband forgets what he has and someone else happens to notice it." It is fun to play with the thought of Mr. Eoghan.

I look at myself in the mirror. I take a long, close look this time. I am *not* a bad-looking lady. My skin is the color of butterscotch. I touch my nose. It has a slight point at the end and provides a smooth transition to my lips, which are full—deliciously bitable, I am told. I laugh at the thought and slightly bite the right bottom lip. "Yes, I concur!" I say out loud with confidence.

My lips are covered in Ruby Woo—a deep red that MAC creates that imprints on the mind of any man who has a thing for lips. There is poetry that flows from these lips, if he can tap into the reservoir of love from which it flows.

I smile a large smile—a smile that remembers its dreams from being a child. I have always had a big smile and hearty laugh. My laugh is untouched by adulthood and untouched by social rules that would have it conform to what is considered polite and ladylike. I have always said that I am a comedian's dream. I will laugh at probably all your jokes, even if they are bad.

My teeth are nice enough. I show all thirty-two when smiling, it seems. They are pearly white against the richness of Ruby Woo.

I move to my eyes—brown, almond-shaped, and framed by full eyebrows. Eyes are windows to the soul, they say. My panes tend to rest pretty low, but they widen with engagement during a good discussion. People used to think I was asleep all the time because of how low they rest. It is now habitual for me to hold them more open than what is comfortable. My eyes are honest and seeking. They hold questions to ask the universe and discover the true meaning of life. They are forever seekers of truth and understanding. They illuminate the joy in a world full of pain. They put in high-definition color what is fuzzy to the injured soul accustomed to grays.

I touch the perimeter of my face.

It is shaped like a diamond. I have a strong jawline, which denotes strength. I move my hands to my neck, long and stately.

My hair is full, curly, and brown with blond accents. It is always big. I have a love-hate relationship with my hair. Considering it is raining today, I love it.

I stand up taller in the mirror. Yes, I am worthy of someone's attention, I suppose.

I straighten my dress. I am a bit vertically challenged, because my five-foot-four frame is a bit curvy. I am not as thin as I would like to be, but who is?

How long have I been in here? My goodness, ten minutes! Without looking, I rush out and run smack dab into someone. I begin to fall backward as arms reach out and pull me near in an attempt to stabilize me.

"You okay?" a baritone voice asks. It's him. Mr. Eoghan.

My bewilderment is evidenced by my clumsiness, which gives way to intense nervousness as I realize I am in his arms for a moment.

This moment seems to go on forever. I dare not look up. What will he think? What am I feeling? Why am I so damned nervous?

Look up, idiot! I literally have to say it to myself internally. I look up, and there are those eyes again—those light brown eyes that soak up the sun, reflecting concern for my well-being.

As I stabilize, I realize how electric his touch was.

His look of confusion returns, and he drops his grip.

"Yes, I am fine," I manage to garble out of my mouth. Get the cotton out your mouth, River!

"You have to be more careful … beautiful," the words fall from his mouth like fluffy snowflakes when people are still in awe of the winter.

"Thank you. I will … Mr. Eoghan," I say with a smile. I know I pronounce it correctly, having earlier been eavesdropping.

His smile is large. His brown eyes widen with surprise and amusement.

I step to the side and walk away to the front of the restaurant.

I am proud to have been able to redeem myself. I walk briskly, trying to look cool, calm, and collected. As I get about fifteen feet away, I look over my shoulder, curious to see where he went.

I am caught by surprise to see that he is still looking at me.

Our eyes meet. He smiles. My stomach forgets that my feet are on the ground, as if I were actually on the last click of a roller coaster. It drops something awful. I lose my breath for a moment. Damn! He knew I would turn around.

The moment seems to carry on beyond comfort.

Unfortunately, a familiar voice jars me from my fantasy.

"River! River!" It sounds so far away.

Why does it sound so far away? Where am I right now?

Eoghan's face falls, and I turn to the voice. It's Jude.

Jude stands average height for a black man. His voice fluctuates from a deep baritone to a higher pitch when agitated. His voice at the moment is grating my nerves. He is gangly in appearance and always complaining about not having enough muscle on his body. He is always talking about protein this and protein that. The house is full of half-used protein powders.

I see him for the first time in a long time. I mean really *see* him. His dark skin glistens when well oiled, and boy does he use a lot of oil. His hair is dark and curly, with just enough length to twist a lock around a well-meaning finger.

His face is full of angles. He has a quick smile, full and large but almost too quick. As a finance manager of a large dealership, his quick smile puts people at ease. However, it is a bit untrustworthy. There is subtle deceit behind his smile.

Jude's eyes, a deep brown, are wrought with pain from a traumatic upbringing. Occasionally remnants of his pain manifest during discussions of his parents.

Pride and selfishness are the Jude's crutches, and he betrays everyone who means anything to him.

Betrayal—a concept Jude knows all too well—was his sidekick growing up.

6

SESSION 5: JOE'S REVELATION

I cannot get my mind off of Eoghan. The idea of running into someone who could look at you and send electricity through you without the pleasure of his touch is amazing and frightening at the same time. All of this…and I do not even know his last name.

Thinking about him, I let my thoughts go wild. I become more alive with a kind of passion that I have not felt in a long time. I look out of my office window to the blue sky. He holds my thoughts captive. I soon realize I am breathing a little deeper than normal. It is like a sudden change in weather during the winter season.

Being from the Midwest, I am accustomed to long, long bouts of cold winter days. There can be months when the sun will hibernate, leaving its worshipers in quiet despair. When it does return, its appearance reminds us that new life is on the horizon.

The sun's guest appearance during the winter months gives the impression that forty-five degrees is blazing hot. Most of the world knows this is ludicrous. However, if you are from the Midwest, you know that forty-five degrees in the winter is a gift from the gods! When winter truly surrenders to spring, tiny flower and tree buds begin to bloom. The sounds of living creatures returning from their winter hiatus fill the air. It is amazing how this reflection of life lights our eyes after months of living in the dead of winter. We remember that we are of the living and forget the months of solitude and reclusiveness.

Wow! The thoughts of him just now felt like the gift of forty-five-degree day during a winter cold snap in the Midwest! Life has returned, and it has returned suddenly—fiercely, even. It's life I did not know was even lost. Spring has come early.

I am slightly dazed by my thoughts and am jarred back into reality when I look up at the clock and see it's almost three o'clock and time for the Riley-Buttons. They are on time again. Interesting. I watch them in the waiting room. I take a closer look and really watch them, because I have ten minutes before I need to bring them back.

For some reason, I need to study them a bit.

They are in their usual uniforms and locale. Joe is wearing his usual work attire, and Belle has her usual mess of papers surrounding her. I watch Joe a little closer. He is watching various women in the office. He would not be a bad looking guy if he cleaned himself up a little.

His cooper skin is complemented by large old eyes. His eyes seem to tell a story of their own. His eyes are a dark steel-gray color. Where did he get those eyes? They are not gorgeous in the way most would consider. However, they are almost lost, and as I look into them, it is as if I were peering into a dense fog. These are eyes that cannot see their way through.

His nose, although symmetrical to his face, makes a statement. It is very broad and flares slightly when he gets emotional.

He definitely notices other women, and he does not seem to remotely notice that Belle notices him noticing them! He is too funny. I chuckle to myself.

Her face provides dichotomous emotion. There is fierceness and disgust. Her suppressed anger is only released by the fiery red clay eyes that burn that through Joe. I am surprised he doesn't feel the hole being seared through his skull.

Her anger is tempered by full, painted pink lips that have a slight smile. It's a knowing smile, a smile that is amused that once again he does not see her.

Many times in relationships, people disappear. Sometimes they actually disappear and leave their current space and place in time. They are no longer emotionally or physically present. Unfortunately, in some unions, the body is present while the heart no longer takes residence. They are physically present but emotionally gone.

The other option is to make the other person symbolically evaporate. Slowly but surely, one loses awareness of the other's existence. The other evolves into shadows. What is worse is that you can lose yourself, no longer knowing who you are. This is tragic. The loss of one's self can only be remedied by taking the journey to reclaim oneself.

"Mr. and Mrs. Riley-Button?" I say as if I did not know they were there.

Her burning gaze is broken by my call. Joe jumps up and helps Belle with her papers, and they come in.

"So, how has last week been?" I ask.

They look straight ahead, not looking at each other or at me.

Here we go.

"Have you guys gone on another date?" I ask.

"Welp!" Belle starts off. "One of us went on a date." She turns her lips up, and the red clay eyes grow wider.

Joe sits up and throws his arms forward. "Damn, just tell her, Belle. Hell, I'll tell her."

Joe sits straight up and looks at me with indignation. "I went on a date, River," he exclaims.

Well, that was pretty damn obvious.

"There, it's out there," he said with a sigh and collapsed back into his usual chair.

Many couples have had to experience the trauma of infidelity, and how it impacts them depends on many variables. At what stage of the relationship did the infidelity occur? What is the strength of the relationship? What are the ego strengths of each individual? Are there religious beliefs or children tied to the union? Was the infidelity a relationship or just sex? Who was the other person? What values does each person hold individually or as a couple? What are their rules, spoken or unspoken? There are just so many variables to consider.

Joe and Belle are married with a child, but they are in a very weak stage of their marriage. On the outside, it looks dead. Saving it will take the desire of both of them. They have to *want* to save it, independent of the child.

"Joe, would you care to talk more about who this was or why you went on a date?" I ask.

He looks at Belle, who will not even look in his direction. She stares at the wall, no doubt waiting for the moment when things become right with world—the predictable minutes starting at half past three in the afternoon.

"I … I … I just liked how she made me feel," he stammers.

Okay, he is going to make me work for it.

"How is that? Specifically, how did she make you feel?"

"Like, like … I do not know how to say it, River. I just know that I feel important when … when I am with her," he says.

Belle turns her head sharply to him. "You choose to not be important in this, Joe. I mean really. You only exist when there is something fun to do—something fun that you have no intention of paying for." She rolls her eyes at him and continues. "That is so old to me! Please. How old is she, Joe?"

Now I'm curious too, although I try to be cool and not to look too curious.

"She is twenty-four years old. What does it matter?" he questions.

"You're thirty-eight years old." She slams the words and her voice into his ears. "It matters." She looks in my direction. This must be my cue to explain to Joe why it matters.

Okay, I am looking for my script.

"Well, Joe, let's begin with the fact that we have to make ourselves relevant to ourselves and to the units we have *chosen* to bind ourselves to. Are you in a relationship with this person? Can we give her a name?" I am really entering rocky waters now. Giving her a name makes her alive—a breathing barrier within their union.

Belle's arms are folded. She quickly glances at me and then the clock: 3:28 p.m. It is becoming time.

Joe sinks in his seat. He is quiet for about ninety seconds. "Her name ... Her name is Delilah."

I can tell that Belle never heard him. It is half past three. Her arms unfold. With a slight smile on her face, she is gone.

"Delilah is a coworker; she really doesn't mean anything. It is just something to do really. We are not an *item* or anything," he snaps.

I am surprised to hear Joe so casually discussing Delilah as if he were a single male and honestly here alone. Joe has an interesting approach to life. I can see how Belle gets frustrated with him. He does not see global issues. He sees issues in isolation.

When we fail to see our patterns, we fail to both identify and change ourselves in a way that is effective and long lasting. Until we are able to see the patterns, we are only dealing with symptoms. We have to attack the bacteria that allow for symptoms to manifest. Joe's issue of womanizing is centered not only in self-centeredness but also in feeling inadequate or lacking self-validation. He has to deal with his feelings of inadequacy in order to deal with his need to seek validation outside of himself.

"Joe," I say as I turn to see if Belle has rematerialized.

Great. She has.

"What was it like for you growing up? Tell me more about how your parents were as individuals and together," I say.

Belle laughs. "This will be interesting."

Joe ignores her sarcasm.

"My mother and father were together until I was about ten years old. My mother got rid of my father because there was some family scandal about who my father really was. She decided that she was going to be with the man who she 'thought' it was," he says as he forms air quotes with his fingers.

"It was so damn awkward. She forced me to call him Dad, despite the fact that I had already been calling my other father Dad since I was eighteen months old."

Joe searches my face, no doubt looking for judgment. Little does he know I would never display it. I have been well trained to not display emotion—even in the most extreme conditions.

However, internally, I am shocked. I cannot imagine what it would be like to try to navigate such confusing waters.

"Continue," I flatly state as I nod my head to grant permission.

"Anyhow, she told me that she could decide who 'the fuck' she wanted to be my father. Besides, he has more money," Joe says at an annoyingly high pitch, mimicking his mother.

"She is such a bitch!" Belle exclaims. My head swerves toward Belle. I give her a disapproving look.

"No, she is! There is so much you just do not know. We could do sessions on just her alone, and we would never have enough time."

"Belle, I appreciate your input, but right now this is Joe's experience. Allow him to have it. He has to have his process."

Belle smacks her lips and rolls her eyes again. "Whatever."

I hide my annoyance.

"Joe, please continue."

"Anyhow, here I am, eleven years old, and my mother moves this man into our house. She tells me, 'This yo' daddy now. He always was yo' daddy! You can forget the other one!'"

That voice. Man she must be a piece of work.

"What was your relationship like with your father ... errr the first one? What is his name?" I ask.

"Lake, his name is Lake. The other one's name is Joseph." He eyes me carefully.

"Well, Lake really just disappeared after he was kicked to the curb. I would try to call him and hang out. He would say he was coming, and he would never show up. I kept calling, and he kept making promises he never kept." Joe's eyes begin to tear; he is losing emotional control. His voice begins to shake. Yet, he refuses to surrender to it. "But before, everything seemed okay. We hung out. I thought he loved me."

Promises. Promises are words intertwined with gold. They are never to be broken. I have my own history with promises, so I understand his feelings of rejection and disappointment. I take promises very seriously, and when I make them they are as good as gold.

I know I am emotionally pushing Joe. He needs to work here. He needs to find the root of his issues and decide what to do with it.

"What about Joseph?" I inquire. Interesting, the name is practically the same.

"Oh, he was in my life for about two years; the black widow got rid of him too."

The black widow? No doubt he is talking about his mother. We'll get back to that.

"Well, what was your relationship like with Joseph? I push.

"There was not a relationship. He was only there for *her*. Once she could not extract anymore life force from him, she let him go too. I tried … I really tried to call him Dad and treat him as one. He always told me I was bothering him. He always had a list of chores for me to complete. When he offered to do something fun, he would then find some bull-crap reason to not do it."

Joe does not realize it, but he has touched on the root of either his inability or his refusal to be dependable. He has also touched on his need to seek the attention of others outside of his own union. Joe has used some powerful words: *life force, black widow.*

The words people choose are important to me. They hold a lot of power. More important is *how* they use words and the nonverbal messages that accompany them. Joe's presentation informs me that he is still in a lot of pain. This experience has not been reconciled in his heart, and we haven't even begun really talking about his mother yet. I am sure there is enough there to fill volumes.

"Joe, do you have a relationship with any of them now?" I suspect not, but I ask anyway.

"No. I don't." He wipes his face. "I am sorry … I got upset."

"That is okay, Joe. That is what this is for. This place is a safe haven for you to explore your pain and decide how to integrate it into who you are so you no longer have to suffer from its bondage," I state.

Belle gets up, walks over to Joe, and hugs him. She says, "We may be in a terrible place, but I do not want you to hurt. I want you to be okay."

I am pleased by Belle's sudden softness for Joe.

She still has compassion for him, so she really does not hate him. Plus, she knows his life story.

Hmm. This is a good sign.

Joe half smiles. He squeezes her tightly. She wipes the rest of his tears from his face.

"What about your mother, Joe? What is she like? What type of relationship do you have with her?"

To my surprise, they both started laughing.

"Can we revisit the black widow on another session?" Belle chuckles. "We need a full session for that. It is almost time to go."

I laugh along. "Sure."

On the way out the door, Joe squeezes my hand. Without his even saying the words, I understand that he is more than thankful for the release.

Belle touches my shoulder and provides a smile that continues to hold the compassion she used to retrieve Joe from his legacy of abandonment.

I watch them leave the office.

Unfortunately, It is hard for many of us to see that our current patterns are often intertwined. They are connected to the historical patterns set within us as children.

I gather my things and get ready to leave as well. It is a short day for me today.

7

DON'T IGNORE THE ALARM

"River, um ... I am sorry, Dr. Meadows!" I turn.

"Mahaley, it is okay. River is fine. I keep telling you, you do not have to call me Doctor."

"Oh, okay. Sorry, Dr. Meadows."

I sigh. "Yes, Mahaley, what can I do for you?"

"Well, your husband Jude called and said he would be late picking you up."

Picking me up? I drove myself. "What do you mean Mahaley? I drove myself here today."

"Oh, I guess he did not tell you. He came and picked up the car. He said there was something wrong with his, so he had a friend drop him off here."

I attempt to conceal my anger. Take my car? A friend dropped him off?

"Oh, okay, Mahaley. Did he come inside while I was in session?" I ask.

"No," her voice and eyes drop.

"I was outside in my car, where I was taking a smoke break."

"Mahaley, you said you quit a long time ago!" I am shocked.

"I know, I know. I did not want anyone to know. I am just having such a stressful time right now. I've been using that smoke spray to throw you off my scent," she says with a smile.

"Anyhow, when she dropped him off, it startled me, and I burned my dress."

Mahaley attempts to show me the burn on her dress, but I stopped hearing her after she said *she*. Who is *she*? Why would he not call or even text me? I work to refocus my attention to the moment. This will have to be put on the back burner until I get more information and then decide how to feel about it.

Of course when Jude shows up, I am a bit apprehensive. I want to question him immediately about who dropped him off. However, I hold off. "So, what happened to your car?" I manage to get out.

Sighing, "Uhhhh … Remember that I was supposed to get that knockin' checked out?" He grimaces while trying to explain the inevitable consequence of his continual negligence.

Flatly I say, "Yes, I remember, Jude. The knockin' that I have been asking you to check up on for a couple of months?"

Before my eyes Jude turns into a child. His voice becomes small and insignificant. Yet, I know that the consequence of his inaction is significant.

"Well, sweetie." Jude is trying to sound sweet and innocent.

Here we go. Sweetie. Let's drop some honey on that nuclear bomb. That makes it more palatable.

"I ended up blowing the transmission. It is going to be a twenty-five-hundred-dollar repair." One side of his face scrunches up as if to avoid being knocked clearly in the eye. "I knew you would be in session. I did not want to disturb you. You know, you get all worked up in the middle of your … your whatever you do. So, I had my boy from the dealership drop me off."

I did not take the time to even address the small shank to my work. *My boy from the dealership. My boy from the dealership. My boy from the dealership.* This statement circles my head like a shark and an injured man.

Okay, okay. We have an issue. Mahaley stated that she clearly saw him dropped off by a woman. Calm down, River. Do nothing yet.

Jude is living up his to past again.

We arrive home, and I am moving in slow motion. I replay the day in my head. I replay his explanation of events. I study my memory of his face, looking for evidence of lies.

Jude has always been a really good liar. That is how I met him—in the middle of a lie.

I met Jude during a softball game. He was a playing for the dealership he works for as a car salesman. Anyhow, my car was on the fritz, and I was in the market for something new.

I'll never forget that day. It was an early Saturday morning in late September. I was finishing up my morning run. The air was crisp, as fall was arriving early. Jude was finishing his game, hangin' out with some of his teammates.

I attempted to start my car, and it refused to turn over. I began to rub the dash and begging Betty to get started. For some reason, I name my cars; I guess I figure that if I personalize them, they will have a positive relationship with me. Anyhow, I was begging her to start. She was wheezing and sputtering but would not turn over. I placed my face on the steering wheel and began to pray.

As I started to pray, a knock on the driver's windshield broke me from my moment with God. *This is not the time to flirt*, I thought to myself. *Can't you see I am in trouble?* I smile the kind of smile you give when you really want someone to go away. "Yes, how can I help you?" I say.

"No, can I help you? My name is Jude, and it looks like you are in trouble."

Well, you're brilliant crossed my mind to say. But instead, I said, "Yes, I am," through my *please go away* smile.

He wiped his face and flashed me a quick smile, "Well, I work at Warner's Auto, and we just finished a game. Some of the mechanics are here. I can have one of them look at your car for you." He offered another flash of a smile.

Suddenly, I did not want him to go away so quickly. I needed the help. I mean, who was I to turn down someone who obviously had access to help!

My smile turned from fake to genuine. "Hi, Jude. My name is River. River Meadows. I appreciate your help." I looked at him with a sigh of relief. "You have quite the interesting name—kinda close to the infamous Judas. I am sure you've been told this."

"Uhh, yeah. Don't hold it against me. Jude Silber," said as he reached his hand in the car.

I shook his hand. "Hi. All right, Jude, let me get out of the car. Can you get your mechanic friends?"

He waved them over. Three guys came over to the car. They asked me all the insulting questions one could ask.

"Do you have gas?"

"Did you leave your lights on?"

"When did it last start?"

I answered all their questions, as I was just happy someone was willing to look at my car. I left them to their project as the machismo took over. They were all disputing what the problem was. *Yes, yes,* I thought. *Please allow the testosterone to flow.*

I was amused, and Jude could see it. He smiled and stated, "Hey, you mind sitting and talking a bit? I've been playing for a few hours, and I am tired."

"Sure."

I walked with him and sat at a bench in sight of my car.

"You should consider getting a new car. I mean a woman like you, should always be safe."

A woman like me, I thought to myself. *Men.* I let that slide. I really wanted my car fixed.

"I know. I am in the market. I just haven't taken the time to look. As luck would have it, the dealer came to me!"

Another smile flashed across his face. Yes, he was a car salesman.

"Are you single?" he asked.

"I thought we were talking cars, Mr. Silber." I leaned toward him, but not too close—I did just get finished running.

"Well, we can talk about cars over … maybe dinner?" His smile flashed again—nice teeth. He had large eyes with the apparent wisdom of a thousand lifetimes. I decided to trust the eyes, although the smile raises a red flag. There was something in my spirit that was a little alarmed, though I couldn't put my finger on it. *It is just dinner,* I said to myself. *I can go.*

There are times in life when we are given direction, and we may call it intuition, a gut reaction, or hunch. Nevertheless, a spirit communicates with us that knows no words but understands the energy that emits from us all.

We are given moments of clarity from the ultimate counselor, but many times we choose to ignore them. These moments are the very ones that resurrect their "I told you so" heads when hindsight is at work.

As I remember it, Jude looked up, his colleagues apparently waving him over. He grabbed my arm, and we walked over to the car.

The cool crisp air became cooler as it began to rain. The tiny drops of life were welcome on my exhausted body. I stopped walking and raised my face to the rain. Eyes closed, I appreciated the cleansing from Mother Earth.

Jude stopped with me but looked as if I had lost my mind. "You are getting wet! You'll catch cold," he said.

"You never heard the quote, Jude? Some people get wet—others feel the rain?"

"No," he said. I could hear in his voice the realization of a world that I experience regularly; he was not connected to it, but he was curious.

I smiled and got in the car.

With a twist of the wrist, the breath of life returned to my car without sputter. I was so elated that my car had been started by the testosterone brothers. I was so grateful, in fact, that I decided to make arrangements to meet Jude later that evening.

Jude tapped the window one more time. I rolled it down and said, "Hey I already agreed to dinner." I laughed. He reached in the car window and touched the line of my cheek.

"No, that is not it," he said. "You know what, River?"

"No. What, Jude," I asked.

"You gave me needed oxygen today. You're a breath of fresh air ... really." He took a pause and finished his thought: "I felt like I was drowning earlier today. I'll tell you more later." With that he walked away and was gone.

I bit my lip. My wet curly hair fell in my eye. I watched him trot away through the space between locks of my hair. That tugging of my spirit returned to me. I chalked it up to paranoia.

I chose to meet Jude at a family-style Italian restaurant located in the neighborhood mall. He met me at the door of the mall. *He cleans up well*, I thought to myself. He opened the door for me and handed me flowers—snapdragons, actually. Maybe there was nothing to really be alarmed about after all.

He chose a secluded corner in the restaurant and told me he never sits with his back to a door. He switched sides with me.

"So," I said. "What were you goin' to say? You said you would tell me later."

Jude began to stutter as he spoke: "Yeah, you caught me off guard with the rain. It showed me that you were a little different."

He struggled with eye contact. As he talked, he looked all over the place. "I am just over a serious a relationship. I mean, it crushed me. I felt as though my lungs collapsed. For a brief moment when you were there, I could breathe again."

Sounds incredible, doesn't it? Anyone would have been in awe of such a powerful statement. I should have remembered he was a car salesman.

Fast forward seventeen years and one wedding later, I made an accidental discovery.

I discovered Jude previously had girlfriend of six years whom he had been supporting down South. He had been with her for three years before me. It looked like his business trips were not all business after all. I suppose it pays to check pockets when washing—I found receipts for room service for two and a crumpled up post-it note with a kiss and the message, "Muah! See you next month, baby."

He did not deny it when I found out. He said he was happy it was all out. He said he was not sure why he needed the attention of other women. He proceeded to recount other relationships he'd had over the years.

Now we just exist. I have tried to work through it, as I try to keep my promise to God.

Promises. Good God. The promise you make in front of God is the ultimate promise. I do not think many people recognize the weight of their wedding vows. You are asking God to join your two spirits to one in His name. If it's done right, God is at the head of the marriage. This allows for the unit to be stronger than any one individual. This means, however, that you must marry with pure intentions. You marry for the desire to no longer be known as an isolate but a polymer. You create a *new* thing. That is awesome. If there are motivations other than the desire to create this new thing out of the essence of God (which is love), the marriage will fail to thrive, as it has been bastardized since conception.

The new unit, the new marriage, will bear defects. This teratogen will cause the DNA of this new thing to express maladaptive genes—the expression of infidelity, jealousy, verbal abuse, physical abuse, emotional abuse, and spiritual abuse. Spiritual death can soon follow. Souls that once saw color are washed in a series of grays.

However, Jude begged for my forgiveness. I thought I gave it to him by staying. I learned, however, that all I did was allow a marriage that was in the middle of a grand mal seizure to enter a vegetative coma. We are on life support. Who is the power of attorney? Who will pull the plug? Who will call the time of death? Who?

8

SESSION 6: THE BLACK WIDOW

I am still reeling from Jude's chronic infidelity issues. it is an effort to make sure that these issues do not color my work with clients.

As clinicians, we work hard to disconnect our personal lives from the lives of those we are privileged to work with. Unfortunately, we would be lying to ourselves if we did not admit to seeing aspects of ourselves in our clients.

Like a kaleidoscope, life is made of many parts. With a slight shift of the scope, the entire picture changes. How does that happen if all the parts are the same? The perception has changed. Often, viewing our lives through the lens of a client allows us to have better perspectives of ourselves.

Understanding who you are in the reflection of another person is a priceless gift. It means you can have an opportunity to live authentically and without apology.

I inhale deep and exhale slow. It is 2:50 p.m., and Mahaley has informed me that the Riley-Buttons are on the way. With a smirk, she puts "just running late" into air quotes.

I peak out the window again, because I want to watch them as they arrive. I need to be able to get out of myself, out of my head, out of my heart.

Here they are. I pull the curtain, allowing one eye to be exposed.

Joe parks the car erratically and jumps out. Belle has her head leaning against the window, staring at the sky. I wonder if he notices that she is not present. Maybe this is her normal, because he does not even look back to see if she is getting out of the car.

She does not seem to acknowledge that she is at their appointment. She takes her hair out of the ponytail and runs her fingers through it. She piles her hair high on her head, creating a loose bun. Oddly, she begins to smile—and not just any smile, either. She is covered by joy. She reaches her hands to the air and then—

"Dr. Meadows?" My head sharply swivels around. What the hell? I am half agitated and half embarrassed. I adjust my clothes and push my glasses up on my nose.

"Yes, um … yes. Mr. Riley, did Mahaley show you in? Where is Belle?"

"As you can see, Belle is in the car," he says with a knowing smile. "As far as Mahaley, she left the front desk, and I wanted to have a few minutes of your time before Belle gets in."

"Um … that is really not a good idea, Joe. I mean, my allegiance is to the unit. I cannot give the appearance that I have aligned myself with a particular person in the union."

Couples often fear that a therapist will align with one or the other person. They are accustomed to opposing teams an fail to recognize the third party in the union. They have failed to recognize the union itself. The union is starving and seeking nourishment. Out of desperation, the union grasps for the placenta of love that has manifested out of two joining souls. These souls that conceived and bore this new thing desperately reach for the umbilical cord that once was the path for nourishment.

This new thing was once bathed in abundant rays of love. Like a bird, it was once able to spread its wings, but now it is grounded … dying. And like the sun, though it was once able to infect everyone around it with passion-filled heat, now only the scent of toxic resentment and hostility remains.

People can recognize the aroma of joining hearts. It reminds them that they are alive. The unit becomes a film to the world, forever a spectacle of desire. Together, the hearts become one.

However, when the fused hearts come undone, the unraveling union becomes invisible to the world. Finally, the death is presented to the world through cold exchanges. *Another star has died*, the world sighs. It has become consumed and extinguished.

"Really, Dr. Meadows. I want to talk about my mom today, but I want—rather *need*—Belle to allow me to talk. That is all I wanted to say to you," he says, seeming anxious. I look at him, wondering why it was important to tell me this.

"She has such venomous feelings for her, and she has difficulty controlling herself whenever I even have to bring her up," he says as he puts his hands through his hair. He looks confused and lost.

"Sure, Joe. Can you go to the waiting room? I need to put away some files from my last client, and I will be right with you and Belle."

He gives me an army salute and an about face and then leaves the room.

I start a self-inventory. What is going on with you, River? I realize that I have been thinking of the baritone often. Why do images of Eoghan appear out of nowhere? He is just a stranger—a stranger with an uncanny ability to shift me off my axis. Okay, feeling check: confused. Thought check: distracted. Oh boy, this is going to be an interesting session. I will have to work a bit harder to focus. I gather myself and walk to the waiting room. I turned toward Mahaley, whose face reads, *Sorry, I know I screwed up!* I smile to ease her discomfort.

In the waiting room, Belle is sitting opposite Joe again. He makes immediate eye contact with me and again looks pretty anxious to get started. Belle does not even turn around to see what he is looking at.

"Riley-Buttons?" Why did I just say their name as if I were not sure they were there? Goodness. Put the script away, River. He already saw you peeking out the window.

Joe jumps up and makes a beeline for my office. Belle is slow to retrieve her things. She is a pretty woman—in a smart kind of way.

They assume the usual sitting arrangement. I sigh. I decide I will address this today. I want to know if they are aware of it, and if they are aware, I would like to process that first.

"Belle and Joe, I hope you have had a good week so far. I would first like to ask a question before we get started."

Belle and Joe both nod.

"Do you notice that when you arrive in my office, you don't sit together? You actually sit far from one another."

Belle speaks first. "Of course I do. We always sit like this, Dr. Meadows. I mean our energy is so negative with one another that it is almost like putting two magnets with the same polarity together. We immediately repel."

Wow. What an interesting analogy.

"Yeah," a hesitant Joe agrees. "It is like we can sense the hostility in each other, so we'd rather just not even feel it if we can avoid it."

"I see." That is disturbing. They will never come together with that mindset.

"I really like the statement regarding similar poles, Belle. Let's go with that for a moment. Let's consider that you both have negative polarity. When hostility settles in your hearts, it will not seek common ground. It is not the nature of hostility to do so. Once a relationship moves from a hostile environment to an apathetic one, it has died. One can return from hostility with some effort. There is still emotion attached to the union. Now it may be negative emotion, but nonetheless, it is emotion. However, when apathy enters the picture, your relationship becomes increasingly hopeless. Here is where having a belief system is fruitful, because it can take a miracle from God to make one care about the other again."

I allow silence to enter the space.

I sit back. Looking at both of them, I do not see any sign of unity.

"It is my assessment that you guys are hostile toward one another. Initially, I thought you were apathetic, but *hostile* is a better descriptor, I think" They are deer in the headlights looking back at me.

"What do you guys think?" I ask.

Joe is quick to comment. "I think that makes sense. I am willing to do anything to make our magnets come together."

Belle turns to Joe and then to me. "Joe's desire not to lose me is greater than his desire to keep me." Her voice reflects loss of hope, but the words are quite profound.

Wow. I have to control my eyebrows. I wonder if Joe knows what she means. I believe I do.

"Belle," I say. "Can you unpack that statement a bit more?"

Belle exhales. The sound of air leaving her body tells of a thousand times she has had this type of discussion. It is breath that begs to be held for a worthier cause.

"Joe wants me to stay in his life. Joe does not want to do what it takes to keep me in his life. His desire to keep me in his life is not about *us*; it is about *him*. It is about loss of a possession not the development and nourishment of our relationship. It is hard for him to see that. He is blinded by the possibility of loss; however, he can only see himself. Does that make sense, River?"

Belle fluctuates between calling me Dr. Meadows and River. The mix of formal and informal address is a pattern I must pay closer attention to.

I lean in toward Belle. "Yes, I understand. But that matters little. Joe, do you understand?"

"I mean … I hear her," he says. Belle's eyes roll. "I do not think that is true though."

"What is the evidence? Why is it not true? Do you believe that you love Belle on her terms or your own?"

Silence.

The silence was loud. It was as if I could see the neuronal connection in the brain that allows for the consolidation of information and hindsight. It was preparing to make an all-too-familiar appearance. It is fascinating to watch hindsight in action. This is also known as an epiphany.

Years of misunderstandings become understood in moments. For some folks, just one piece of a one-thousand-piece puzzle is necessary to see the whole picture.

Joe just got his one piece, and he can now see the picture.

"Do you understand, Joe? Do you love her as *you* desire to love her, or do you love her as *she* needs you to love her?" I persist.

"I never thought of it that way." He looks over at Belle. Belle is smiling, as she finally feels heard. It's fascinating how you can talk to someone for years, and they never hear you. God grants us the biology to hear, but we listen with our hearts. That is something we have to develop. The ability to listen is not innate; it is something we learn from our upbringings.

I smile, as I feel some real work has been done so far. We haven't even gotten to his mother yet! I am not sure if we are going to make it there. I look over to Belle and notice the time. It is 3:28 p.m. She pulls her hair out of the ponytail again and begins to twirl her finger around her hair. As she is getting lost, she remembers that I know her secret. She looks up at me and asks if she can go to the restroom.

The conversation our eyes have with one another is significant. I know her truth—at least that there is some truth to be known. Joe has not brought it up as of yet. Does she do this at home? I suppose if they have so much hostility built up in their home, he would not notice when she disappears because he is used to her not really being there anyway.

"Sure, Belle; you know where it is." I point across the hall.

"Thanks, Dr. Meadows." She scurries out of the room. I chuckle. My eyes widen, and I cover my mouth, as that was supposed to happen *inside* my head.

I turn my attention to Joe. He is lost in his phone. I sit back and wait for Belle.

No doubt she is having her invisible tryst in the bathroom, away from knowing eyes.

Three minutes later, Belle returns. She almost skips like a kindergartener back to her seat.

Well, she's awfully happy. I will get that secret. I just need her to get comfortable enough to want share or to provide the information unknowingly.

As a therapist, one must be able to endure secrets. One must be able to have the patience of Job, some might say. People protect their secrets, sometimes even from themselves. Those are the worst secrets to have—the ones one does not know lie within. They are parasites to an unknowing host. They can be in the driver seat of one's life. Tragedy, which results from these secrets not be integrated or acknowledged, can operate a GPS, calculating routes that are self-destructive.

Belle will release her secret in due time—in her time.

After Belle returns to the session, Joe looks at her. "I never thought that I was loving you on my terms only. I just do not know any other way."

"It has been years of me trying to tell you, Joe. You refused to listen."

"It is not me not listening. I guess with my mother and the way she raised me, we had a different language. Belle, it's like you would be speaking English one second and suddenly switch to Chinese."

I can hear the confusion in Joe's voice.

This is such a great exchange. This is work—the simple act of being willing to seek understanding.

"Joe, that is such an excellent analogy you used," I state.

"What analogy?"

"English versus Chinese. That was good. Often we do speak different relationship languages. We must speak *each other's* language. If not, we are setting our relationships up for failure. That is where I come in as the 'interpreter.' It becomes my duty to translate until you guys are able to do it on your own. Or at least it is my duty to provide you with the script that will assist you with translating each other's love language. We did some work today but missed discussing your mother, Joe. That is important too, because you will be able to see where you developed many of your life patterns. You will need it to do this exercise as well, Belle. We are also going to talk more about Delilah, as I am sure this has been the talk of your household."

"No, not really," they both retort.

Hmm, not good. They are far too nonchalant about this.

"Well … okay. We will talk about that as well next time."

9

TRIANGLES, PARKS, AND CROISSANTS

Eoghan McGhee is a man of decisiveness. He is clear about his decisions and his desires. As a city councilman, he prides himself on his ability to set clear expectations and execute his decisions. In moments when most would suffer great distress in ambiguity, Eoghan has always been able to see a clear path. This is what has made him unique in his district. He is the alpha in a room of omegas. He does not wallow in moments of weakness but enjoys the challenge to his spirit. As of late, Eoghan has not been himself. He notices that during meetings he is doodling, lost in thought. His mind seems to wander back to the random moment that seemed an eternity—a moment that reminded him that he is not as complete as he once believed.

Being complete.

It is interesting how there are moments when we hear or read the words, "You complete me." It is imperative for us to remember that two broken people do not create one. They are only fragments with jagged edges that hurt each other when they meet. There are times, however, when someone can enhance who you currently are. Someone can breathe new life into a soul that had been prepared to accept the reality that the other did not exist.

When one inhales the spirit of a love for the first time, it is as though they had never breathed before. The lung's capacity expands, filing each lobe with the purest oxygen.

Eoghan chuckles to himself and starts thinking in the form of a monologue: *Bob, my assistant, has been really on me about missing appointments. He actually asked me to see a therapist, as if I am having some sort of midlife crisis. For a forty-four-year-old man, this crisis is lite. I am just a little distracted. I cannot understand why I keep thinking about this River chick.* Eoghan stirs the cream in his daily coffee. He gets lost in the stir, gradually slowing down. *The energy we have.* He laughs. *Funny how natural that sounds. We. How can I think of the concept of a "we"? Here I am, dedicating thoughts to a woman I don't know at all. I mean I only ran into her, and now I feel some odd connection to her. She reminds me of something that I just cannot place my finger on but must have.*

"Eoghan!"

Jolted out of his trance, he turns, spilling his carefully stirred coffee.

"Man, where are you? I've been calling your name for a couple of minutes now! You are supposed to be in a meeting in five minutes!"

"Bob, dude … man, I do not know what my deal is. It's this girl. Anyway, I'm on my way. Lemme clean up this coffee."

"What girl? Your girl? Or that chick you bumped into after dinner at a Prima Vista?"

A small smile creeps over Eoghan's face. He draws his hand his face and sighs. "*Yes.* That one, *River.*"

"Look, you gonna get yourself in a world of trouble. You are always involved with multiple women. How do you juggle them all? That shit gonna catch up to you one day! You need to settle down … again," Bob says with a chuckle.

"Settle down *again*? That is not funny. But there is something about this one."

Bob's face speaks a thousand skeptical words.

"Man, I know. I know. Let's go to this damn meeting. What is it about anyway? We have these meetings every week, it seems!" Eoghan says.

"Well. You are the city councilman. You set these meetings up, dude. Let's go."

As they walk down the hall, Eoghan's mind wanders back to River. She is the memory of childhood. Nostalgic. *I've known her forever … despite the fact that I don't know her at all*, he thinks to himself.

****

"Belle, I am going to take Jasmine with me to the park. I need to get some air. We need to get some air." Joe takes his phone, checking his messages. *Yep. Delilah,* he thinks to himself. *Always seems to know when to hit me up.*

"Joe, I do not care where you decide to go. If you are *really* going to the park, take Jazzy. That is fine. I cannot keep arguing with you about these damn bills anyway."

Jasmine sits on the top of the stairs. She has been listening to the argument for at least twenty minutes. Her ears perk at the sound of her name. Her stomach drops as if she has been caught listening in. She quietly gets up and shuffles off to her room.

Pretending to be reading, she notices her bedroom door opens to a crack. "Jaz … you wanna go the park? Maybe go get some ice cream?" Joe asks.

He looks desperate to her. "Sure, I'll go."

The ride is silent. Joe periodically looks at his phone and over to Jasmine. Jasmine's mind is lost on the passing scenery.

She turns to Joe when she realizes the path they are taking differs from the usual route to the park.

The car stops in front of an apartment. It's an old six-unit building with battered doors and porches.

Joe sees that Jasmine is confused.

He takes her hand. "Sweetheart, there are times when grownups struggle. I am sorry that you witness some of Mommy's and Daddy's problems. Sometimes it means that we need someone to talk to. We need to have friends who will help us through the problems. Delilah is a good friend of mine. She helps me talk about Mommy."

Jasmine's frustrations mount. She cannot believe that again. He is not following through on what he said he was going to do. "Daddy, is that why we are here? I thought we were going to the park. You told Mom we were going to the park." Jasmine's face is a mix of confusion and disgust.

"We are parked in front of Delilah's apartment. I just needed to talk, Jazzy."

"Dad, you can talk to me ... why not talk to me? I heard Mommy talking about Deeli Deela—whatever her name is. I don't think she would be okay with it. I thought we were friends, Dad." Jasmine's voice trails to a whisper. Her arms are crossed, and anger begins to form on her face.

Far too often children are casualties of the war between feuding parents. They often become referees, sounding boards, or worse, chosen allies. Many couples fail to realize that the home is where children first learn how to negotiate *any* type of relationship—platonic, romantic, or familial. We are their models. Parents who lack proper support will utilize their children as support systems. This is not negative if it means that parents will buffer the stress of the relationship by spending quality time with their children. However, if their relationship is built on creating an ally, which means developing an enemy, this is ineffective and cruel. If parents are our first relationship models, then children need to see relationships that are healthy.

A negative result can develop if children are bought up in homes that have high amounts of hostility and unresolved conflict. It is possible that a child can move from a citizen in his or her own home to a refugee, feeling as though he or she has no place and no one to turn to. These "refugees" will become "asylum seekers," looking for a place to belong. Unfortunately, many of the places they will claim are usually the ones parents have cautioned them against. They will seek solace with poor influences. This only creates more distance between the child and the parent. It is imperative that parents recognize when they are "infecting" their child's ability to honestly love another person.

"Well, I tell you what, Ms. Jazzy. Why don't you stay in the car? Here, use my phone to play with. I will only be a few minutes. Pinky swear?" Joe holds out his finger, smiling. Jasmine smiles back. She holds our her small finger and wraps it around Joe's, sighing. "Pinky swear," she says. "Remember you promised!" She wags her finger at him.

Joe, chuckles, "Yes, yes ... I know ... I know." He gets out of the car and shuts the door. Turning around to Jasmine, he smiles and gives a quick wave.

Joe approaches the buzzer to Delilah's apartment, number 731. He has been here several times before. This time, however, there is a heaviness to his approach. He cannot place his finger on it, but with each step he takes toward that door, regret begins to settle inside his chest. As he lifts his arm to the buzzer, a voice tells him he is making the wrong decision. Today is not the day to be here. Joe's need for instant gratification overrides the voice of reason in his head. He begins to justify why it makes sense to be at her apartment when he is supposed to be spending time with his daughter in the park. He raises his arm to push the buzzer, acknowledging the weight of his regret.

He pushes.

"Hello?" a small voice screeches over the grainy buzzer.

"Hey, babe, it's me," Joe says with a smile.

"Hey! Come on in." The door buzzer seems abnormally loud this time. *What is the deal with me today*, he thinks to himself. He shakes it off and double-times it up the stairs to the elevator.

Jasmine pulls out the phone Joe had left for her and begins to look for games. *I really wanted to go to the park*, she thinks to herself. *I hope he is really only going to be a few minutes at this terrible place.*

Jasmine begins to review the pictures in Joe's phone. She sees many pictures that they all have taken in the past year. Some she likes, others not so much. Those she does not care for she takes the liberty to delete.

She checks the "recently deleted" folder to make sure she gets rid of the photos—or, more importantly, to get rid of the evidence that she has deleted photos. She notices one photo she hadn't before: it is Joe wrapped in the arms of another woman.

She stares at the photo for a long time. She traces the outline of the woman's entire body with her finger. She experiences multiple emotions—anger, confusion, and sadness. It's a recipe for the act of betrayal.

She goes to the text messages and looks through the messages to see if her name shows up. "This must be that Delilah chick," she says out loud to herself.

Looks like there are not any text messages from Delilah, but Dad certainly seems to get several messages from Randy, she thinks to herself.

She opens the messages. Almost dropping the phone, she realizes that either her stepdad is gay, or this is not a guy.

She begins to read them out loud.

Randy: "I can't wait to wrap your legs around me."

Joe: "Babe, I plan on doin' that all night. Soon as that bitch leaves, I can leave out of here.

Randy: "Hurry up. I got a surprise for you."

Joe: "You do? What is it? What you got for me?"
Randy: "I got a new teddy for you."

Joe: "You don't need it! LOL. I'll see you soon."

He called my mom a bitch, Jasmine thinks to herself. She goes back to that text, feeling the pit of her stomach line itself with rage.

There are several other messages outlining their meet-ups, which seem to happen almost everywhere and multiple times a week.

She can tell the days he "forgot" to pick her up, because he was with *her*.

She sits and cries for a while in the car, confused on what to do next. Before she knows it, she is getting out of the car and walking toward the apartment. Jasmine is on autopilot, not sure what she is doing or even aware that she is doing it. She looks at the phone and notices she has been waiting for thirty minutes already. Looking over the names, she notices one that has meaning: Delilah Samson. 731. She instinctually knows not to push the button. Instead, she pushes multiple buttons. Several hellos come through the box. However, one magical person does not check: he or she just buzzes her in.

She walks in and looks around. 731. She figures it must be on the seventh floor. She makes her way to the elevator. She is on a mission, though she is not sure what the mission is. She just knows she has to do this. She leaves the elevator, checking the wall for apartment 731. Once in front of it, she stands there for what seems like hours. She can hear sounds on the inside, but not clearly. She raises her fist to knock, her heart pounding. Her heart seems to want to leap from her chest. She can barely breathe. Her breaths become increasingly shallow as fear grips her. She knocks, her head just below the peephole. She gets as close to the door as she can.

She is afraid but knows she needs to do this. She must understand her father's actions of betraying her and her mom. She wants—no *needs*—her father to say why he is really there. This needs to make sense.

The sounds cease.

Jasmine can hear footsteps near the door.

"Who is it?" She hears a woman's voice.

Jasmine says nothing.

"Who is it?" The voice is more stern this time.

Again, Jasmine says nothing. Her breathing is almost nonexistent. *Can she hear my heart?* she thinks to herself.

"Damn fool kids," the voice says, and footsteps walk away from the door.

Jasmine sits on the floor against the door. The sounds begin to start up again. After about five minutes, she does it again: three knocks. This time, she is more forceful.

The footsteps return. This time she hears Joe. "I'll get it, baby. You go back to bed."

"I'll teach these assholes a lesson," Jasmine hears her stepdad say.

Unbeknownst to Joe, the other side of the door offers an experience so painful—the look of a child betrayed.

He swings the door open, wearing just a towel. His look of rage turns to utter surprise when he sees Jasmine.

Jasmine says nothing. She looks at the hand gripping the towel on his naked body.

The most painful question leaves Jasmine's mouth and nothing more: "Why? Why are you doing this? You pinky swore!"

With that, Jasmine bolts down the hallway.

"Jazzy wait!" Joe attempts to run for her, but the towel is a reminder that he is naked.

He quickly reenters the apartment.

Jasmine takes the elevator and exits the apartment, sobbing. She does not get in the car. She runs down the street. She just needs to get away from everything and everyone.

Not sure of where she is going, she just runs. She fails to pay attention to street signs and eventually begins to realize she is not quite sure where she is. Her running stops, and she looks around to make an assessment of her layout.

Wiping the tears from her face, she begins to walk.

"It doesn't matter if I am lost. I got his phone still. I can get home. I'll call my mom."

Jasmine meanders around the unfamiliar shops, restaurants, and cafés. The rest of the world seems to slow down. She is so lost in herself that the sense of not being in sync with the rest of society has settled in her heart. Images seem to jump at her. Families, couples, and children all appear to be immersed in a sea of connection, and she is disconnected, apart from everything. She is a refugee in a nation of loved citizens. There has been a constant buzzing in her pocket. *The phone!* She remembers: she has her father's phone.

Randy.

Randy has called several times. *How funny,* she thinks to herself. *Dad is trying to reach me through "Randy"—or more like Delilah.* In disgust, she declines the call.

The smell of coffee attracts her. She turns her head and sees the local coffee shop. Jasmine ducks in. It is quaint and cozy.

This is not your typical cafe. It seems to attract couples with its low lighting, close seating, and aroma of coffee and lavender.

No one appears to notice her. Her hands glide over the tops of the plush chairs. She feels the soft fabric in her fingers—the feeling of soft fur. It is almost like rubbing a new kitten. It begins to soothe her. She is interrupted from her tactile trance by a short, stocky woman asking, "How can I help you, lil' lady?"

She turned swiftly. "Oh … oh, yeah … a croissant?" Jasmine is not even sure if she has money. "Croissant with apricot preserve?"

Jasmine chuckles to herself. She digs in her pocket and is relieved to find ten dollars.

Happy with the monetary discovery, she sits and waits for her goods. She looks out the window of the café and can see her reflection. She studies her face—sad and heavy. Her large brown eyes look weighed down by the troubles of the adult world. Her hair is wild from running. She decides to put her long curly hair into a ponytail.

She gazes into the reflection to straighten her hair. She notices other patrons' reflections. However, only one reflection seems all too familiar to her.

She squints to clear the image and focus. She hushes other sounds, and she can hear a laugh that brings warmth to her heart.

It is the laugh of her mother.

She turns around to find the woman who bore her.

Turning toward the back of the café, she can see her. Jasmine's body feels light and warm with the relief of reconnection. Her pace quickens to approach the solace she ever so needs.

Jasmine slows as she notices that not only is her mother not alone, but her mother's eyes are lit by an unfamiliar light—a light that one only sees in the romantic movies. It is the light of love.

Across from her is a man—it's neither her father nor her stepfather. She is embracing his hand, tracing his fingers with hers.

"Oh, Eoghan … you are too much!" she hears her mother say.

Yo When? What kind of name is that? Who is that? Jasmine thinks to herself, horrified.

"Croissant for Jasmine!" the stocky woman yells through the café.

The familiarity of the name jars Belle from her immersed experience. She returns to reality and turns her head around to see, standing before her, her creation.

Mortification has entered the room.

"Hi, Mom," Jasmine states flatly with slight wave to only enhance the discomfort of the moment.

61

10

SESSION 7: THE CANCELLATION

Hmm … it is 3:15 p.m., and the Riley-Buttons have not called to say they were going to be late. I check my watch again and walk over to Mahaley.

"Mahaley, did you get any calls from the Riley-Buttons?"

A confused, wide-eyed Mahaley responds, "No, ma'am. No calls here."

"Hmm … I'm worried. I will call them."

River walks back to her office. Digging around in her calendar, she finds their number.

Hmm, whom should I call? Joe or Belle?

Belle is kind of interesting with her half past three checkout. I will call her. Why am I so concerned about them? There is something about them that I connect to—something that captures my attention.

I decide to dial Belle first.

"Hello," a whimpering voice on the other end responds.

"Mrs. Riley-Button? It is Dr. Meadows. You guys had an appointment today. I wanted to check to see if everything is okay."

"Um, no. Dr. Meadows … River … can we talk for a minute?"

I can hear tears in her voice.

"Yes, Belle. Please … are you okay? What is going on?"

"No … my daughter caught me and my husband with other people."

What? At the same time? My eyes pop. Thank goodness she cannot see my face.

"I … I don't know what to do. I was with my boyfriend at the café yesterday, and she walked up on us." She sniffles in the phone. "Also, she saw her stepdad with his girlfriend. It's a mess, River." Belle attempts to talk through her tears.

"Belle, I know. I can only imagine how hard this has been for you. I can see how you guys did not make it in today, although today would have been a perfect day to work through some of this.

"Your daughter will survive. Right now she is probably in shock. She has entered an adult world that she was probably not ready for. She has seen betrayal manifested, Belle."

There is silence on the other end for a long time. I allow her the space. After a minute or two, I can hear her slightly say, "I know, I know ... I agree, actually."

"So, Belle. It's time to put on your big girl panties and Joe to put on his big boy undies and make some decisions."

I am shocked that I am so blunt with her. I hold my ground. She needs this.

Many times in relationships we are stagnate because we choose to be. We fear the decisions that we must make. We believe that we can just create extensions of our problems by seeking our needs outside ourselves. Our problems become murkier by our need to self-satisfy rather than deal with the issues head on.

In order to grow as couples and individuals, we must decide to deal with a problem in all its glory. We have nothing to fear except the refusal to change.

"Belle, call Mahaley and make an appointment for you and your husband for next week, okay? You ... both of you ... will make it through this if you so choose to."

"Okay ... River. Thank you. Will do"

I sit in the office for a moment after speaking with Belle. I am still trying to understand why I am so stuck on and so concerned with the Riley-Buttons. Maybe I need to know the details of Belle's half past three checkout moment.

Maybe it is my own stuff that I see in theirs. There are some eerie similarities that I wish did not exist. However, although I wish they did not exist, I need to acknowledge they do.

My mind wanders back to my own Jude. A distracted husband and frustrated wife are living parallel lives that do not seem to meet anywhere or have a common destination.

Since my last session has been canceled, I have extra time in my schedule. Considering I do not have to pick up Jude, I decide to go to the restaurant where I first met Eoghan. A Prima Vista is about an hour and a half away from the practice. I want to spend some time absorbing the energy that Eoghan left me with. For a Wednesday, it would be nice and adventurous. It is calming just to think about getting away from the office for a while anyway. However, walking to the car I realize the air is damp and smells like a pending storm. Additionally, the sky is bit of overcast, but none of this matters. I love that smell. I love the smell of knowing something greater than myself is looming in the unseen. It is the smell of Mother Earth caring for herself, without human assistance, and it is intoxicating. Life's vital energy is out of our control and will soon be visible if she commands it.

It's the time of day when traffic moves smoothly, and with the radio off, my mind wanders. These moments remind me of how small I am and how big the "big picture" really is. They are moments that allow the imagination to wonder about what is going to happen and to slow down and reflect on what is. I am so involved in my thoughts and calmed by the scenery that I am disconnected from such awareness.

Before I know it, I arrive at A Prima Vista. The first raindrops appear as I park my car. I reach my hand outside the window to feel the touch of Mother Earth's vital life source. It is cool and heavy. I am aware that I need to seek shelter very soon.

I collect my thoughts before I leave the car. What the hell am I doing here again? To absorb Eoghan's energy?

What the hell? Who have I become? I must admit that as crazy as this is, I like it. It is almost as if I have always been this person who has finally realized herself.

I shake my head and chuckle to myself. Walking toward the door, I have hopes that I will see him. I know it is ridiculous to hope for something that is virtually impossible. I do not even have his number.

I walk in, and the front door staff enthusiastically greets me. As I proceed in, I understand why. This place is almost empty. The pending storm may have chased the patrons away.

Little do they know, I am not here for food. I am here to re-experience something akin to a defibrillator. I am jolted to life by the sheer presence of another human being.

Few times in life does someone make you forget everyone else. When we were here some weeks ago, I felt like we were the only ones here.

I wanted to capture that again.

As I slowly walk down the foyer of the restaurant, I look over to where Eoghan was sitting with his friends. I take a moment to enter the memory of him. I remember taking comfort that I could watch him without his awareness. I could see the corners of his eyes crease as he laughed.

The signs of years of joy swelled in his face. His eyelashes were long and wrapped around eyes so brown and gentle they instantly warmed the heart of this beholder.

I touch the area he sat in. The tips of my fingers swirl small circles against the back of the booth. A smile instantly appears, one that seemed almost reflexive rather than intentional. Who can do that? Who generates reflexive responses from an intentional process? It is like … arriving home—home after days, months, or years away. I think of the movie *The Wiz*. The song "Home" enters my mind.

When I think of home,
I think of a place where there is love overflowing.
I wish I was home.
I wish I was back there with the things I been knowing …
Wind that makes the tall trees bend into leaning …
Suddenly the snowflakes that fall have meaning:
Sprinklin' the scene makes it all clean.

This is interesting, as I am living in the memory and the current moment. I can have dual experiences in which the past and the present become one. I love this.

A pair of feet arrives in my view and forces my eyes to search for their owner. I look up, and the hostess is confused. I realize that she has been asking if she could seat me several times.

I laugh out loud at my own "checking out," much like Belle.

"Yes, please," I say.

"Are you expecting someone to join you?" She sounds irritated. After all, this lunatic entered her establishment completely spacey.

"No... uhhh"—I look at her name tag—"Diane. I am dining alone tonight."

"But of course. Follow me," she states.

I follow but realize that I might have been insulted on the low.

I have a seat at the bar.

"What can I getcha?" a male with a strong Spanish accent asks.

I ask for a Riesling—"something that I can still get myself home with," I say.

He chuckles.

"You mind talking with me for a second?" I ask. I need to distract myself from this fantasy I am living in.

He checks his watch. "Sure, we have a quiet evening tonight. It will be my honor," he bows.

I smile. "Why, thank you!" I say and pretend curtsy. "My name is River. River Meadows, and you?"

"My name is Conrado. Like Conrad but with an O at the end. You have an interesting name, River. River Meadows, I like that. It's calming."

"Thank you ... what does your name mean? Was that your father's name? I hope I am not getting too personal."

"No," he states while cleaning glasses. "It actually means something like counselor or something. I got the right job for it, don't I?" he says as he laughs, spreading his arms to highlight the liquor displayed behind him. "Listening to people discuss their lives while they drink is pretty much what I do for a living."

I damn near bellow. I laugh so hard I can barely catch my breath. "Are you serious?" I scream—which is a little inappropriate considering my environment is a quaint romantic restaurant.

Conrado looks quite confused. This confusion causes me to really laugh. I mean, he thinks I am laughing at his statement. In a way, I am, but also at the coincidence of the situation.

I gather myself. "Conrado, please forgive me for laughing. I am not laughing at you. It is just that is what I actually do for a living. I am a counselor. So a counselor seeking a counselor just struck me as funny."

He understands and laughs along.

"So, you hear the good, the bad, and the ugly all day too, I suppose?" I ask.

"Yes, I do," he chuckles. "Some of it I love to hear, some of it is so tragic that I go home and kiss my family, thanking God for my position in life."

"Tell me about it." I sigh and perk up. "The fun thing is you are not bound by any laws that keep you from talking about it! So tell me, what is the worst thing you ever heard?"

Conrado leans against the bar. He looks up so as to search his memory.

"Well, I know. This was terrible. I came in one Sunday about five years ago right after church. There was a man sitting not too far from where you are sitting who looked dead inside. His eyes were—how do I describe it? Zombie-like. I initially treated him like a regular customer. I kept his glass full, which is what he wanted. His voice, River ... may I call you River?"

"Sure," I say quickly. I want to hear his story.

"Okay ... you can call me Conrado," he says.
Makes sense considering he only told me his first name.
Jesus, man! I want to say. *Tell the damn story.*
I smile, nodding my head and accepting the informality.
"Cool, anyway. Where was I?"

"His voice?" I try not to sound irritated. Wow, the counselor is so impatient! I laugh at myself.

"Ahhhhh, yes ... his voice. It was difficult to listen to."

"Why?" I ask. "Because it was annoying?" I lift my glass to drink.

"No. You could clearly hear pain in his voice. It was the sound of *la muerte.*"

"What is that? What does that mean?" I ask.

"Death." He looks at me without expression.

I am intrigued by his need to go to his native language to make a point. English is not enough to describe his thoughts, and Spanish increases his statement's resonance.

"His heart was exposed. He talked of a woman—a woman he loved deeply," he says. Then he picks up another glass to clean.

"Tears slowly rolled down his eyes. He did not even care that he was in public and everyone could see him. Love is very powerful, River. It is the birth and destruction of all things. Our love for something will either allow us to come alive or kill us. Love is something that we have no real respect for. I sit behind this bar every day, and all I hear are stories of love found and love lost. I watch the birth of love as people meet each other for the first time courtesy of a shared drink or meal. Love is our salvation and curse all at the same time. But I am sure you already know that, counselor!" He laughs.

I am anxious to get back to the story. But I entertain the discussion of love.

"You are correct. Love is a very powerful force. However, I believe it is our mishandling of love that is the destructive force. I do not believe its mere existence is a curse. When we perverse love, we cannot help but be destroyed in the process. Love, in my view, is one force that gives us all purpose. I enjoy watching the 'budding' of love, as you stated, when you see people meet. I love witnessing the initial excitement of a first date or early romance. It is funny how your brain treats the beginning of love akin to a cocaine high."

He busts out laughing. "Cocaine! Are you serious? Explain that one."

"Well, really it does. Your brain has chemicals in it that are responsible for a number of things—for example, pleasure. So, when a person uses cocaine, these particular chemicals hang out in the brain longer than usual and at greater amounts. This makes a person feel extremely good. Love operates the same way in the beginning of a relationship."

"So," he says. "Are you telling me these people are high?" His pitch goes up.

"In a matter of speaking, yes, Conrado. They are ... high as a kite!" We both laugh.

"Okay, okay ... but I am assuming that you will eventually crash and not feel the high anymore," he says.

"Correct again. This is why it is so important for couples to recognize that relationships have transition periods. It is important they are able to see changes and to respond positively to those changes to keep the fire burning in their relationships."

"So, okay ... okay ... back to this brain thing. Does that mean the person no longer brings you pleasure when those chemicals disappear?"

Are we going to finish his story? I decide to entertain this interlude a bit longer and say, "No ... not disappear, but the type of chemicals in the brain changes. This change creates a bonding that strengthens the relationship. However, if we no longer feel that first high, then we will believe all is over, and we will not respect the transitions that relationships tend to experience," I explain. Then I transition back to the story: "So, is that what happened to this guy?"

"Oh ... yes! It was the loss of his love, because he had just left her funeral." The sadness came back to his face again. "He said that as he peered into the casket, all he could see was himself. He said he died that day. She took his heart with him. He vowed to never love again. I wish I could really share with you how tragic it was, but you had to be there. He was wearing *la muerte* like a heavy coat. He was broken."

"Like a heavy coat." I could feel the pain ease its way into my heart as I slowly repeated his words.

"Yes, it was heavy. As a man, it was not easy to see another man in such a broken state. I have seen lots of breakups, River. I've seen enough tears to equal the meaning of your name. However, there was something different about him. It was his fearlessness in being in that place in front of *everyone*. Exposed. He kept saying, 'I'm just a man' while staring at her photo, which was covered with his tears."

"That is a terrible story. I must admit that as I hear it, I can feel his pain through your retelling of it. I could not even imagine being there and bearing witness to it," I say.

"Yeah ... tragic, as you said," he says with a smile.

"Did you ever see him again?" I inquire.

"Yes, but there is good news in that story. He perks up as he goes on, but it is your turn—your story. What would your tragic story be, counselor?"

"My story?" My eyes widen. I am operating on my third glass of wine. I have to make sure I do not spill too much of my clients' private issues. "Ha! Well, I am not technically allowed to share the stories that I know."

"Okay … well give me yours," he persists.

I did not anticipate this. I raise my glass to my lips. Hell, why not? I sit there and reach for a place I vowed never to return to—a place where I struggled to breathe. A place where I could feel my blood pressure drop and my heart rate drop to the zone where a time of death could be called.

Why do I feel compelled to release this? I can feel a murmur return to my heart even as I contemplate repeating this to a total stranger. Maybe this is what my clients feel. There is safety in a person whom you do not know. Yet there is something dark within us that we all want to let go, and of course someone comes along and knocks on the door.

He waits patiently as if he can see the process my mind and heart must goes through. *A true counselor.*

"Okay … um, I remember there was a time I was home from work. I was doing some work on the computer. You know how you are watching TV, but not watching it at the same time?"

He nods.

"Well, it was on, and this movie was on. It was a movie about two women who were both unsatisfied with their lives. One woman fell for a guy while on vacation. She was telling him about her life as a kid. She was an only child, and when her parents divorced she was only eleven years old."

Drumming my fingers on the bar, I am trying to figure out which direction to tell this story. I can feel the welling of hurt.

"Well, she said that was the most painful part of her life. She said she'd never cried again since that time. She would never let anyone else get that close again. She said she and her parents were the three musketeers. They did everything together—and now nothing. Her entire life changed. She said if her parents' love could not be forever, then she could never love."

I inhale deeply.

Conrado leans forward, "Go on."

This guy is really pushing it. I look around to see if he has any other customers. Damn! No one. He is acting like I do in session.

"So ... they go to his house. Now remember, Conrado, I am kind of half listening. They meet his little girl. So, they build a fort and play around with her. They decide to lie down in the fort, as they were all tired from playing. They are all quiet briefly. The little girl, so innocently, says, 'We are just like the three musketeers!' At this part of the movie I look up and am giving it my full attention. Something grabbed me and made me watch this unfolding. Anyhow, you can see her go to a place that hurt her so deeply. Her eyes become dead ends, and she loses all color in her face. Her mouth falls open, as she is fully exposed to this child who is none the wiser to the scab she has ripped off this woman. So here it is, Conrado. At this point the man reaches for her fingers and interlocks them. He never even saw her face, because he was lying on his back, but he knew. He *connected* to her pain!" I say emphatically.

"Okay, but this is a movie. What does that have to do with you?" He looks confused.

"Well, I could not stop crying at this scene. I was sobbing. It was as if I was watching myself outside of myself and was confused by my own behavior. I instantly wanted my mother. I wanted her to soothe my heart by brushing my hair. It was at this time I realized that I had no connection—that no one was connecting to me. I realized exactly at that very moment how lonely a person I truly was. The worst part of it was that I was in a relationship at the time. I had never felt so lonely in my life. I was so busy with school and working that I never really paid any attention to it. I was able to cover it up. The pain never made its way to the surface. It was as if the cabin pressure had left the plane, and all the seats and people were being sucked out and hurled into the sky. It was something I could no longer ignore, Conrado. That was the moment my soul communicated with me. My soul was suffering from negligence. I had become a different person. I became aware of myself more fully, and I did not like what was there. I was without love—just duty. The lack of love, the lack of connection, and a life of obligation were killing my soul. My soul reached out to me that day."

Conrado is silent for a minute. He sits back and rubs his hand through his hair.

"It is still there isn't it, River? That disconnection you speak of?"

"Yes," I mumble. Then my eyes light up. "But! Something really strange happened to me a month ago. I met someone whom I wish I could really see again," I tell him.

"Tell me about him. I have a lot of experience with people who have missed connections. People will ask, 'Did you see this guy about yay tall?' Jeez, I wish they would just talk to each other when they have the moment," he sighs. "Carpe diem! Isn't that what they say?"

"The mere thought of him really just makes me come alive. That dead space becomes smaller just at the thought of possibility. Who knew the word *possible* holds so much power." I pause, and then I start in on my investigation. I can feel how wide my smile is. "I was here with my husband about a month ago."

"Wait, wait … the person is not your husband?" he asks.

"No. That is a different story. Let me tell you this. I am so excited. I'll get back to him. Okay … you ready, Conrado?"

"Si! Si!"

"Okay—why do I keep saying that? Okay." I start laughing. "I met him about a month or over a month ago. He was here with some friends. I noticed him, more like his energy. I felt strangely drawn to him.

"I was later leaving the bathroom, and I bumped into him. He caught me, and I knew it was the same man. I struggled to look up at him, and as his hands held my arms, they summoned me to fall into them. I looked into his eyes and could feel him through me. I felt connected, like I was supposed to know him. Like I already knew him."

Conrado looks taken aback. His looks me up and down with his mouth hanging open. He slowly states, "I cannot believe it … I just cannot believe it. This cannot be real. You met him about a month ago? You cannot be serious," he starts to laugh. "It is you! River, it is you!"

"What the hell are you talking about, Conrado?" Whoops! This third glass of wine has caught up to me.

"Okay, about two weeks ago the man I told you about came in here. He kept asking about a woman. That is not usual really, not at the bar," he says while shrugging. "What is unusual is that the very thing that you just described is what he described. He really did. As I look at you, it was you he described the whole time. My God, River. It is you. The man spoke of a woman who captured his heart without saying a word—a woman whom when he touched her, he was compelled to hold her forever. A woman he needed, I mean absolutely needed to find. He talked about the spiral of curl in her hair." He takes one of my locks and allows it to bounce back in place.

I do not even mind the momentary intrusion. I am lost. I am found. I am all of these things. I never thought that I would actually find him. He was elusive to me—something just out of my reach. He was the dream I could not quite capture to retell, and here this man is telling me that he wants to find me too—that he has been looking for me and has felt the same since we first touched.

Suddenly I feel lightheaded. But I need to focus, because I need to hear what Conrado is saying to me. He is still talking with expressions of disbelief.

"River, he said that the width of her—rather, *your*—smile was his Sunday morning. A day meant for rest. That you brought him rest. Can you believe that?"

I just nod. "Rest." I repeat with my mouth hanging open. "He brings me life."

"You are the ying," he says. "to his yang."

"I know," I say. "How is it possible to see a lifetime in a person you have … haven't spent a day with?" I clasp my hands on my face.

"Oh my *God*! It just hit me … *his wife died*? That was *his* story you told me?"

"Yes. He bought that up too. He said you bought him rest when he had none, that he knew everything was going to be okay again. He'd encounters with other women—stupid attempts, I guess, to dampen the pain left by the loss. You were not an encounter, according to him. You did not dampen the pain; you created new space for love and desire for life. This was not an encounter with you, River. It was … it is … destiny."

Tears come to my eyes, and I am not sure what type of tears they are. I am elated but also saddened at the pain in his heart, pain I now feel.

"River, he will be here in two days—Thursday, like clockwork, 7:45 p.m. Was that around the time you were here before? A Thursday at 7:45 p.m.? And do you think you can come?" His voice sounds hurried, anxious. He looks so hopeful, as if it were him I was coming to see.

He reads the expression on my face.

"I know. I know I must look excited, River. I am just happy to be part of something that seems pure. That seems true. That is destiny. You will tell this story, and I will forever be a part of it. The honor is all mine," he says as he places his hand on his heart.

"I will be here," I tell him as I bite my bottom lip. I know now that everything will change. Nothing will ever be the same. I have decided to step out on faith and enter the train of destiny. The train that forces one to relinquish all control and actually live. I glance at my watch—it is almost ten o'clock at night, and I begin to panic.

"I … I have to go. I cannot believe that it is almost ten o'clock at night. Jude has not called me once!" I say as I rise and gather my things.

"Jude? Oh, River … you owe me that story!" He says as he chuckles. "I really hope to see you Thursday—it is *our* destiny," he says emphatically.

"Yes! Yes, okay. Thank you, thank you!" I reach to hug him over the bar.

He embraces me and kisses me on the cheek. I whisper to him, "Thank you, Conrado, for standing in the hallway of destiny to help me open the door." He smiles, and with that I leave.

I run to the car and call Jude. On my first two attempts, the call just rings and then goes to voicemail. I text, "Jude. Where are u? I tried to call. Please answer."

I wait to see if he opens the text.

Read.

Hmm. No response? I call again. An agitated voice answers.

"Jude—hello? Can you hear me?"

"Yes. I hear you. Where are you?" he asks.

"I went back to that restaurant we went to about a month ago … the Spanish one. Remember?"

He chuckles—almost a sly chuckle. It does not match our discussion. I am so excited about Eoghan that I ignore it.

"Yes, River. Boy do I remember. What made you go out there?"

"Oh, nothing," I lied. "I just really liked it. I had some time and wanted to check it out again. I had a couple of glasses of wine and was talking to people. You know how it is with me. I turn into the neighborhood counselor no matter where I am. Time just got away." I wince at the end of my lie. I mean, it is sort of the truth. I had been talking ...

"Whatever, Riv. I'll see you when you get here," he says.

"Okay ... can you cook something to eat?" I ask.

"Sure, what do you want?"

"Anything. Okay, talk to you later," I say. I begin to put the phone down and hang up when I hear his lingering sentence.

"Wait a minute—you did not eat *at* the restaurant?"

Too late.

I disconnect.

11

SESSION 8: PANDORA'S BOX

It is three o'clock in the afternoon, and I am awaiting the Riley-Buttons. This day has been dragging, considering I am waiting to meet Eoghan tomorrow. I am just so anxious, and I cannot believe how slow time moves when one is anticipating something.

It is interesting how the perception of time changes depending on the incident. Time is not static. It is always moving forward, but its perception is very dynamic. It is a relative experience. We can anticipate something positive happening in our lives, and time will just seem to drag on. It will seem as if everything and everyone is moving slowly.

It also seems as if everyone knows that you are waiting for something and chooses to take their sweet time moving along. However, if we are anticipating something negative, time seems to fly right on by with no problem. You seem not to be able to get your bearings straight. You glance at the clock, and it seems that hours have jumped over each other, bypassing minutes.

Wanting something that's in the future can make us seem to lose the ability to respect the journey. We spend most of our time during this anticipatory stage chronically worrying about things that are out of our control.

This means we lose the gift of the present. We spend a good amount a time in the future or in the past. If only we could enjoy the current moment. This instant. If only we could process what is happening and savor it. How awesome that could be! How much more at peace we would all be.

The moment I am savoring is this feeling, the excitement of something that seems bigger than I am. It is almost physiological. There is a sense of belonging that I just *cannot* explain. He belongs to me, and I to him. I laugh at the thought. It is just ridiculous. Shaking my head, I walk toward the lobby, and there they are.

The Riley-Buttons.

As usual, they are seated apart. Joe is distracted. His eyes seem to wander at every woman who enters the room. It is not a normal kind of look you give people to acknowledge their presence. It is more of a sexual kind of look.

Belle has her head back on the sofa. She is looking up at the ceiling. I wonder what her thoughts are, considering our last phone call.

This is sure to come up in session today. I need to check my calendar. I am sure they will need more time. The discussion of how both of them were caught by Jasmine is certainly not going to go very fast.

I wonder if Belle will check out today at half past three as usual? I walk to Mahaley.

"Mahaley, dear?"

"Yes?"

"Do I have anyone scheduled after the Riley-Buttons? This may take a little more time today," I say.

"Hmm … no, ma'am. Not today. Yeah, you're right. They look like they have been through the ringer."

"Okay, thanks a lot."

I walk over to them. "Okay guys, come on in. I am looking forward to our session."

Their eyes meet and share a somewhat horrified expression. They walk with me toward my office.

With a slight smile, I about face and open the door.

I am not sure if I should mention the phone call from Belle, so I begin with, "So, where should we start? Seems like there has been a lot going on lately."

Belle and Joe are sitting in their usual spots and seem to fumble with their hands. Even their eye contact is erratic.

Belle gestures that she will begin. She is twisting her fingers around her slightly messy ponytail. She is in workout gear and takes advantage of its comfort by putting her legs up in the chair, hugging her knees.

"Our daughter, Jasmine. She … she … found out we both were seeing other people. She found out on the same day." Belle's voice begins to choke. "I just cannot believe it. I do not know what to do." Tears begin to slowly trickle down her face.

I switch my attention to Joe. His head is hanging low. His hands are keeping it from dropping into the abyss that regret resides in. His hands hold up what shame will not allow him to do.

"Okay, let's back up a bit. Take me to the day it all happened."

"Well, Joe will have to tell you his story. I can only tell you what Jazzy told me. It is better to start there," Belle sputtered out while looking at Joe. A look of quiet desperation is on her face. I highly doubt she will check out today, considering the pain she is experiencing now.

Joe raises his head slowly. His work clothes seem unusually clean. He does not look as though he has been out in the field. His eyes, his old eyes, suddenly deepen with an inevitable sense of loss of control.

Far too often we believe that we have control over things we actually do not have control over. This mere illusion gets us in webs so tangled and abysses so deep that we become like children when we realize that we lied to ourselves. We lied to ourselves about our ability to navigate situations we were never meant to be in. The delusions we hold only feed our egocentricity.

We become consumed by our perceived losses. We seek to fill them at all costs. The true issue is that we believe we have control over all the variables. That is the true tragedy. When we realize we cannot control everything, we begin to see the devastation left in the wake.

The Riley-Buttons have left devastation. All is not lost, however. Far too often we are caught up in our feelings of shame, which poison us, causing us to believe all is lost.

We must be willing to face the *thing*—the thing we all want to run from or cover up with all sorts of home remedies, such as liquor, sex, attention, gambling, drugs, eating, and all sorts of self-administered medicinal agents.

When we return to base, when we return *home*, only then can we fix the broken thing within us. I don't mean the home where you lay your head and eat your breakfast. I mean the home that is the core of who you are. The home that knows the *truth*—not the truth that we tell ourselves; that one is covered in self-deception. No, I do not mean that one.

The real truth is the one we face at three o'clock in the morning when we are alone. It is the one we choose to mask as part of our daily rituals, almost like brushing our teeth. We enact a ritual of justification, cover-up, denial, escape, projection—the list goes on.

When we decide to uncover and face the demons that live within us, only then can we be really free. Only then can we be liberated. We allow God in, who exposes those truths and sets us free. We can be embraced by the love of God, which buffers us from the pain of shame. Only then can we move forward. Other than this, we live life sentences in a self-imposed prison with the key locked inside the cell.

Joe sits up a little straighter and begins. "I did not go to work today, because I knew I would have to talk about this."

Belle lifts her head from her knees slightly and exposes one eye, which is focused squarely on Joe.

I appreciate his honesty. I tell him and ask, "Where did you go?"

"I went to the very park I was supposed to be at with Jazzy. I walked around and sat there for hours today. I just could not believe how selfish I was. I was so consumed by my own needs that I did not concern myself with hers. Belle's stuff ... Belle's stuff ... I cannot even speak on it yet. I just know that ... I betrayed that little girl in a way that is familiar. My mother betrayed me for the momentary affection of a man on a regular basis. I cannot believe I repeated the same pattern in my own life.

"I was supposed to take Jazzy to the park. Belle and I were arguing about money, I think. It seems so stupid now. I asked Jazzy if she wanted to go to the park and for ice cream. I suspected she was listening to us, so I wanted her to go. She said that she would. When she got in the car, I could not stop thinking about how I knew someone else who would be willing to keep me warm—someone who would tell me everything is okay and *make* everything okay … for a few minutes. I can drown in her for a moment and not see or feel anything real. The reality of my life is filled with pain. So, I went to her apartment. I knew I should not be there. I could feel myself being pulled back toward the car. Something kept making my steps heavy. My arms could barely lift to push the buzzer. Something told me to stop, but I just would not."

I glance over at Belle. It is half past three. She is not gone. She is present in this moment. The pain of her daughter has consumed her. She is not lost in the abyss of another but instead in the one who was created within her. I am happy about that.

She still has one eye on Joe, expressionless. She releases a sigh that signals exhaustion.

"So," Joe continues. "I give Jaz my phone to distract herself. I tell her that I will be only a few minutes. At least that was my intention. The time went by so fast. I … we heard a knock at the door. The first time Delilah peeked through the peephole, and no one answered. We thought nothing of it. The knock came again—three hard, forceful knocks. This time I decided I would answer. I thought it was kids acting up. I swung the door open, wearing just a—" Joe looks over at Belle apologetically and says, "Just a towel."

Belle's burrows her face in her knees.

Joe sighs but continues. "Jaz just looked at me. It felt like forever. I did not know what to say. She asked me why, and then she ran away. I was running after her until I remembered I was not dressed. I was wearing just a towel. Her face … I will never forget that. It was of disbelief. I came back to the apartment and tried calling my phone several times, trying to reach her. I called from Delilah's apartment, but her house phone comes up as 'Randy' on my phone. She never picked up. I started to get dressed to look for her. I guess Belle can pick it up from here."

Belle fits her chin in her knees, never looking up. She begins with, "I never, never, never want to hurt my daughter. She means everything to me. I cannot believe we both did this to her. Anyway, I guess she ran into a café when she was running from Joe. She saw me there with my friend. We were having coffee. I did not see her at all, but when the cashier called for croissants with apricot preserves for Jasmine, I looked up and met her eyes. She did the same to me. She said, 'Hi, Mom' and that … that was it. I was choking on my selfishness, and Jazzy ran out of the café."

"This may be a hard time for this, but we know Joe's counterpart. May we have the name of yours?" I ask.

Belle begins to form her mouth to say the name—the name that will become the physical manifestation of her infidelity.

Joe interrupts. "I do not want to hear his name. I just cannot handle that right now."

This confuses the both of us. I ask, "Why? So that I do not make assumptions based on my own experiences."

Far too often we make assumptions about others based on our own experiences. We see the world through lenses colored by our own lives. Unfortunately, this makes our interpretations of others distorted. We have to work as much objectivity as possible into understanding what is being brought before us. This means that we must not act on what we believe but we know.

"Because," Joe says. "I just do not want to know. I want to be in this place we are in right now. I need him to be nameless. I cannot let this break me by knowing who he is."

Nameless. That is pretty authentic of him. He is not only saying he wants him to be nameless, but he *needs* it. That is honest. That, I can respect.

Belle continues to rest her head on her knees.

I feel bad for them both. I understand they seem to be stuck and not know how to become unstuck or even if they want to be unstuck. What a confusing place to be. They will need to do some soul searching.

"I am just worried about how we have damaged her. How will she see relationships?" Belle begins to cry. She looks around the office—for tissue, I presume. I pull my chair near her, gently reminding her that she needs to go ahead and experience this pain. She needs to allow it to unfold so she can deal with it.

Joe gets up to sit next to her. He pulls her to his side for her to lean against him. She initially refuses but surrenders.

"I understand that you both are probably worried about how this will impact Jasmine, and I am glad that you are, actually. I would be more concerned if you were not. As you know, we are the first role models for our children for everything. This includes relationships. They see how we are with one another, and then they either will emulate us or completely do the opposite. Therefore, it is imperative that you fix this situation with Jasmine." I look at both of them, but they cannot look back at me.

"She will need support from *both* of you. Now, the desire to see other people is something that you guys will have to work out. You will need to determine what the rules are regarding your relationship and abide by those rules or change them."

Both sit quietly, as if they are siblings who just got cussed out by their parents.

"Now, as it pertains to Jasmine, has either of you spoken with her about this?"

"Yes and no," Belle replies.

"What does that mean?" I ask.

"We pulled her aside when Mr. I'm-Going-to-the-Freakin'-Park came home," she says as she rolls her eyes.

Joe looks at her incredulously. "Really, Belle? Really? You got something to say?"

"I'm just sayin'! I did not lie to her and tell her I was taking her to the park and then actually took her to some chick's house that I doin'," she says and actually laughs. It's not the kind of laugh in response to something actually humorous but more the laugh of disbelief and slight disgust.

"Mr. and Mrs. Riley-Buttons, you both failed your marriage, each other, and Jasmine. The faster you acknowledge that, the better you will be. You can decide if you are going to go further in this process. Spending time blaming one another about whose infidelity is greater is a waste of time. The difference is what happens from here! What do you want?" I ask emphatically.

"I will be honest, River, I just do not know. I have so much pain in my heart that I do not know if it can heal. The place I am in, as it pertains to this marriage, is dark. My heart feels like a box of matches in a tub of water. There is no way that it can light up." Belle throws her hands in the air.

Joe's head is to the ceiling. "I just do not know what I am doing anymore. I am just a buoy without purpose, without destination."

I look back and forth between them. "No way it can light up, Belle, or is your heart floating in the Dead Sea? A purposeless and directionless buoy, Joe? Your marriage seems to be in the Dead Sea—a sea that cannot sustain life. Bear with me through these examples, guys. It will make sense soon.

"Many times during surgery a person's heart will stop. One would believe that it is time to stop the clock and pull the sheet over a warm lifeless body. However, the surgeon knows better. He or she will compress the heart with one or both hands, preferably both, at a rate of sixty to seventy times a minute. The goal is to maintain circulation of the blood to the brain. Imagine you have to count on yourself during such a time. Imagine you are lying on that cold table, Belle and Joe. Life is becoming a past tense. There are people all around you, and all it takes is that one person willing to go all in—that one person willing to take the most delicate part of you and squeeze it. The most delicate part of you is the part that exchanges something useless, such as deoxygenated blood, and restores it to the life force it has always had the possibility of becoming. The massaging of the heart reminds it that it *is* alive, that it has *more* time, and that if fails to beat, it has to return to the earth. Has someone massaged either of your hearts? Are you alive and just dead to each other? Are you willing to massage each other's hearts?" I ask, pleading for their connection.

There is a long silence. Belle looks at her watch—3:54 p.m.—and she looks disappointed. A deep sigh slowly leaves her. She runs her hands through her hair.

Joe looks to her. A look of adoration followed by grief crosses his face momentarily.

They are stuck. They are stuck in a sea of uncertainty, a sea of not knowing if they want to even want their relationship anymore. There are traces of hope. That is all one needs. A trace.

"I will let you guys think about this for the next session. You will need to have a response the next time we meet. You cannot continue to hold each other hostage, because familiarity has got you captive. Let's do more work next week."

They look relieved. I smile and walk them to the door.

I walk slowly to the car. I think of the one more day I have to wait until I see him, the one day until I sense the magnetic field that draws me to him. There is something I just cannot place, something that energizes me. I bite my lip and smile in anticipation of the experience. I suddenly realize that I have been lost in this mental space for more than a few moments. I am standing at my car, holding the car handle, with a smile across my face.

"River! Dr. Meadows!" I snap out my trance. It is Mahaley. "Are you okay?" she asks. "I just saw you standing there. I came out here to tell you that your husband said he was not going to be home when you get there. He just called. You just missed him. He said something about a finance managers meeting. He asked that you pick him up something on the way home."

"Mahaley, is that a cigarette in your hand?"

Sheepishly, she puts her cigarette hand behind her back and giggles. "Sorry, Dr. Rivers, it is. Anyhow … yes that's his message."

"Thanks, Mahaley. I'll see you later—tomorrow, actually." I smile pleasantly in an attempt to disguise my irritation. I have to pinpoint what I am upset about. Am I upset because she interrupted my daydream or because I do not believe Jude? I suspect it is a little of both.

I sit in the car and turn on the radio; the playlist titled - love.

Yes, I can immerse myself in this.

12

JUDE'S TIE

"I called her already, sweetie," Jude says as he circles his fingers around the steering wheel of his car. Jude feels a pang of anxiety as he looks at the phone to insure that he has disconnected the practice.

"Yes, yes … I can see you tonight. I am on my way to the office. Come by there. Jezzy, Jezzy, Jezebel! Sweetheart, I am on my way. Stop rushing me. Yes, I miss you too. Okay, see you soon. Muah!"

He cannot wait to see her. He starts to think about her to himself: *That girl knows she can please a man. Not that River is bad; it just is not enough. She always gotta work or is upset because of something. I don't feel like dealin' with that shit. I'm a damn man. I want more. I want all I can get. Hell, I'm getting older—better work it out while it still works!*

Damn this forty-five-minute ride. Well, playlist time.

A voice on the radio sings "ninety-nine problems, but a bitch ain't one." Jude chuckles. "Yea, a bitch ain't one," he whispers to himself.

River is good for a few things, Jude's inner monologue continues. *I mean, she is hella smart. I like her company, but she wants too much. I cannot keep trying to meet her expectations. That day at the park, I just thought we were going to be kinda cool, and that's it. Hell, what happened? How did I end up married to her? I woke up to forever, when I thought it was going to be just for a little while. I feel my eyes open wide at the sheer thought of forever.*

What is actually forever? Nothing lasts. Nothing good stays around. That is such a lie people sell themselves. That is all I do all day—I sell fantasies. People have dreams, and the cars I sell become part of those dreams, part of people's belief in who they would like to be. It is the image—the mask we wear every day. All I need to understand is what mask you wear, and I got you. Dudes are the easiest. Usually, their car is an extension of their "lil man."

Jude throws his head back and laughs out loud at his own private joke. *They buy for "her." Any "her" will do. It is all about status to most of us. Women eat that crap up too.*

Now with her, it can be a combination. She wants to be sexy, look smart, or look family oriented. I just need to know which one.

An annoying ring interrupts his train of thought. "I really need to change that," he says aloud. "Hmm ... who is this? I don't know this number." He answers it. "Umm, hello?"

"Jude?" a female voice on the other end says hopefully.

"Yes, this is Jude. How can I help you? Did I sell you a car?"

"No, dear. You did not," the voice responds. "I gave you a life."

"What? Who? Who are you?" Jude's right hand is shaking.

"It's your mother, Jude," the voice says, trembling. "Your father passed away last night. Somebody needed to call you."

Jude drops the phone, swerving the steering wheel, which causes him to drift into oncoming traffic. He pulls over to the shoulder and stares out the windshield.

"Hello? Hello?" a faint voice from the phone cries. "Jude? Hello? Answer!"

Jude takes a breath. Robotically, he reaches for the phone. "Yes, mother. I need to call you back."

Jude drives the rest of the way to the dealership in silence, trying to sort out feelings. He needs to find them, figure out what to do with them. As he gets closer to the dealership, his mood shifts back to the pending pleasure-seeking session with Jezzy.

"I need not to feel anything, and I know just the person to help me with that," he says out loud.

As he pulls in the driveway, he sees the familiar little sporty Mazda. Jezzy. He waves to her. She beckons him to her, biting her lower lip.

Boy, won't he be surprised when all I am wearing is the tie he left over here last week, she thinks to herself.

Jude walks to the car, each step slower, heavier. He attempts to push back his mother's conversation on the telephone and concentrates on disappearing from all things that matter for a little while. Needing this momentary high, he climbs in and wipes his eyes with the palms of his hands.

"I see you are ready."

"I am always ready for you," she responds.

He looks around, making sure he is properly hidden from public view.

He touches the tie. It is blue with small white squares and slightly textured. River bought him this tie. He remembers. She bought this for him when he got his promotion.

Jezebel, sensing something is different, asks, "What is wrong, baby? What is wrong, Jude?"

He rubs the tie with his between his finger and thumb, slowly increasing his grip. "Come here. I need this *now*," he says, barely audible. He pulls the tie, yanking her in his arms.

A small gasp escapes her mouth.

13

THE CONSTRUCTED REPRESENTATIVE LIVES

"Jazzy, can we talk?" Belle calls over the kitchen counter. Jasmine sits at the table with one ear plug in, bobbing her head and pretending not to hear her.

"Jazzy! We need to talk!" Belle says.

Jasmine lifts her head, raises one eyebrow, and looks back down.

Frustrated, Belle leaves the kitchen and yells up the stairs.

"Joe! Joe! Come down here. We have talk to Jaz." *I cannot keep up this silent treatment*, she thinks to herself.

Jasmine, captured by the byproduct of betrayal, bobs her head to the sound of nothing. Her mother believed the staged front of listening to music, but she had actually been looking at a photograph of her family at the park. Her grandmother had captured the candid image. She traces their smiles with her finger. She remembers the bellowing laughter of the day. There was a quality of oneness about them then that she has not seen in a long time. The picture captured a reality that did not exist—a reality that was manufactured for the benefit of outsiders.

Her family is "the great pretender," one might say. We all pretend at times—some more than others. Many times we do not even know that we are pretending, which is the most dangerous. Johari's Window speaks to this very concept. A window, typically has four panes. These four panes, symbolic of our lives, are not equal in size. The extent of your self awareness determines the size of each pane.

The first pane is what we know about ourselves and what others do not know about us. This pane is about the secrets we keep from others. It is composed of the constructed representative. The second pane covers what others know about us but we do not know about ourselves. This pane is demonstrative of the blind spots about ourselves. These are things our friends are willing to tell us to help us understand where we are going wrong or need developing. The third pane is what we know about ourselves and what others know about us. This pane is actually the healthiest pane. You are living an authentic life when this pane is the largest. You can be who you are unapologetically. You can be who you are without hurting others. You will live a full life. You do not need a representative. You have arrived at this point. This fourth pane is the most damaging to our lives. It is the black hole of panes, the pane that can consume us and rob us of an authentic and liberating life. It is the pane of what we do not know about ourselves and what others do not know about us. This is the most damaging pane, as we are not even aware of why we think as we do. We do not know why we behave as we do. We act largely like animals, seemingly instinctual. However, in actuality, we are marionettes. The puppet master is our destructive past. It is the pattern of emotional and relational instability symptomatic of the infection that is unresolved trauma.

How does one remove the infection, you ask? Simply begin by acknowledging its existence. Sometimes we need the help of a professional in order to weed out the destructive parasite that lives within our hearts.

****

Peering out the window, I am able to see Jude pull up. It is after midnight. It took the strength of Samson to keep me awake. I am interested in his lie.

He sure is taking his sweet time getting out of the car. I can see him through the streaks of rain that have kissed the windshield.

He is slowly getting out of the car. Leaning against the car, he is running his hands through his hair. My anger begins to dismantle as I sense that something is wrong. This is not how he is. This is not his usual way of being. I am not too happy about my anger dissipating; sometimes I want to be able to discharge it.

My spirit of compassion does not allow me to wallow in anger. I walk into the kitchen and pull out a glass of wine to prepare for both of us. Apparently, there is something I need to learn about and help him with.

It is so quiet I can hear a pin drop. I only realize this because I cannot hear my own breath. I begin to realize that I am holding my breath. Why am I holding my breath?

The lock slowly twists, preparing me to receive the world of hurt I suspect.

"Hey, sweetie," he says dryly.

"Hey what is going on? Are you okay? I can tell something is wrong." I hand him the glass of wine.

Jude brushes past me and sits. He leans back and closes his eyes.

"My father died today."

"What are you feeling?" I ask.

"Like the bastard I always knew I was," he says flatly.

Wow. Such a simple sentence holds so much power. I know exactly what he means.

Jude has never had a relationship with his father. His father fathered multiple children with multiple women. His father never learned the concept of commitment for anything; he couldn't even commit to the extension of himself—his seed.

I sit and reflect on his pain. His eyes are closed, and soon he will be asleep. He is the direct reflection of his pain. Jude does not realize that his life's record has a scratch. He does not realize it continues to replay the same song over and over again. He commits to nothing yet wants everything to commit to him.

I sigh and sip my wine. I think of Eoghan. What is on the other side of this? It is exciting to think there is something more … possibly. The sheer thought of a possibility is exciting—the sheer thought that I might see what is on the other side of myself just by meeting him.

Yet, I see him, Jude, sitting here. He is the safe bet—he will always be dependable in doing the same things, even though they are horrible things. He cannot hurt me anymore. I have become acclimated to his level of pain, and I am numb.

To feel the electricity of Eoghan would be a reminder of the deep wound that was ripped open when I watched that movie so many years ago—the movie that reminded me that my soul was dying.

He will never do right by me. We are only holding spaces for reasons unknown.

****

Tomorrow is the day, at 7:45 p.m. I cannot wait.

My mind switches to my clients, the Riley-Buttons. I wonder how they are doing. They called the office earlier and said they were going on a family vacation and would not be back for a session for at least three weeks. They are trying to smooth over a crisis—who knows, it just might work!

Anyhow, back to tomorrow … what shall I wear? I smile slowly.

Wait! Jude! I'll see if he needs me and then go from there. He'll probably cover it up with alcohol and say he has a meeting so he can meet whomever it is this time. I shake my head at his need to constantly violate us.

I am the bigger problem, though. Hell, I know he'll never change.

I will support him through his pain. However, I need to decide what to do with mine.

14

THE FLINT'S STONE

The next day goes so, so slowly. I can feel myself pushing my clients along as if I could really rush the day along. I am so nervous. I am sure my clients have been a little confused, as I had very little to say and ended some sessions early. I chuckle at my ploy to rush the day. I mean it still only means I can leave fifteen minutes early, which is not much prep time.

Considering I am a planner, I decide to bring a change of clothes with me. A simple black cocktail dress will do.

It is 6:45 p.m. I run to the restroom and change my clothes. I check in with Jude, and he appears to be okay. He says he's decided to work late—whatever that really means.

I can barely get to my car fast enough. Mahaley runs behind me—I know because I can hear her voice calling me. I ignore the first two calls. I am afraid it will be an emergency. I am not prepared to hate whomever this emergency person is. At her third call, I turn swiftly around.

"Yes?" I almost yell.

This stops Mahaley in her tracks. "Oh, sorry, River! I mean Dr. Meadows. I wanted to make sure you were okay. You ran out so fast that you forgot your purse on the counter."

I apologize for such abruptness. "I am sorry. I am a little all over the place." I hug her. "Have a good evening. Lock everything up."

"I always do … I always do," she says as she hugs me back.

The drive seems to last forever. I mean absolutely forever. I cannot even listen to music. I need my head. I need to calm myself. There is a symphony playing in my heart. There is a tsunami happening in my mind. There is a cataclysmic event happening in my entire body. Bottom line: I'm a little nervous.

I pull up to A Prima Vista. The building seems bigger. It is intimidating. As I approach, I cannot seem to keep objects in my hand: I drop my purse, keys, lipstick, and change as I walk toward the door.

I am twenty minutes early, thanks to a brick otherwise known as my foot on the gas. I wanted to be early. I wanted to have time to remember to breathe. I spot Conrado at the bar and brush past the hostess. He smiles a grin so wide I believe that I can no longer see his face. It is pure joy that I see. I smile knowingly and offer a quick wave. He beckons me to come to the bar.

"River, River … you beautiful woman!" he says as he comes around the bar and offers a hug.

I embrace him. It is so crowded tonight. Even though it is crowded, I can still feel the mystery that is to come.

"I am excited to see you too, Conrado!" I say with a laugh as I rock side-to-side, hugging him like a friend I haven't seen in twenty years.

"I am so nervous, Conrado!"

"Me too, me too!" he says as he laughs. "Okay, get a table. I will bring you … a Riesling?"

"Yes, good memory!"

He finds me a wonderful table in the corner of the restaurant. It is dimly lit, but the baroque wallpaper is worn and faded. It has seen better days. It seems like a table that has witnessed the magic of love being emitted by the people it hosts.

Will I ever see her again? Eoghan thinks yet again to himself. He is on his weekly drive to A Prima Vista in the hopes of even getting a glance of her caramel skin.

He hopes to smell a hint of her—the flowers God meant to decorate the Earth with which seem to emit so naturally from her.

This is ridiculous, Eoghan thinks to himself. *I keep going back there.*

Everyone keeps telling me how dumb this shit is. I am drawn there, just cannot help it. I will meet her. I will know her.

This feels as though it is bigger than I am. I am supposed to know her. She is supposed to know me. The God in me needs to be reunited with the God in her.

"Dammit! It is crowded!" Eoghan curses aloud.

No matter, Eoghan's thoughts continue. *I appreciate Conrado, anyway. He always has been good to me. He has always lent me an ear when all I wanted to do is drown in my sorrow. I'll go in and do my weekly inquiries about her.*

Eoghan decides to wait in line for valet.

Conrado changes the table setting and sits River's drink in front her.

I am so excited to be a part of this, Conrado thinks to himself as he walks back to the bar. *This man deserves to meet her. Love is such an elusive thing, yet it is available to all. It's all around us, yet like the pollen falling on a breezy fall day, it is difficult to grasp.*

I have seen friendship, lust, and love all in the same moment, but this one is different. This one is destiny. To be part of something that is orchestrated by something greater than both individuals is an awesome thing. This is the kind of story that gets handed down to your descendants.

It reminds people that despite all the material things in the world, despite all the troubles and distractions, something as fundamental as true love is alive and constantly waiting to be discovered.

Eoghan walks into the foyer of the restaurant. *The colors look richer today*, he thinks to himself. *Is there a holiday, some event going on? Why is it so crowded today?*

Eoghan catches a glimpse of his reflection and chuckles. He thinks to himself, *I cannot believe I am always doing this—searching for this soul I do not know and wondering if I will ever lay eyes on her again.*

Walking toward the bar, Eoghan looks for Conrado.

Conrado catches a glimpse of Eoghan and waves him over.

"Hey, man! What's up? Why you grinning like that?" Eoghan asks with a laugh.

"Are you ready for a moment that you will never forget?" Conrado asks.

"Man, what are you talkin' about? Moment? You know why I am here. Let me get a glass of cabernet."

Conrado hands him the glass and nods to the corner of the restaurant.

Eoghan loses his breath for a moment. He has to catch himself as everyone in the room disappears: he can see only her. He watches her profile as she lifts the rose from the small unassuming vase. She rubs the velvet petals against the slight upswing of her nose.

"My God," Eoghan says, barely getting the words out.

"I know. Go to her," Conrado whispers to him.

"Wait, I need to watch her for a moment. I need to have this all to myself … if just for a moment," he responds.

Eoghan absorbs the vision before him. The light perfectly causes her hair to glisten. She is biting her lip and tracing her fingers along the rim of her wine glass. She leans her head back and begins to smile. *What is she thinking? Is she waiting for me? I have always been waiting for her. I can feel her now. She may not be looking this way, but the spirit in me knows the spirit in her. The spirit in her knows that I am here.*

"Go to her," Conrado's insistence breaks Eoghan's internal dialogue.

As Eoghan walks toward the table, each step becomes lighter. Each breath becomes shallower. His mind is focused and confused at the same time. He cannot seem to process this moment as something he can understand in language. Her eyes are still closed, and she is still leaning her head back with a slight smile. He cocks his head to the side in curiosity. What is she dreaming of? He is behind her now. As he begins to lean toward her right ear, River abruptly sits up. Eoghan stops mid-lean, holds his breath.

He is here, she thinks to herself. *I can feel him. I can smell him. The electricity generated by the trillions of cells in his body is short-circuiting me. I cannot move. I cannot breathe. I can hear nothing but my heart. The dub-dub is deafening. I dare not turn.*

Eoghan smiles. *She knows I am here*, he thinks to himself. He continues to lean forward. Closing his eyes, he pulls her hair away from her ear and whispers, "Hello, beautiful."

Eoghan swiftly stands, taken aback by just touching her again.

She bites her lip. Panic ensues, followed by an unfamiliar calm. *His voice is a melody to me*, she thinks. *The vibration of sound generated by his words sings a song as it twirls in the cochlea of my ear.*

She starts to turn around to lock eyes with the brown-eyed soul she has been thirsting for.

"Not yet. Do not turn around just yet. Let me have this moment. Let us have this moment. I want to continue to experience the mystery of you and you of me. I want only a few senses operating now. The sense of sight dulls the others, and this is a moment we will never have again. Let's savor it, like tasting a meal after a long fast," he says.

She instantly complies. Turning around, she shudders. *Who is this guy? Who is he?* she thinks to herself.

He kneels behind her, taking a lock of her hair and tucking it behind her ear. She can feel his breath. He is breathing slowly. Tears well up in an anticipation of his next touch.

"You intoxicate me, River. You intoxicate, and I haven't even had the pleasure of consuming you. You somehow infiltrated my being with your energy when I ran into you a while ago. I have not been the same ... and I suspect neither have you," he whispers in her right ear.

Her breath is heavy as his words continue to play a melody in her ear. She can feel his lips gently caress her earlobe with an occasional brush.

"No ... no, Eoghan. I have not been the same. You have been on my mind, and I felt compelled to see you again. Not because I wanted to—because I needed to," she says with her back still turned to him.

"I can feel your smile, Eoghan. I can sense the energy from you, which has passed through every barrier that I have ever erected as if it were water easily making its way, not *forcefully* but without hesitation or recognition of obstacles. Water does not recognize obstacles."

She is surprised she can even say that much. The anticipation of seeing him and just being is making her feel crazy.

"You are a living lyrical poem, with language of indirection that only I can decipher. I know this without knowing you. There is language beyond words, River—a language of the spirit."

A small gasp enters River's lungs as her eyes widen. She says, "I know this. I know that although the flesh of me has just met the flesh of you, the souls that inhabit our bodily temples in this temporary realm know each other well. They were separated by death in another time, only to be reunited and recognized as the counterparts of the other."

What are these words that are leaving my mouth? River thinks to herself. *I do not recognize myself.*

"My God, where have you been all my life?" he says in quiet desperation.

"Waiting. I wanted to see you. Will you sit down with me," River asks.

"No, will you *stand* with me?" he responds.

He pulls her chair back for her to stand. She slowly rises and turns to him. They stand, watching each other, for what seems like hours. He grabs her hand and pulls her to him. "Come back to me," his voice says, cracking with emotion.

Her face is within inches of his. She can feel the anticipation that exists within the crevasse dividing them. The world they know as individuals will no longer exist the moment they become one. She cannot take this any longer.

"What are you doing, Eoghan? Are you going to kiss me?"

He chuckles.

He takes his hand and, with his fingers, gently brushes her face. "Close your eyes. Not yet, beautiful. Can you feel this? There is something so beautiful about being so close to you but not consuming your kiss."

The room is full of people, but River hears no one. It feels as though no one else is there. The sounds of the world are drowned. She can only hear the sound of his nervous breath.

Holding River's hand to his chest, Eoghan laughs. "I can feel your heart beating, River. Are you nervous?"

"Yes," she manages to whisper. She looks up to him. "We are standing in the middle of a restaurant. We must look crazy."

"Yes, we do," he whispers in her ear. We do look crazy. But they all envy us. They envy this moment we are having. How many people get an opportunity to return to their counterpart?" He pulls his head back, opens his eyes for a moment, and smiles. "I may not be Greek, but this is close to it. I should not be so familiar with someone I do not know. We are more powerful together. Don't you feel the energy in this space now?" he whispers.

Return to their counterpart? River thinks to herself. She remembers the myth. According to Greek mythology, humans were originally created with four arms, four legs, and a head with two faces. Fearing their power, Zeus split them into two separate parts, condemning them to spend their lives in search of their other halves.

It wasn't quite a laugh, but the sound of delight leaves River. "You found me."

"We found each other," Eoghan says. "We were drawn irresistibly to each other."

With that, Eoghan leans forward and ever so softly kisses her lips. "Welcome home, love."

His kiss wakes up a trillion cells that have been dormant. She feels more alive than she ever has in her life. As soon as they kiss, they both open shocked eyes in a feeble attempt to understand. Electricity is increasing and pulsating, exchanging power—the positive to the negative and the negative to the positive. The dead battery from the remote of life has been replaced. They both laugh at the experience without having to even talk about it. Eoghan beckons for Conrado, who has the biggest possible grin. His face must hurt. He has been watching this exchange the whole time.

Conrado practically skips over, and they all laugh. With tears in his eyes, them hugs us both. "You guys have given me faith in something I had lost faith in—the idea that something as beautiful such as true love can be real. The idea that you met at A Prima Vista is just cosmic. 'At first glance' is the translation of the restaurant's name, River. You loved at the first glance. Do you understand this?"

Eoghan pulls River closer to him. "Yes, I do," he says as he brushes his cheek against River's.

She cannot handle his touch. It raises the hair on her body! She turns to Conrado and asks, "So, Conrado … can you get us a bottle of wine and a menu? We have lots of catching up to do. We have been apart … a lifetime."

"Oh yes! I am so glad to be a part of this. You must invite me to the wedding!" he jests.

"Of course," they both chime in and then look at each other.

What is happening? River thinks to herself. *What is leaving my mouth? I cannot remotely understand where any of this is coming from, but it feels natural to me. It is the knowledge that is within me—the knowledge that is part of the collective unconscious of love that all humans have the capacity to give and yearn for.*

They sit for what seems like days, sharing every aspect of their lives—their hopes and dreams, their love and tragic stories. They share the complete and incomplete anthologies of life. Roberta Flack's song "Killing Me Softly" plays in the background. How appropriate. "Killing me softly with his song, telling my whole life with his words," she sings. This is magic. This *is* magic.

Eoghan listens with intensity as River describes her marriage with Jude. She searches his face for a trace of irritation or confusion. He does not provide a drop. He looks actually relieved for some reason.

What an odd expression, she thinks to herself. *After I explained that Jude's father just passed, Eoghan looked lost. This lights up on my radar—a small alarm goes off in my heart. I have no time for this right now. This I will not lose.*

Eoghan tells River that he is dating someone and that they are close.

"Is it serious?" River asks.

"No. It is not serious. I care for her."

"But, do you love her?" River asks.

"I could."

River feels sick. Eoghan reaches for her hand. "Baby, there is not a word to describe what this is. This is uncommon. This is too big for such a word that mere humans use so loosely. This is a gift. We will have many loves in our lifetimes. Only one will become the definition of love. This one will set the standard for everyone else. This one you will love for all time and will bring pain and glory to your life. Only surpassed by Christ and all His glory, this one will inspire you to heights of greatness and also have the ability to bring profound lows of despair," he says looking deep into her eyes.

He continues, "The amazing part of this is that you know the risk, and you take it anyway. River … you are that definition. I know that, without doubt. I know I am that for you too. The people in our lives are not barriers to who we are destined to be. Do you notice I have not asked if you love Jude? Of course you do. This is not something I feel threatened by. What is for me will always be for me. Nothing can stand in its way. Do not ever feel threatened. Let us be us. It will all come." River looks to him and believes.

****

Eoghan walks me to my car and places a kiss on my forehead and softly on my lips.

The drive home is hypnotizing. While driving, I listen to my "love" playlist, and Roberta Flack happens to be next. I want to close my eyes, but I am driving.

So, I sing.

The first time ever I saw your face, I thought the sun rose in your eyes …

Your face
Your face
Your face

My head is spinning. I feel intoxicated. Well … I just might be, after all that wine! I think of Conrado and how I thanked him immensely for being the bridge to us. He hugged me when I was leaving and thanked us for helping him believe in something so beautifully pure.

We make love so complicated. There is nothing complicated about love. Humans are complicated. Love is pure. It does not care for social rules. It cares only for itself. It is selfish—meaning, it only wants to grow, express, and give itself. Humans complicate it by adding toxic ingredients to it. We add experiences, ego, past, trauma, and poor models to the mix. What was once love is no longer. It becomes a reflection of something darker within us. Once so transparent, it becomes murky.

I look at my phone, something I have been ignoring for the past two hours. Jude has called at least ten times. At the light, I look at his text messages. Ah! No emergency. He is going to be later than he originally thought. That is okay. I put the phone down and am lost again in Eoghan. I pull up in the driveway and see the lights are on in the house.

I start to feel heavy as the cloud I am on seems to descend into reality. The idea that when I turn this key it will be all over is painful. I know this is not true, though, as Eoghan and I made plans to see each other next week.

The click of the key is so loud. I take a deep breath and walk in. Jude is lying on the couch.

"Where you been?" he asks. "I went to get something to eat," I respond. I ask about his father and what he plans to do.

"I just don't know, River. I don't want to care, but something in me does." He leans his head against my shoulder. "These are dark times, River. I do not even fully know why, but I know it." He looks up to me. "You know what I mean?"

"I do not know if the times are dark, Jude, or if it's just that the illusions we are consistently perpetrating will be destroyed—the illusions that we have become comfortable in. Sometimes we run from the light, because the illusion begins to define who we are, and to lose the illusion is to lose ourselves. Unfortunately, that itself is an illusion, as it never was who we were destined to be."

Jude smiles. "That is why I love you. You have such a way with words."

"You had a father, Jude. Whether or not you had a dad is irrelevant. You have to determine if you are willing to live with regret in your heart. You have to determine if you want to do what your ego wants or the honorable thing. I love you, and I say put the ego down. Embrace the pain of losing the dad you never really had and the finality of never having reconciling that relationship."

Jude falls in my lap and sobs. I run my hand in his hair.

"You need this, Jude. You have to let go of the pain of it all."

There are people who are supposed to play certain roles in our lives, be they mothers, fathers, sisters, brothers, grandparents, or others. We all have prescribed ideas of what each relationship should look like. Unfortunately, the human beings in these relationships operate according to their own ideas, traumas, and belief systems, which can destroy the truth in these bonds. What is "supposed to be" never really *is*. When we learn to stop reaching for love that will never be returned, our hearts become harder, dimmer, and more cynical to the world. We begin to believe that we do not care for the love lost or love never returned. So, we bury it. It is okay to grieve what was never there. That is the beginning of releasing the bondage.

This next week has been simply amazing for me. I have spent nearly every day with Eoghan. I have canceled out part of my days in order to spend more time with him. We have been inseparable. The days have been a whirlwind. I cannot concentrate on anything else. I am drunk on him.

I feel bad when I leave home early in the morning just to have coffee with him. My early runs have turned into early coffee runs to see the sunrise with the love of my life.

We sit in silence in the hour after half past six in order to watch the light of the world lift above, gracing us with the elements we need for existence.

My head rests on his shoulder. Is this real? I fear this is akin to the brightest burning star. Most think the sun is the brightest star in the sky. We believe it is the brightest because it is the closest. However, Deneb is much farther from Earth than most of the other stars you see, and this giant is around one hundred thousand times brighter than the sun.

Deneb pays a precious price for shining so brilliantly. It is using up its stellar fuel at a furious rate, and it will burn itself out faster than the sun. It is sad that at some point it will die a spectacular death.

Are we Deneb? Are we shining so brightly and furiously that we will die quickly? I most certainly hope not.

15

SESSION 9: BELLE CROSSES A RIVER

I have been having difficulty concentrating on my clients since Eoghan has been in my life. I do not even mind that Jude has been having multiple "meetings" at all hours of the night.

I have missed Belle and Joe during these three weeks they took off in order to get their house in "order." I look out to the lobby, and Joe is sitting in his usual spot, dressed in work boots and fresh out-of-the-concrete wear. I study his face. He looks perplexed. I feel a bit sorry for him. How hard it must be to want something so badly that is in front of you, but you cannot seem to grasp it. Belle has a messy up-do, glasses falling toward the peak of her slightly pointed nose. She seems preoccupied. Her usual mess of papers surrounds her. She looks up to the ceiling, rubbing her eyes—stress maybe? She rises, walking toward the bathroom. I have to shelter myself to avoid being seen. She is crying. I see the tracks of tears on her face. What is going on?

I go to the bathroom quietly and let myself in. I can hear her controlled cry in the stall. She is sputtering, "Where are you?" over and over again. I cannot tell if she is on the phone.

I slip out of the bathroom and wait for Belle to return to the waiting room. I am not sure if I am going to talk about her crying. I have to play the session out and see if it feels right.

"Riley-Buttons?" I call out as if I did not know they are here.

They come and sit in their usual spots. Belle looks withdrawn. I can understand, considering she is probably in the same mental when she was in moments before.

I sigh and smile at them. "Well, it has been some time, huh, guys? You must tell me what the last three weeks have been like. What is going on with Jasmine?"

Joe starts. "Well, there is a lot to tell you, River."

"Okay, where would you like to start?" I ask as I glance over at Belle.

"We took Jasmine to Montana. We wanted to spend time with her— not just any time. We needed her to see that we are strong." He amplifies those last words while looking over at Belle.

"Wow! Montana. How was it?" I ask.

"It was great. We were at the Absaroka Mountain Range." We camped and stayed in cabins," he responds.

"Okay … that sounds great. How did the experience impact the three of you?"

"Did you want to talk, Belle?" Joe asks.

"Go ahead, Joe. I will jump in," she says. She never looks up.

Agitation washes over Joe's face. I kind of want Joe to answer the question. I want his perspective without input from Belle.

Joe rubs his hands over his concrete-dusted work pants and sighs.

"Okay, well … I think it helped *all* of us. We were able to spend uninterrupted time with one another. There were times that Belle seemed lost, at least to me. Jasmine seemed to have a lot of fun. She liked having her parents together, not just in the same room but interacting. At least, that is my take on it. What do you think, Belle?"

"I agree. I mean she was actually *watching* us. It was as if roles were reversed," she says with a laugh.

"What do you mean?" I ask.

"Well, I mean most of the time, we are watching our children. We make sure they are okay. We look for little nuances in their behavior to make sure they are safe and okay. I could tell she was watching us in the same way. It was kinda funny. Regardless of what is happening with us, I need her to be okay. Sometimes that takes sacrifice. It's an unexpected sacrifice, but it is worth it." A small smile manages to come through.

What is great about the Riley-Buttons is that although they have such internal problems in their marriage, they both really want to make sure that their daughter is okay. That is their common denominator. This is where I know they can come together for now.

"You are right, Belle. They do watch us. We have spoken about this in prior sessions. Our children want to make sure that we are okay. They are also learning how to love and navigate relationships in all their glory and despair," I explain.

"Right," they both say.

I look to the clock. It is 3:28 p.m. I almost forgot about Belle's usual mental and emotional disappearance at half past three. She pulls her hair down and allows it to flow into her face.

"So, you told me how you feel and how Jasmine responded to the trip. How did you guys like it as a unit?"

Joe looks over to Belle and then to the clock. "You okay, Belle?" he asks.

Hmm, this is interesting. I wonder if he knows now.

"I'm fine," she says. However, with her hair draped over her face, he is unable to see the tears welling in her eyes. She allows one to fall. It descends slowly down her cheek.

"Anyway, Belle and I seemed to be okay. Like I said, there were times she seemed to disconnect, and it is usually about now that it happens. I think it has to do with that guy she was or is seeing." He says the last phrase sarcastically.

Belle does not look up. It is half past three. While she once seemed lost in something beautiful at this time, today she seems lost in something darker.

"I loved the time Belle and I had otherwise. We were able to laugh and connect in a way we have not in a long time. We were present for each other, if that makes sense," he says.

"It does," I respond. "That was a great explanation. Be present for each other. I like that. You have to be able to put your ego and all the transgressions down and decide to just be. That is the challenge, guys. When you decide to put down what is owed to you, you can allow the oneness of who you are supposed to be together to grow. We spend a lot of time protecting ourselves.

"Consider two countries that border each other. Let's say they have a misunderstanding. Instead of working on the misunderstanding, they begin to increase their defense systems. For example, they increase armies, surveillance of each other, and walls along the border. This does not allow for the countries to connect in love and peace. It is preparing for war. Each country is reducing its risk and refuses to be unprepared in case of an attack. On the surface, this seems like a really positive thing. However, the undercurrent of this is fear. Fear breeds hostility, and hostility breeds apathy. Apathy, my friends, not hate, is the opposite of love. Apathy means we no longer care. In protecting ourselves, we build barriers to the very things that will allow us to grow closer. We are afraid of vulnerability. It is a risk. There is the chance that you will experience pain. That is the beauty of it—the thing worth hurting for. There is always an inherent risk in love. However, the beauty of allowing yourself to love and be loved is far greater than the risk. The only true risks are not loving at all, loving with restrictions, or loving only to possess."

Belle looks up abruptly at me, and the tears puddled in her eyes flow freely.

"I thought he loved me!" she blurts. She jumps up, falling over herself and walking toward the door.

"I do," Joe yells at her, looking extremely bewildered.

"Not—" Belle doesn't finish her sentence. Instead, she runs out of the office.

"You." Joe says, finishing her sentence. He puts his head in his hands.

"Joe, I will be right back. I am going to check on her, okay?"

He nods, not even looking at me.

I go to the bathroom and can hear Belle sobbing in the bathroom stall.

"Belle, can we talk? Can I come in there with you?"

Belle manages to gurgle, "Yes."

I walk in, and she hurls herself at me to hug. I am caught a bit off guard, but I hold her.

"I do not understand. He has not been calling me or anything. I do not know what happened to us," she cries.

"Belle, tell me what or who you are talking about."

"The guy I was seeing. I mean I just cannot understand what happened. See, at half past three it was our thing that we would think solely of each other. We do that for a full minute. It is our way of connecting, even if we cannot talk. Lately, I have felt no connection to him. He has not even been calling me. I do not know why Eoghan is disconnecting from me."

My mind explodes. I cannot have heard her right. "What did you say his name was, Belle?" I ask. I am feeling sick. There suddenly seem to be sirens going off in my head. Here I am holding her, and I barely can feel my legs now.

"Eoghan," she unfortunately repeats.

I need to get out of here. *I need to get out of here right now!* I am trapped in this space and moment with Belle. The man that feels like my *everything* is seeing my client!

Oh my God! That is the woman he was speaking of, my damn client! My God—I need to get out of here today!

I am trying to talk, but I am having difficulty getting my mouth or even my brain to formulate words. I have to regain control of myself until it is safe to not have control. I manage to get out, "Belle, do you love him?"

"Yes," she whispers.

Oh, God. I lean against the wall.

"Belle, do you love Joe?"

"Yes, I do," she says as she wipes her face.

"Okay, what do you want? Who do you want?" I ask.

I can barely keep myself focused. I am dismantling inside.

"River, I remembered that Joe and I could love each other when we left town. I also want what is best for my daughter. I am just conflicted."

"Does Eoghan—" Oh, God. I cannot believe I am even saying his name right now to this woman. I can barely keep standing. I manage to choke out, "Does Eoghan know you love him?"

"Yes," she replies.

Who is holding my legs up? I do not know how I am still even standing.

"Does Joe know that you love him?" I ask.

"Probably not anymore. I distanced myself from him, but I do."

"Do you think he should know?"

"After what you said about the countries, I was able to see how I built walls and would not let him in. I could see how I was becoming increasing hostile and apathetic," she says, managing a smile. Suddenly there is banging on the door.

"Umm, yes? We are in here!" I yell out.

"I know that. I came to get my wife. Belle, I love you. I know you are caught between something. But I love you, and I want you. I want us. I want all of us. I know I am a fucking mess. I know I have cheated and have cheated you out of a love that you deserve. I cannot afford ... I will not afford losing you to another man. I ... will ... not ... lose ... you. Come out. I want to hug my wife, even if she is mourning someone else!" Joe yells.

I am at a loss. Belle looks up at me and walks toward the door.

She opens the door, and Joe rushes in and grabs her. She sobs in his chest.

Wow. I am not sure of all that is happening. I cannot even really appreciate this moment. Little do they know that secretly I am crushed. I am dying on the inside. Only the professional me is acting like the master puppeteer, directing my words and body.

They stand holding one another for what seems like an eternity. I touch Joe on the shoulder.

"Let's end this session. This has been a heavy session. There are some wounds that must heal. Let's talk through them next week," I offer.

Joe does not even look up to me. He manages to nod and mutter, "Okay." They continue to embrace.

"Take care," I say as I exit the bathroom.

I have to remember how to walk. I have my own devastation to deal with.

I hope they realize they are in the bathroom.

"Eoghan," I cry out loud to myself as I walk back to my office with tears falling down my face.

I peek through the blinds and watch the Riley-Buttons exit the office toward their car.

They are walking hand in hand. It's funny how tragedy is the proper medicine. This is far from over. There is a string of hope and love that is still connecting these two.

Time to turn inward. I lie on the couch and burrow my face in the pillows. Eoghan. *My* Eoghan is *her* Eoghan? I play back the conversation we first had in the restaurant.

"Do you love her?" I had asked.

"I could," he had replied.

I felt sick then, and he grabbed my hand and told me all his wonderful beliefs about love. I remember it ended with him saying, "Do not ever feel threatened."

Do not feel threatened? I cannot help but feel threatened! I am trapped! I cannot tell either of them about this, I cannot tell him about her, because she is my client, and it is unethical. I cannot tell her about him, because it is *my love, my life.* It could also devastate her.

I am in my own private hell. What do I do with this? Who can I even talk to? Why does the most beautiful thing in the world have so many strings attached?

"Eoghan." I whisper his name over and over through the tears streaming down my face. "Eoghan. I love you, Eoghan."

What will I say when I see him? Can I even be the same? Is our love now tainted by this secret?

We cannot have this secret. He has to choose!

How can I *say* that? I am married! I have to choose too! I am not in a position to tell him what to do with his life. My God. What am I doing? What am I supposed to do? I do not want to leave the office. I just want to sit in this bubble and grieve, because a meteor has destroyed our world. In a matter of seconds, it was demolished. Belle is crushed that the "love" of her life has distanced himself from her. He is doing it for me. He is defecting for me. Oh, my God! I rest my head in my hands. What the hell am I going to do?

Okay. Okay, River. You can do this. You can face the world. You can face … him. I think. Yes. Yes.

I stand to my feet. *Yes!* I can do this. I can face him. I can see him!

Then what? Suddenly the courage evaporates from my body. See him and then what? Talk to him? Ask him about the woman he is seeing? Stop seeing him? Tell him who "she" is?

No.

None of that.

"Continue as normal, and allow the process to unfold," a voice within me speaks.

My spirit. *Listen to her,* I convince myself.

Worry and fear have always been road dogs with me. They have stymied most of my personal and professional growth. It is high time I give them a rest, especially with this. I am not prepared to lose the purest thing I have ever loved because of fear.

Life is a series of moments. Moments strung together make a life. Lives connected together create a legacy.

I look in the mirror, and my face is puffy and tear-streaked.

"Clean it up, River!" I say to myself. I am glad that I do not have anyone else to see today. I do not think I could handle it.

I walk to the bathroom and look at myself again. I study myself as I studied myself the night I was exposed to Eoghan. Taking a paper towel, I drench it in cold water. I fold it slowly and wipe my eyes clean. I slowly wipe my face dry.

Let's do a test.

"Hey, River! How are you?" I say out loud to myself.

"I'm good. Real good! You?" I respond.

Nope. No you are not. The pain is written all over your face.

I take a deep breath and sigh. I am going to have to sneak out of here. I will not fool anyone with these eyes. I hurry to the door. Mahaley is locking up tonight. She will be okay without saying good-bye to me.

"Dr. Meadows! River!" I hear her yell. I pretend to be engrossed in my phone and keep walking. I can hear the steps of her feet increase. Oh, well. *Good try*, I think to myself.

"Yes?" I turn to her

She stops abruptly. "Are you okay?"

"Yes. Yes … allergies. You know how they are with me. I forgot to take my medicine the last couple of days."

She squints. Surely she does not believe me, but she knows well enough not to probe.

"I just wanted to tell you that Jude picked up the car again and wanted me to take you home. Is that okay?" she asks.

The grip increases on my phone. The anger wants a place to go.

What? No, it is not okay! I think to myself. I was prepared to have a full fledge crying session in my car while torturing myself with love songs and love lost songs.

"Sure, Mahaley" is what actually leaves my lips. "Are you ready?"

"Yes, lead the way," she responds.

She opens the door, and I sit. I instantly want to choke.

"Mahaley?" I gasp.

"Yes, Dr. Meadows?"

"Stop smoking! This is gross."

She laughs as she buckles her seatbelt.

****

Jude turns to Jezebel. "Sweetie, I gotta go. My wife is expecting me to be home soon. Plus, I have to talk to her about my father. She has been awfully accommodating lately." Jude throws the covers back, exposing Jezebel's thighs. He lightly circles his fingers on her newly spray tanned legs.

"Jude ... I really do not want to hear about your wife while you are with me. I mean, it is disrespectful." Jezebel says as she interlocks her fingers with Jude's.

Taking her face in his hands, Jude states, "Sweetie ... honestly speaking, being here with you is disrespectful. You must know that. You must know that I am caught between two worlds—a world of obligation and a world of fantasy." Jezebel's face turns to disgust. Jumping from the bed, she begins yelling.

"I suppose I am your fantasy! Do fantasies ever become reality? Or will we just be what we are—sneaking and hiding ourselves from the world forever?"

A familiar ring emits from his phone.

"That's her. I know her ring. Answer, Jude! What is the excuse this time? What will you tell her? She probably already knows about us."

Jude rolls his eyes and picks up the line. "Yeah, River, what's up? I am finishing up here at work. I'm sorry I am late. I'll pick you up something to eat on the way. Whoa, wait ... what's wrong? Yes ... yes, there is, I can hear it in your voice. You sound upset. Mahaley with you? Well, okay ...

okay. Tell me about it when I get home. I want to tell you about my father. About what happened after the funeral … Okay, talk to you later."

****

"Lying bastard," I mutter to myself as I throw my phone into my purse.

I can tell that Mahaley is a little uncomfortable. I must have muttered a bit too loud.

"Dr. Meadows, I want to ask your opinion on something," Mahaley asks.

"Personal or professional?" I ask. This is good distraction.

Mahaley bites her lip, cocking her head to the side. "Probably a little bit of both."

"Well, I'll do my best."

"You always do. You *are* the best!" she cheers.

I laugh. One thing Mahaley is good for is for bringing sunlight to a dim room.

"Okay, so … " she begins. I can hear the excitement in her voice.

This sounds like it will be a relationship discussion. God knows I do not want to have one of those right now. I deeply inhale, not sure if my collapsed lungs can carry oxygen to a heart that is no longer functioning in a body that feels like it has lost its soul.

So I fake it. I am good at that. Dr. River Meadows shows up.

"Go for it … I am all ears!" I exclaim.

"Okay … well … I kinda like this guy," she says with a laugh.

"Kinda? How come it is only kinda?"

"It is not really kinda. I guess I am not sure what to do. I mean, I've been hurt in the past. I just want to make sure that I am safe. I mean, you know how it is. You remember when you were single, right? How do you know when it is the right one? How do you know who to give your heart to?"

I am fighting back tears. I really do not need this right now. I can do this though. I have to be able to do this.

"Mahaley, you will not know if he is the right one or not unless you go all in. See, we spend so much time protecting ourselves that we do not experience the fullness of love. Love has pain, Mahaley. You will not be able to avoid it. The purpose of love is not to avoid pain. The fullness of love is finding the one worth hurting for. You do not have to suffer. That is what we do when we build artificial walls around our hearts: we allow only the windows to be cracked. Why have only the experience of a sandbox and a kiddie pool when you have the option of a beach and an ocean?"

I continue on this thought. "The ocean is scary, Mahaley. I know this. However, it is far more beautiful than the sandbox and kiddie pool will ever be. You may be safe there, but is that what you want? Do you want to be safe, or do you want your soul to be touched?"

Images of Eoghan manifest in my mind over and over again. I am talking to myself just as much as I am talking to her. What the hell is going on?

Tears are leaving my eyes, and I cannot stop them. They are warm and begging to be released fully.

Mahaley pulls over. "Dr. Meadows, are you okay? I am sorry to get you so upset. I was watching you, and for a minute I could not tell if you were talking to me. You seemed lost in yourself."

"I'm sorry. I just got caught up. Love is beautiful, Mahaley. You do not know if he is the right one. Nothing on this earth will guarantee that for you. The only guarantee is that you will get hurt during the process. You just have to determine if he is worth it. Not everyone is."

"You are right, Dr. Meadows. I appreciate your words. I want assurance that I will not be hurt. I understand that is not possible. He is a good man. I have to open my heart to him fully in order to fully experience his goodness."

"Yes, and he will then be able to experience fully the goodness of you. Third house on your left, Mahaley ... Well, we are here Mahaley. Thank you so much for the ride. I appreciate it. What would I do without you?"

I manage a smile. My cheeks feel as though they weigh a ton.

16

SHARED DILEMMAS

Eoghan's alarm clock goes off for the third time.

Jumping out of bed, he grabs his phone and runs for the bathroom.

"Dammit … I am late again. What is going on with me?" he says out loud.

Picking up the razor, he smiles. *That woman*, he thinks to himself. *That woman. She is everything to me. She defines me.*

How can that be? How can this human being excite me to a level that is cellular? The human body is autonomic. It responds without explicit instruction from its owner. When she is around me, my body does not know what to do. It seems confused, and neurons fire and misfire.

But at the same time, all is right with the world. I know that my soul aches for her. Our spirits, once separated, now have returned to one another. I am drained when I cannot be near her. I need that woman. Somehow she has me on life support, unable to inhale fully unless she is in my presence.

After Eoghan turns on the water, the room quickly steams. Hot water rolls down his face, and images of River flash before him—before images of Belle interrupt the sanctuary of the moment.

I care very much for Belle, he thinks to himself as the guilt begins to consume. The nights he shared with her come back to him. He remembers the nights he's spent caressing her body—the softness of her skin and the scent of sweet lavender that would lure his body into a deep sleep after making love to her.

I have not called her in weeks, he thinks to himself. *I am sure she feels my distance from her. I was ready to just live on the periphery of life, to sit just outside the gates of elation, catching whatever seeps out of the edges.*

River, River … my God, I have not even been with her one time. Already she has not only let me know that I have not been breathing for all of these years, but she also actually has given me breath. Never mind standing outside the gates, scavenging for remnants of joy. No, River is joy. I do not have to scavenge for something that I become when I am with her.

I know Belle loves me.

I know River loves me. She has not said it, but her soul has already confirmed. Those eyes of fire that operate as flint in mine … I love her. I more than love her. Is that possible? I cannot describe what this is. It is belonging. She belongs to me. Not in some crazy stalker way, but we belong to each other. We are one. Once we become one, she will see that. She will need to decide how to handle her marriage.

In the meantime, I have to handle Belle.

"Shit! How long have I been in this shower?" Eoghan yells out loud. Reaching out of the shower, Eoghan grabs his phone.

"Damn! Twenty-five minutes?"

Scrolling down he sees six missed calls from Belle and four missed calls from "home," also known as River.

Sighing, he puts the phone face down and returns to the shower.

"What the fuck am I doin'? I cannot even sleep. One woman who I do not want to hurt, but I know I will hurt her. I *am* hurting her," Eoghan whispers, putting his head down and allowing the music of the beating water to soothe his torn, achy heart.

****

I walk up to the front door, trying to hold myself together. The lock seems unusually loud as I unlock it. Maybe I am hypersensitive because of what took place in the session. Jude's crap did not even faze me today. He is just doing what he does best, which is satisfy his carnal needs.

I slowly slip off my heels as I enter the house. Taking my keys and dropping them in my purse next to the coat tree, I stand in the foyer as a stranger would. I walk around, gently grazing my fingers on the surface of every item in my path—couch, chair, table.

Something needs to feel real, because certainly this does not. I do not feel as though I am having this experience. It is as if I am on the outside, a watcher who is doomed to struggle to rewrite the story for it to make better sense or for it to at least be more digestible.

I find myself in the kitchen. Without thought, I grab one of my favorite tulip wine glasses and pour a glass of wine. I manage to find some chocolate and strawberries, and I head to the quietest and most personal room in my house.

There is small space located on my third floor. It's quiet, and I can be alone there. It may seem useless to some to seek quiet time to ponder, but it is important to me. I found a small couch and filled the room with candles and pillows. It has to be one of the unmanliest rooms in the whole house. I purposely set it up that way to keep Jude out of the space.

I check out the playlist options; it is unfortunate that "broken" does not exist as a playlist title.

The closest I got to "broken" is "love." Oh, how ironic. My itinerary until Jude gets home:

Press play.

Drink.

Cry.

Repeat.

I immerse myself in the sadness of love lost with an array of music.

"I've got Chinese!" I can faintly hear Jude yelling. I have released as much pain as I could release in an hour. I also called Eoghan at least four times, and he did not answer.

What is he doing? What is he thinking about? I crave to lay my heart on his chest in order to hear and feel his heartbeat.

I think of the weeks we spent together, and I feel like I lost a piece of myself today.

I remember the lullaby his heart makes while sustaining him. My heart syncs with his. My breathing syncs with his. We breathe the same breath. I love him.

My God. I love him.

I cannot lose him.

I will not lose him.

I wipe my tears as I hear the steps of betrayal approaching. "River … you okay? I have been calling you. I've got Chinese. Are you doing okay? You only seem to come up here when you are troubled. What is going on? What's up with this playlist?"

"Lots of questions, Jude." So many questions. "Where were you today?"

"Um, well, I had to work. Nothing major. You know how it is. I am always trying to make sure that we have the deals and making the money! Never mind me … what is going on with you? You are obviously upset. What is going on with the chocolate, strawberries, and wine? It is me? What have I done to deserve your drawing inward?"

I smile a knowing smile. "Nothing, Jude. Nothing outside of what you usually do."

Jude's eyes shift past me, through the window to the backyard oasis, for what seems like forever. I allow the silence to be. Sometimes we need not fill the air with words but just be present in the moment. He seems to be seeking assurance for what comes next.

"I am not sure what that means, but okay. I need you to be okay. Things are weird between us. I know. I can feel it. We are here but not here. You get what I'm sayin', Riv?"

I deeply inhale air thick with regret and confusion. We have to eventually address the alternate realities we are living. I nestle my head in the cup of his arms and reply, "Yes, I get it. I know it. We are not here. We are wrestling with ourselves."

We sit in silence, watching the large snowflakes gently cover the earth. Tears slowly stream down my face. I am not completely sure what my tears are for—fear of losing the love of my life? Grieving the inevitable dissolution of my marriage?

17

A KISS DENIED, A BODY FULFILLED, AND A GUILTY SOUL

Belle is ecstatic that Eoghan wants to meet with her. She has made sure to be just sexy enough for him to salivate when he sees her. She has missed him, but this time it is different. She feels guilty pains about the secret she has kept from Joe.

She arrives at his house around seven o'clock in the evening. Joe is spending time with family out of town; he left just this morning.

I am dying to spend time with him, even though I feel the duality of guilt and excitement, she thinks to herself.

Eoghan opens the door. Belle is surprised that he is only wearing sweatpants and a tee shirt. Usually he dresses up for her, knowing she loves him cleaned up.

"Hey, sweetheart. I am sorry I am not cleaned up. It has been one hell of a day. Come in."

Belle is a bit bewildered, as she is accustomed to his pulling her in and kissing her as he says hello.

He seems colder—more distant.

Walking in, Belle offers her croissant, purchased from their favorite café—the unfortunate where place Jasmine saw them.

"Thanks, baby. Sit down."

"Okay ... what going on? We usually go right to the bedroom, Eoghan. Do we need to talk? I haven't heard from you in weeks, and I was dying inside. I do not want us to not talk anymore. Did I do something?" Belle asks.

"Yes and no. You are a beautiful woman, Belle. I am having some things going on in my life, and it is just so complicated. I don't know what we are doing. Are you staying with your husband? Are we just playing around with one another? You talk all this shit about leavin', yet you still there. You cannot give me *all of you*. You can only give me moments—moments that are stolen or left over. So to answer your question, yes you did do something—I got close to you; and no you did nothing—I complicated my own life by choosing someone who has chosen another," Eoghan responds.

Belle grabs his hand. "Why haven't you kissed me yet? You would never let this amount of time pass without touching me in some way. There must be someone else—is there someone else?"

"Did you hear anything I just said?" Eoghan emphatically states.

"Sure, I heard you. I just wasn't listening. This is not about me, Eoghan. This is about you. This is how it has been all this time. Why now? Why now do you have an issue with me? You've known my circumstances each time you've wrapped yourself around me. Who is she? Can she love you the way I can?"

Belle approaches Eoghan, slowly wrapping her legs around him as he sits in a chair. She kisses his face. "Can she?" she repeatedly whispers as she gently caresses his face, placing lingering kisses closer and closer to Eoghan's mouth.

Eoghan feels the monster of desire consume him. The thoughts of restraining become weaker. Belle's hands lift the flimsy tee shirt covering the expansion of man, which she cannot wait to have her arms around.

Eoghan's thoughts manifest an image of River. Her smile, her scent reminiscent of Sunday morning ... Her scent welcomes—no, beckons him to fall without thought.

The image becomes weaker as Belle's kisses intensify. Feeling weak, he gives into the battle and gives into Belle's delicate touch.

He quickly jerks his head up. Belle startles and opens her eyes. No words are exchanged between them. None are needed. Eoghan's eyes turn animalistic as if he is ready to consume his prey. With one hand, he traces the lines of her shirt, making sure to make contact with each button. Tracing his hand back from the bottom of her shirt, he snatches the helpless fabric from the stitch. Belle's eyes widen. She has not experienced this Eoghan before. Her right breast exposed to the sudden change in temperature, her nipple constricts.

Not taking his eyes off Belle, Eoghan leans her back, forcing her body at an angle that her abs struggle to maintain. Taking his free hand, he aggressively moves his hands up and down her chest. He lifts her in one move and stands up. Her loose skirt falls to the sides of her legs. Instantly, without instruction, Belle knows to wrap her legs around him. She brings her face to his, as she wants to taste his mouth and feel the softness of his lips. Eoghan pulls back—a barely audible no leaves his mouth.

Taken aback, a sudden feeling of submission consumes her. He carries her to the bedroom. They never lose eye contact, the fire between increasing as the rise and fall of their chests intensifies, forcing them to breathe from their mouths.

Reaching the bedroom, Eoghan leans Belle's back against the wall. One hand at a time, he places his hands on Belle's butt and lifts her. Gasping, Belle is frightened and excited. He rests her legs on his shoulders. Her legs parted allow for her aroma to increase his sexual aggression. He needs to have her.

Sensing what is in store for her, she leans her head back, willing and waiting. She can barely catch her breath. Her panties, barely covering her sex, are pushed aside, and he begins to slowly devour her.

Belle loses herself and can barely hold on to keep her balance on his shoulders. She does not even realize that he has walked her to the bed.

Often when we are involved in complicated relationships, namely forbidden relationships, it becomes difficult to untie the tie that has bonded us to our lovers. Much like a drug, the person can become a habit— especially if the tie is sexual. The instinctual drive of sex can be difficult to deny. The limbic system, an ancient part of the brain that is the seat of those primal drives and emotions, needs to work with the thinking part of the brain, the part of the brain that cares about future consequences. There is a flood of dopamine that hijacks the brain during sexual stimulation. This surge, which increases lust, is difficult to ignore.

Dopamine is a chemical in the brain responsible for stimulating the pleasure we feel. Imagine how difficult it is to ignore pleasure and follow straight and narrow path of righteousness. It is imperative to not allow yourself to be alone with someone else in situations that tie you to consequences that you do not consider during a few moments of illicit ecstasy. Regret is not an easy emotion to live with.

Eoghan is the first to wake up from his sex-induced coma. He looks over at Belle, and the pain of regret takes root in his heart.

Little does Belle know that Eoghan was thinking of River while becoming one with Belle. It only made him want her more. Frustrated, Eoghan wakes Belle up, handing her the phone with five missed calls from Joe.

"You're being missed, lady," he says as he dresses himself.

"Good God! Okay, let me get myself together. You were crazy and amazing, love!" Belle reaches over to kiss Eoghan, who turns allowing it to land on his cheek.

"All right, sweetie. Talk to you later." Eoghan's voice has a tinge of despondency.

Belle is busily consumed with the several missed calls and yells "Okay!" while running out the door. Only when sitting in the car does it hit her hard: *He never kissed me. He is saving the most intimate part of himself. He can only be saving that for someone who has touched his heart more than I. Who is she?*

"Who is she?" was a question Belle never got the answer to.

Getting dressed for work, Eoghan thinks of the night's events. The ride to work is filled with contradictory emotion. *Why did I allow myself to sleep with Belle? I know what and whom I want in my life. I will lose her if I am not careful. I absolutely must contact her.* Eoghan thinks to himself. *I cannot risk losing River. Ignoring her calls was a mistake.*

Eoghan walks into his department meeting only to hear the vibrations of his phone. "Home" crosses the screen.

"Guys. I will be with you in a moment. Please get everything started. I will be right there."

Seeing her name across the screen is like new air entering his lungs. A shadow of trepidation develops in Eoghan's spirit as he remembers Belle. Residual betrayal begins to pierce the anticipation of the sweet melody of her voice.

Just before the anxiety overwhelms him, Eoghan manages to exhale and whisper, "You," in quiet desperation.

"Eoghan, we have to talk," River says, managing to navigate the murkiness of her despair.

"Anything for you, beautiful. I am sorry I missed your calls. I have been a bit … occupied."

"Okay, dinner tonight? A Prima Vista?" She asks.

"Sounds good. I cannot wait to see you. See you at 7:45," he says knowingly.

Biting her lip, River smiles.

"Yes, see you then."

Hearing her smile in her voice, Eoghan returns to the meeting with new life.

18

THE INTRODUCTION OF THE IRREGULARITY

I hang up the phone with a series of conflicting emotions. Even the vibrations of his voice are the right frequency for my soul. Yet, shame manifests and quickens my nausea, as I remember that I am in love with the lover of my married client. Not to mention that I am married too! What kind of joke did God play on me? What kind of joke did I play on myself? There has to be something I need from this experience. If I do not figure this out, I will be back in my personal space accompanied only by chocolate and wine.

The ring of my phone disrupts me. Jude. Great. More lies. Let me act as though I do not know the lie that he will sell as the truth.

"River, I am so glad you answered the phone. I really need to talk to you. My mother called, and she needs me to come by. She wants to talk about some issues with my father. I want to use your car so I can quickly escape if I want to."

"Jude," I ask, "what does that have to do with you leaving?"

"Well," he replies, "I will tell her that I need to come pick you up or something. That ... um, my car is in the shop. I just need the escape plan ahead of time."

"You make good use of those, huh?" I ask under my breath.

"What? I did not hear you."

"Um, nothing, Jude. I am at home. Come and get the car."

"Okay, sweets. See you soon," he says with much enthusiasm.
I fail to reply.

I set the phone on vibrate and wait on Jude's arrival and Eoghan's call. I process the emotions I am experiencing. I think of the Riley-Buttons. I think of Belle and Joe and how our lives have been intertwined in this cosmic matter. I need to see the purpose of our interconnectedness. It exists, but I just do not know why or how.

I go to my sanctuary with a bottle of wine, chocolates, and strawberries. I am indecisive about listening to music. I just need to *be* for a minute. I am having a hard time understanding this "new thing." What am I becoming? I know that I am in the middle of a dramatic change. I search my mind and heart for predictability—for answers. However, I fear the truth is that I will have to wait for the unfolding. I will have to introduce God into this new thing.

There is a concept in mathematics called chaos theory. It operates on the simple premise that complex systems' origins lie is simple equations. These equations operate on a feedback loop, allowing for the repetitive development of structures on a smaller and smaller scale. The system replicates itself ad infinitum.

Point? Consider your belief system, which is impacted by your self-talk. You are what you think. You are what you say. You will repeat and be attracted to things that support your belief system. This, in essence, only strengthens your system, creating a network of negativity or positivity. There is hope!

If you are looking to change this fractal, this repetitive self-destructive nature, you have to introduce the irregularities within it. If these irregularities support the desired new belief system, you will continue to repeat them, producing a new fractal. The key? You must truly want a new belief system. Oh, God exists in the irregularities, and the irregularities create a new thing—a new you.

What is this new me? Who is this new me? Where is this new me going? I satisfy my answer with a sip of Riesling, and I give in to the unforgiving texture of the strawberry and the lullaby of its sweet nectar.

****

Eoghan returns to the meeting with a swirl of excitement and trepidation. He is aware that he is approaching a culmination of events. Soon he will have to end one thing to begin another. No longer will he be able to hold onto Belle's safeness. He will have to dance on the ledge of life and risk the multistory drop that love lost provides.

Then, and truly only then, do you actually live.
This thought utterly frightens him.
Eoghan allows himself to return to the real world to distract himself from the anticipatory pain of heartache.

"Bob, listen, I have been sitting here in these meetings for the past six months on this community development center project. I am confused about why we are still just in the planning phase. It does not seem like such a large project. What is the holdup?"

"Well," explains Bob, "we are trying to time this project just right. We know that when election time arrives we need to have leverage. Our connection to the neighborhood during the unveiling will only help the campaign."

"I understand that, Bob." As he continues to speak, River's voice enters his head—a discussion that she'd had with him some time ago. She had shared a moment that she'd had with her spirit. He quotes her: "Life is a series of moments. Moments strung together make a life. Lives connected together create a legacy."

He pauses and then continues. "Bob, we are creating a legacy. We are in this moment now. If we operate in truth, we will prevail. There is no need for us to manipulate the thoughts and hearts of the people. Be true to yourself, and the truth will be true to you."

The team looks at Eoghan in amazement. Very rarely a man of metaphors or analogies, even he is a stranger to this new voice.

River is entering my soul, he thinks to himself. *I was right when I told her, "Welcome Home."*

Tapping his pen on the conference table, Eoghan gets up, and as he turns to leave, he says to Bob and his team, "I gotta go for a minute. I've got my own truth I have to deal with. I have to go home."

Little do they know he is not talking about his house.

19

SHANGHAI CREATES A PLACE OF CHERITH

It is 7:30 p.m. I pull up to A Prima Vista, and my heart has been racing for the better part of fifteen minutes. It is not about seeing Eoghan again. It is that I know I have to find a way to talk to him about Belle.

How do I talk to him and not break my professional oath? How? Why is my heart being betrayed by my mind? I know it is not the right thing to do, but my soul brings the truth forward.

It is bad enough that I had to use Jude's raggedy car. I had to give him mine so he could do what he does best: lie.

I bet Jude does not even realize that I know that he carries an extra set of clothes in a bag in the trunk.

Yet, who am I to even have this discussion? Look at me. I am here waiting to see the one I call the love of my life! Oh, the hypocrisy!

Despite the hypocritical nature of this, it is still the truth. The truth does not have to make sense. It just has to be.

Conrado sees me and waves me over to the bar. He is smiling so hard that he might have an aneurism if he is not careful.

"Conradooooooo," I say as I extend my arms to embrace him.

He hugs me tight, kissing me on the cheek. "River ... River, you lovely lady. You and Eoghan inspire me. I talk about you frequently to other souls who bare their naked, damaged hearts to me. Your story gives people hope for and more importantly faith in love. Love is so elusive yet so available, despite your situations, and you both managed to shanghai it."

"Shanghai?" I begin to protest.

"No, no, no ... wait. Let me explain why I say that," Conrado replies. "You tricked the system of love. You did not mean to. By accident, you obtained something very few people on earth obtain," he explains.

"Go on," I say with my arms folded, not exactly convinced.

"Well, we spend a lifetime seeking. One of the things we seek most is love. Now, we color it in all types of things: money, power, sex, status etc., but is it love nonetheless. This process of seeking allows us—if we allow it to—to grow. It allows us to *become*. We constantly stay in a state of becoming in order to be worthy of something that we will not obtain fully. It is like the wind: to be felt but never held onto."

"So, what is different about us?" I ask.

"You are soul mates, River. You both found your soul mate. Through his pain and your suffering, you found each other. You have something that is unusual. That is a gift, River. I hope you can see this. Not everyone can withstand or is even ready for the very thing they ask for. Most people live substandard lives, outside their purpose or with people who have outlived their usefulness or beyond their season. They don't feel settled." Conrado scratches his chin. "You ever really wanted something to eat and could not get it? And so you then decided to replace it with something else?" he asks.

"Like, I want cheesecake and have to have applesauce because it is lower in calories?" I ask.

Conrado's faces crunches up, eyes squinting, as if the worst odor on earth came into the room.

"Yes, but that was a *terrible* analogy. Or if it was close, it was just okay. Well, River, that is what life is for many of us, 'okay.' You get to have your cheesecake. That is awesome. There is power exchanged when you both look at each other. You transfer each other's power. The yin to the yang. This is not what the world experiences. Love is not able to do its trickery on you to make you consistently seek it. You have shanghaied it. It is now you, and you are now it. You are both one. You are both one with love."

I feel more at ease with Conrado's assessment, and I allow my arms to rest. I succumb to new feelings of adoration for Conrado. I love him for who he is and for what he has done for me. I reach out and touch his arm, and he lightly squeezes my hand. Spoken words cannot say it any louder.

****

"Belle, what is taking you so long?" Joe yells up the stairs.

Lying across the bed, Belle manages to respond through controlled tears, "I'll be down ... in a minute."

Eyes swollen, she reflects on the new distance that now defines her. No longer does she feel the soul connection with Eoghan, nor does she feel the marital connection with Joe.

Belle stands, looks in the mirror, and analyzes her reflected image. *A million shards of glass*, she thinks to herself, recognizing the degree of brokenness that has taken her heart hostage.

"A place of Cherith," she says out loud to herself. Cherith is known as a cutting, a separation. In the Bible, the prophet Elijah hid himself there during the early part of the three years of drought (1 Kings 17:3, 5). The Lord told Elijah to flee and hide there, where he would be taken care of. God promised him he would be provided for there. The important aspect to understand is that Cherith is a place of isolation. It is a place where you are completely cut off and are totally dependent upon God and His resources. One may ask, "Why would God cut me off? Why would God take everything and seemingly everyone from me?"

There are things we acquire during such a separation period that we could not get at any other time. Elijah had to obtain three things during this separation. First, he had to learn obedience. He needed to go where God asked him to go without debate. We follow God out of love, not out of fear. The degree of our love for Him will determine our obedience. Now, do not misunderstand, struggling in areas of your life is not indicative of your love for God. However, you do need to pour yourself increasingly into Him so it becomes increasingly effortless to obey.

Second, he had to learn where his provision came from. Where did Elijah's provision come from? It came from the brook and the ravens who brought him meat. Ravens who feed on meat gave Elijah what they would normally use to sustain themselves. Therefore, take note: when you are in Cherith, you may be surprised by who God allows to provide for you.

Lastly, and more importantly, is faith. Elijah's provisions began to dry up—specifically the brook. This "drying" can put us in crisis mode and make us extremely fearful. We must always have faith that God will give us what we need the moment we need it. This forces us to consistently rely on Him. This place of Cherith is not a punishment. It is an opportunity. You are being strengthened through your brokenness.

Joe is connected to the frequency of Belle's spirit, so he senses she is in pain. Confused and angry, he walks up the stairs to try to rescue her from it.

First, I'll have a cigar, he thinks to himself. *Belle has never liked that I smoke them. Right now, she is a bit occupied, so I doubt if she'll notice. Delilah never seems to mind. Hell, I can smoke them in her face.* He chuckles.

Joe revisits his emotions, a kaleidoscope of confusion, love, and anger. Unsure of what to do, Joe cannot separate himself from Belle. Through the haze of the cigar, he sees Belle come down the stairs. He attempts to quickly put out the cigar, but through the thickness of the smoke, as he watches her, he realizes he can clearly see the truth.

He sees the truth of the living dead. The truth of a cadaver breathing oxygen she will never use. A tornado of emotions begins to weigh upon his heart. *I cannot watch her walk away without fighting a good fight*, he thinks to himself.

Joe submits to the truth that burns his eyes greater than the cigar smoke. As he watches the love of his life approach him with eyes swollen from a pain of severed love that is not his own, he shakes his head. The words tremble through Joe's heart: *I don't have the tools and don't know where to start.*

He walks toward her. Belle senses his presence and anticipates he will touch her in a way that makes her cringe. Her head falls to her chest, and shame and pain reflect in her eyes.

With the tip of his finger, he lifts her head. "Open your eyes, Belle."

"No, I … I can't," she says with a whimper.

Joe places small kisses on each eyelid. As the pressure of his flesh meets the delicate skin, tears fall, staining her face.

Neither Belle nor Joe addresses the cause. "Let's go. Jazzy is in the car. I know you are hungry. Don't forget we have to see Dr. Meadows tomorrow," Joe says, touching her tear-stained collarbone.

****

Conrado walks me to the table, where Eoghan and I will reunite.

I am drunk in anticipation of him.

A few minutes later, Eoghan arrives. I see him walking toward me with *that* smile. I cannot even see the other people in the room, they are now in shadows. His recessed brown eyes provide the antidote to my tipsy anticipation.

He stands before her.

His eyes draw her to stand.

Her eyes snatch the breath from him.

I need to touch him, I think to myself.

Eoghan reaches his pinky finger around mine. "I need my air back," he manages to say.

My chest caves as the oxygen leaves me. I seek his lips—the softness, the taste, the texture. I love every line on his lips. I have memorized the grooves and the curves of them. They are a gift to me.

"Hey, beautiful," Eoghan says.

"Hey, love," I say.

"I have been thinking of you all day. We have a lot to talk about."

"I know." I rest my head on his chest. I feel safe. My chest expands to inhale deeply his kiss.

Conrado brings over drinks, winks, and smiles at me.

We talk of all things except what we need to talk about. I laugh to myself, because it is the elephant in the room we have refused to let join.

It is as if choosing to face the truth will end us. However, I am having such a wonderful time I cannot bring myself to end the magic we both feel. Debates over Captain Crunch versus Fruity Peebles dominate our time. We debate the difference between spirituality and religion over dinner. We debate cable versus satellite television over dessert. We debate the advantages and disadvantages of culturally defined gender roles over more drinks. We discuss the different types of love and how they manifest in our lives over coffee. We are the same but different. We are complementary, not competitive. He is the puzzle piece that makes the picture make sense. I see lines and he sees truth during our exchange. Or He sees lines and I see truth. We are both vessels willing to give as well as receive each other's truths and boundaries. Our discussions over the different types of love were based on a book he read called *Colors of Love*, and this subject yielded the most fruit during our encounter. I was curious if he was in ludic love with me, but in my heart, I know that not to be true.

It is imperative that we understand the concept of love and the various degrees it exists in. Not only must *we* know the different types of love that exist, but also we must know what love our partners seek. If we fail to learn before the fall, great pain can ensue. Often we know what our partners want, yet we still believe we can change them. This mindset will end in tragedy, as we need to believe others when they tell or show who they are and/or what they really want.

J.A Lee's 1973 Colors of Love defines six varieties of relationships that might be labeled as love:

Eros love is romantic, passionate love. Ludus love is uncommitted love where there may be manipulation. Storge is slow developing, friendship love. This love allows for a long term relationship. Pragmatic love is often about mutual benefits. There is a purpose other than the relationship for both partners. Mania love is different. This is the crazy love, full of possessiveness and jealousy. This person truly only loves themselves. They see potential partners as someone own. Agape, is selfless love. It is a caring love that seeks to pour into others. This the of love is rare, as it hold no conditions and does not keep account wrongdoings. It is a Corinthians 13 kind of love.

More importantly, we need to determine the type of love we have for ourselves. If we do not love ourselves, and love ourselves well, we cannot adequately love someone else. If we are broken, we seek out others to *feel* and *fill* the cracks of our soul. Unfortunately, this can drain the life force of the filler/feeler, leaving that person vulnerable to internal and external negative stressors. This person is not able to replenish what is lost, as the broken vessel only knows how to plug in. Additionally, the broken vessel never learns self-love or how to heal. We all need to support ourselves. However, we need to have the desire and willingness to do the work and to truly love ourselves, as well as another person. The broken vessel will always need help being held together. It is never held together on its own.

"Eoghan, there is something I really need to talk to you about."

Eoghan, apparently anticipating River's question, interrupts her. "It's about Belle—I mean *her*, isn't it?

"Yes."

"I've been wanting to talk to you about her as well. I also need to talk to you about something important," Eoghan says as he traces River's hand with his fingers.

"Jude."

"Yes."

"So?" I ask. "Ready?"

Eoghan looks up at me, beginning to smile. Sensing his mood, I begin to laugh and exclaim, "Me neither!"

"Let's make that tomorrow's problem. Tonight, my love, I just want to experience you," he offers.

Agreeing with him, I answer, "And I you."

With that, he reaches over the table and traces the line of my face, ending with his thumb lightly rubbing my lip.

I close my eyes as I feel the warmth of his hands.

He is water, and I am dehydrated.

20

SESSION 10: THE GOLDEN MOLLUSK, JOE'S BONDAGE, AND THAT HONEY VOICE

It has been quite some time since I have met with the Riley-Buttons. At least it feels like it. I check with Mahaley to make sure they have not canceled. I check my feelings and my thoughts. I have to be able to separate what is happening with me from what's happening with Belle. This is an extremely delicate time.

I sit back in the wingback chair and trace my fingers over the metal buttons. Leaning my head back, I think of a time when life was much simpler.

I was seven years old. The one-thousand-square-foot apartment felt more like ten thousand square feet. I smile at how the world was so big to me then. I remember running down the hallway in my blue and white jersey shirt and powder blue jeans. My hair was flowing behind me as the googly eyes of my Cookie Monster slippers rolled around. Playing hide and seek, I was pretty determined that I would never be found. I hid under the dining room table, and my blue Cookie Monster feet were sticking out. My hands covering my eyes, I was sure I would not be found. See, I assumed that since I could not see, no one else could see me! I smiled at my genius. I could hear my mother calling my name, and I wiggled my feet in excitement. She would never discover my hiding place. Unfortunately, in five minutes I was discovered. I could not believe it! Somehow she'd found me.

I laugh out loud at the memory. I was in plain sight the whole time! I mean, my feet were sticking out from under the table, for crying out loud! I was the one blind, yet I believed that because I could not see, neither could she.

Life can be a very similar to this, because many times we only fool ourselves. You think you can hide from the truth about yourself, but those who know you can see the way you interact within your world. You are only truly hiding from yourself.

I jerk myself out of my memory in order to check the lobby for the Riley-Buttons.

The Riley-Buttons are actually sitting together. This is interesting to see. I am very much surprised. Belle once again has her hair in a high ponytail that is kind of messy but cute. Papers surround her, and she is reading with a pen in her mouth. Joe sits with her, a victim of a paper burial. His usual work clothes are dirty. He watches her. I am not sure if she knows she is being watched.

I wonder what he is thinking. I can see the adoration in his eyes. It is almost like trying to figure out a puzzle that you can envision being completed, but you have no idea what to do with the pieces.

I call them back.

Little does Joe realize the fight is within him but does not belong to him. Sounds kind of crazy, doesn't it? Well, I suppose that it is, to a degree. See, Joe began his journey without direction, purpose, or a shepherd. Sheep without a shepherd will wander aimlessly. Joe is a great example of the aimless wanderer. He is not guarded, fed, directed or tended to. This causes him to not understand the importance of nurturing relationships. A feral child, if you will, will only seek to self-gratify. A feral child turns into an instinctual, selfish adult.

Joe's mother did not assist him in creating a value, or better yet, a space for the type of love that matters most in life. She created in him the desire for a possession, not a lover. He only knows how to own things and people. He feels entitled to all things.

Entitlement. That is such an interesting word. There are only a few things we are entitled to in reality. We are entitled to the right to be treated as human beings. In the United States, we have unalienable rights, according to the Declaration of Independence. We also have the right to life, liberty, and the pursuit of happiness.

The use of the word *pursuit* is significant, because it informs us that happiness is dynamic, not static. Happiness is ever evolving, and we must evolve with it. We must make an effort to be happy. Happiness itself is not an unalienable right—merely the pursuit of it is.

This changes the idea that one is entitled. You must make an effort, and sometimes the pursuit of happiness is painful. It is painful, because the seeker must delve within and understand the darkness to appreciate and seek the light.

Anyhow, back to Joe. Here he is, fighting for something, and he does not have the weapons, tools, or plan to win. Worse yet, he does not know what or whom he is fighting. Joe has to recognize that the real war is the one within.

How can Joe complete the puzzle in his marriage when he does not understand the importance of his own constructed image? Integration of his truth begins with Joe piecing himself together first. The integration of his truth is understanding his traumatic past. Will it stop manifesting itself in his present and poisoning his future?

Joe cannot fix what he does not know is broken.

I tremble at the thought of looking Belle in the eyes. I fear that she will know. The saying, "Eyes are windows to the soul," is so true. My soul feels as though it has betrayed her. Yet, I have betrayed Jude, and she has betrayed Joe.

Betrayal is the hallmark of our stories. It is the theme that holds us in bondage. Shining a light on the betrayal will release its constriction on all of our hearts.

A seven year old was unaware that she could be seen in plain sight in her Cookie Monster slippers, even with her eyes covered. A woman many years later is unaware that she can still be seen, even if she shrouds the truth in justifications.

The Riley-Buttons sit together this time on the loveseat. I am elated.

However, I am not sure why. Am I elated because I am happy for them or for myself? Maybe it is a little of both.

I check my purse for my glasses. It is easier to veil the pain behind a set of spectacles, and it helps avoid feeling like a spectacle.

"So," my voice trembles. "It has been quite some time since we last met."

They both nod.

The silence is eerie. Do they know? How could they?

"First, let me ask about Jasmine. How is she doing?" I inquire.

Belle speaks first. She looks so ashen. Her face looks exsanguinated, maybe due the hemorrhage in her emotional heart.

Her voice seems barely audible.

"Jasmine is Jasmine. She has good days and not so good days. She still can probably sense that we are not in accord. We have invasive species in us and through us. Until we deal with it, it will destroy us." Belle collapses back in her seat.

I feel uneasy. Is she talking about me? Why am I so paranoid? She cannot know!

"Wow. That was powerful, Belle. Invasive species? Can you unpack that a bit more?" I ask with my best poker face.

Belle sits quietly for a moment. She cocks her head to the side and looks up inquisitively. She is searching for the right picture to paint, I think.

I look over to Joe. Joe seems preoccupied. He is not even really here, it seems. His eyes scan the room, not connecting with any one thing. I am interested in what is going on there, but I need to understand Belle first.

"Okay … I think I got it!" Belle's voice seems to pick up momentum. "So, have you ever heard of the golden mussel?" She asks.

"Is that a movie?"

"No," she states flatly, acknowledging my ignorance.

"It is a mollusk. Let's say *clam* to make it easier. So, these clams come from Asia, and over the past sixty years or more, they have moved through various waters. In the Amazon, where they were introduced some years ago, they are destroying the ecosystem. They are so many of them and those waters will no longer be able to survive." She smiles, obviously proud of her smartness.

"So, what I am hearing is that you both introduced invasive species to your ecosystem, therefore destroying it?"

"Yes," Belle replies.

"Hmmm." I take my pen and start to chew the tip. "Joe, what do you think of Belle's metaphor?"

Joe pulls out of his distraction, and he looks bewildered, as if someone just dropped him into my office from the sky.

"Well, I think I understand. We both put people into our relationship and messed it up?" Although phrased as a question, his raised hand and high-pitched voice actually declare there is a much easier way to say it.

"Sounds about right. However, let me challenge you both. The introduction of this invasion was/is a symptom of a larger problem. Just because you get rid of the symptom does not mean the problem is solved. I believe we have talked about this before."

They are both silent.

"Joe, honestly … what do you want from Belle?" I plead.

I am taken aback by the mild desperation in my voice. I can feel my own stuff beginning to be involved in the session. I am conflicted, as I am not sure of my motive anymore.

He looks to Belle. "I want her to love me. I want her to *want* to love me."

"Now let's sharpen the focus. Do you want her to love you as the man in her life or as a fellow human being?"

"As her man," he states, as if it's obvious.

"Okay, I am going to say something that on the surface is painful but needs to be said. Do you trust me?" I ask.

Oh my God! That came out so fast. I did not want to ask that question.

"Umm, yes? Where is this going?" Belle asks. Joe says yes too.

I turn to Joe. "Then you have to act like the man who is at center stage in her life and not an audience member. You seem to put yourself in obscurity as it pertains to the relationship but demand the screen time of the main character."

I allow them to sit with that. Belle's head cocks toward him in a "what will you say to that?" sort of way.

"What does that mean, exactly?" Joe can sense Belle's nonverbal message. He does not even look her way.

"That is for Belle to answer," I say as I point over to Belle.

Belle is not quite ready for that. I assume she is prepared to take ownership of making her needs clear, even if she is caught off guard, so I watch her and wait.

Belle adjusts her clothing, takes a deep breath, and begins to speak.

"You are not my partner, Joe. You orbit my life rather than being in my life. You are in the back seat of the car rather than helping me drive it. I am struggling to swim with you hanging on my heels. It's all the same statements I have been making about you over the years: We are not a couple; we are just existing. What plans do we have? Financially, we are a mess, and you do nothing about that. I feel as though I am your mother, who handicapped you. I mean, what is our future? What do we do to move this 'marriage' forward? I can no longer operate as man and wife. For you to cheat on me was insulting. For me to cheat on you was not payback, as you keep thinking; it was different. I was and am dying in this, and you cannot see it. I need to feel alive. He made me feel alive." She turns to look at me.

I drop my pen and begin shifting around in my seat. What the hell? I cannot handle this guilt. I did not do this on purpose. It was and is destiny. I mean, I did not *take* her man.

"Made me feel alive," she says again.

God, I know what that feels like now. I had no idea how shallow my breath was until Eoghan's introduction into my life expanded my lungs. I can never go back to that restricted and constricted place. I just can't. What am I doing? I am supposed to be in this powerful space with Belle and Joe, and I cannot get out of my own stuff. Okay. Let me refocus.

Belle has stated some powerful words: "I can no longer operate as man and wife." This resonates with me, as I have the same issues in my own marriage.

Joe looks despondent. "So, this all rests on me, huh? She takes no responsibility, huh? She did not *have* to cheat. Made me handicapped? What the hell is that?"

"Wrong focus, Joe. Now is the time to look at the each other and determine how it impacts the unit. Belle's theme of operating as man and wife in this union has been consistent. What I see from her is her reaction to how she feels about the marriage. What I see from you is what is done *despite* the marriage. Belle needs to own the fact that, for whatever reason, she has chosen for this marriage to. She could have left. Instead, she reacted to her environment rather than changing it." He looks at me with a bewildered look on his face.

I continue. "That is hardcore truth right there. You, on the other hand, became complacent, as you can see that she will just complain and stay. Your infidelity, however, requires a bit more work. The underlying reason is far more intertwined with your past and must be dealt with. A famous quote by Buckminster Fuller is, "You never change things by fighting the existing reality. To change something, build a new model that makes the old model obsolete." Once you get a grip on the *why*, you must decide to completely change. It is a scary endeavor, but it also an adventure. It is not just the fate of your marriage that is at stake. Is the fate of Joe as a man. Now, Joe. Now is the time. Understand it, own it, and change it," I exclaim.

Joe, recognizing the intensity of the situation, sits back. He seems to have been absorbed by the fabric of the loveseat. He fiddles around, patting his chest and pockets for his phone.

Belle's face grows increasingly agitated. I can tell she wants him to connect, to simply respond or acknowledge what she said.

She sits up to speak, but I raise my hand, stopping her. I want Joe to go through this process. He will have to be a bit uncomfortable, and he will not be able to hide. He has used Belle's tirades as a smokescreen to not do anything about anything.

Belle and Joe have engaged in cyclical behavior for a long time. She screams, he folds, she screams, he folds, and on and on. He has never truly had to be accountable for his actions, because Belle has been too busy telling him what his actions are. Therefore, Joe has never had to feel the true impact of his behavior. She has grown accustomed to him doing nothing, and he has grown accustomed to her screaming and withdrawing behaviors. This has caused a numbing effect for both parties. Neither truly has to deal with the problem, as they are constantly dancing out of step to music that is out of tune.

After locating his phone and checking the time, Joe looks to Belle, who is looking at me. He takes his cap off and runs his hand through his hair. A deep sigh leaves his body.

This time, Joe needs to feel the full impact of this moment. I allow the silence to fill the room. It is excruciatingly uncomfortable for them. I can tell.

After a few minutes that feel like a few hours, Joe responds.

"I do not know how to be a man to her. I know what she deserves, and I can see myself being that person. I just don't know how to become that person or, really, if I can handle it."

"Joe, do you think maybe you deserve being that person not for Belle, but for yourself? That you deserve to be the best man you can be because *you* deserve it?" I ask.

"I don't get what you mean, River. I deserve it?" he responds.

"Yes, because you deserve it. Let me follow this up with a more important and even more probing question. Why do you see other women?"

Joe looks over at Belle, who is looking at me with eyes so hard and glassy it unnerves me. Is she doing this because I asked her not to talk, or because she knows that the heart that has been ripped from her chest is resting in my hand?

I shake my head at the thought and return my gaze to Joe.

"I get the attention that I need. I do not get any attention in this relationship. Belle simply, as I stated before, does not show physical affection or even that she is interested. So, I get to feel wanted."

"That's honest," I add. "Now I am going to push the envelope a bit further. Have you ever felt wanted?"

"By whom?" he asks.

I lean forward.

"Just period—in life, growing up—have you ever felt truly wanted or like you really belonged somewhere?"

I know that this is a pivotal moment for Joe. I suspect that he never has felt wanted or connected. His traumatic upbringing saw to that. Joe was the result of a secret no one wanted to claim. This feeling has lived with Joe his whole life.

Cue the dramatic music. What a horrible thought. Sometimes in the most serious moments, one can have the most inappropriate thoughts.

Joe stands up. "I do not want to talk about this anymore. I am ready to go." He walks to the door, grabbing the knob.

"Wait!" Belle yells, reaching for Joe without looking toward him.

Belle's head swivels sharply to Joe. She speaks in the most heartfelt way I have ever heard her talk to Joe. Her wide incredulous eyes seek understanding. She softens her voice, but it is laced with slight agitation: "Run again? Run from truth? Run from the very truth that can help set you free? You are a prisoner who wants to remain a prisoner because you have been institutionalized. It is all you know. You have chosen me to be your warden."

I watch the beautiful work taking place before me. This is what counseling is all about. It is about revelation before institution. Joe is being emotionally pushed, and it is scary. It always is. Anytime we have to face the demons in our lives, we run away. It is easier to live possessed by the demon than to face it head on.

This moment is not just about Joe. It is also about Belle, who recognizes what her role in the marriage has been. Both will have to choose new roles.

Joe does not turn around while Belle is talking. He begins to respond while facing the door. He offers a few hums and heavy sighs. I suspect talking to the door is safer. How do you face the world while admitting you have never felt you belonged in it? I sympathize with Joe, because he must know that I know he feels vulnerable and exposed.

"Joe," I ask. "Before you answer the question about feeling wanted, can tell me what your experience is right now. What are you feeling?

"I ... umm ... I feel trapped right now," he mumbles, still facing the door.

Leaning forward toward him, my glasses slipping to the tip of my nose, I say, "Yes, I can imagine. Do you know that you can free yourself? Do you know that leaving this room right now will keep you in bondage? I am curious as to what this trapped feeling is. I suspect you do feel trapped or cornered. Who are you trapped or cornered by?"

Joe's hands are trembling.

Years of burying pain and truth can come up like a geyser. Someone you trust can reach in and expose the real you. He or she can snatch the unknown part of Johari's Window away from you and make you face what's there. This is an extremely scary prospect. It is not slow, as it does not allow for you to justify and clean up. It is raw, unedited, and unpurified truth. Many times in life, we only are willing to look at the truth once we dress it up. In such cases, it is no longer the truth we are looking at. It has become perverted.

Joe must experience this pain in order to be free from it.

"I ... I don't know. You?" he says, still facing the door.

"No, not me, Joe. You have been cornered by *you*. You are facing *you* right now. You are facing reality. You are facing truth. If we were in a boxing match, you would be facing yourself. You would be facing the truth, all the pain that comes with it, and the imposter. The imposter acts as your representative to the world. Navigating around your pain, it also manifests its destruction at the same time," I explain.

Then I continue. "You have been living with what I call 'the nothing.' The nothing is the despair and emptiness brought on by historical pain. Some people allow the nothing in their lives to absorb the only 'somethings' they have or create. We are not only acknowledging the presence of the nothing but also crowning it with power. It becomes increasingly difficult to create something when we have given so much power to the nothing. Do you understand?" I ask.

"Yes," he says as he turns to me.

"Good. Now that you are walking through the murky swamps of your despair, you have an opportunity to arrive at its birthplace. When you dare to trudge through the swamp, risking being consumed by the pain, you can shine your light. This allows you to name it, use it, and grow from it. If we choose to absorb the darkness, we transform, joining forces with it. We are then destined to darken the lives of others in our paths. We have to stop avoiding the pain. It has to hurt if it's to heal. You do not have to travel through the darkness alone. Belle, take his hand." I point over to Joe.

Belle seems confused but complies. She rises, walks over to Joe, and grabs his hand.

"Are you willing to walk with him as he unravels his story?"

"Yes," she says in a cracked whisper while gazing at Joe. Her eyes say, "I am here with you."

"Joe, now is the time for you to start being the hero of your own story. This is a story you know. You may not understand it, but you know it, as those chapters were laid prior to today. What you don't realize is that you can rewrite each one. You do not have to be consumed by the nothing by being nothing. You do not have to prove that your father or mother's behaviors were just, and you do not have to accept that you do not have value. You belong. Create a space for *yourself* in your heart."

Tears stream down Joe's face. He is at the source of his pain and fear, and Belle is with him. She is *actually* with him while he acknowledges the nothing that he has allowed to consume and employ him during his life. I smile inside. Belle then does something that practically teases my heart. She squeezes his hand! She says absolutely nothing and everything at the same time. This immediately takes me back to my discussion with Conrado. I flash back to the moment when I felt the sting of loneliness and neglect while I was watching a movie years ago. It reminds me of the vulnerability I felt retelling Conrado how my soul cried in desperation that day.

Instantly, my eyes well with tears. I need to get out of the room. I need to talk, no—to see Eoghan. Immediately, the walls begin to close in on me. My lungs constrict, holding hostage the source of life—breath. I abruptly get up. Both Belle and Joe's moment is destroyed by my inability to control my personal and professional manners. I apologize and ask to be excused for a moment.

Belle and Joe move toward the couch. I desperately try to hide my face as the tears become too heavy to hold. My own pain has reeled its ugly head unexpectedly. The clicking of my heels is the only sound I hear as I race to the bathroom. I fall into the stall, cupping my right hand over my mouth. I fold over, holding my stomach with my left arm. Oh my God, it hurts so much! The tears flow freely as I work to regain control. I cannot risk anyone knowing. My cries are deep heaves as my body shudders, fighting me to release it all. I can hear footsteps enter the bathroom. Damn. I have to work extra hard to maintain. I try to hold my breath. The pain is at the surface, and I hold my shaking hands, trying to control the pain. I hear the sink turn on. Good, she is almost out of here. The door opens, but no footsteps.

"You okay, hun?" An older woman's voice pours like honey over the walls.

Mmhmm," I manage to get out.

"No, baby, you are not okay. Anything I can do?" the honey voice asks.

"Mmm, nooo," I manage to crank out.

"Well, baby, nothing in this life that got you hemmed in that bathroom is going to last unless you let it," the honey continues.

Geez, will she not go away?! My eyes grow wide with irritation.

"Mmm … k," is all I can manage for the moment.

"Come on out here, baby. Let's get you okay." I needed to hear that: "Let's get you okay."

My heart ignores my mind, and I unlock the door and walk to the sink. "Okay, just a sec." I struggle to clean myself up before I see her.

"Come on. Nah, don't go cleaning the very thing you need to do to clean your soul. Come, let me see ya." Her voice is calming, like a warm breeze during a brisk fall day.

I see her. Her eyes are a warm hazel brown. She's an elderly woman; she can't be a day younger than seventy-five. She looks as though she should be preparing morning biscuits.

"I'm Earnestine O. Banks. What is your name?"

"River … Dr. River Meadows." I try to be as professional as I can, extending my hand.

"Girl, if you do not get that away from me … Give me a hug. I'm Mahaley's mom." She reaches her arms and embraces me.

I fall into her arms, and I mean *fall*. I begin to sob.

This is horrible, but it feels so good.

"Sweetie, let it out. I read something a long time ago. Suppose to be something written by the Buddha: 'Suffering is not holding you; you are holding suffering.' Just let it go."

I sob even harder. I am damn near convulsing in this woman's arms. What about Joe and Belle? I have no idea. I cannot face them at the moment. The reality of it all has removed its protective shell of professionalism, justification, and repression.

What felt like an hour was no more than ten minutes. Ms. Banks attempts to reach for paper towels while holding me. She is successful at folding the towels and putting cold water on them.

"Lift your head, sweetie." I comply. I have an extraordinary trust in this angel of a woman. She dabs my eyes and cleans the streaks of pain from my cheeks. I stand on my own, trying to resurrect the professional me. I need the professional me to stand in for the broken me.

"Now, I want you to tell me what is going on. I want to help you. I know you help others. It is now your turn," the rich honey of Ms. Banks emits.

I feel as though I am gathered enough to see if my clients are still in my office. "I am okay now. Just some mess I am going through," I say, attempting to reassure her.

"Yeah, the rock always turns down the help. River, baby, you cannot carry this. You should not carry this. I can see the pain in your eyes. How will you be able to continue to help others? I hear so many good things about you. You should come by for tea this week. I'll tell Mahaley to put it in your schedule. Now, I gotta go get that husband of mine out the lobby. I won't take no for an answer. Remember, it may be hell right now, but the good Lord wastes no pain on the weak. This is for you," she says. And with that, she is gone. I lean against the door and remember a word I gave to Joe.

"You do not have to travel alone."

I leave my "session" with Earnestine, and my mind turns back to Joe and Belle. I am appalled by my inability to control, to separate, and navigate my emotions. I look in the office, and they are gone. I walk over to the front office where Mahaley is sitting and scrolling through her phone. Does she not have enough to do?

"Mahaley, the Riley-Buttons—did they leave?"

"Uh, yes, Dr. Meadows. They made another appointment and told me to thank you," she responds, all while staring at her phone.

"Oh!" Mahaley exclaims after a pause. "My mother made an appointment for you! She's like that. Ernie has quite the effect on people. She told me you and she had a great talk," she says as she starts to laugh. "I tell ya, my momma has more clients than you will ever have. She frequently has 'tea,'" she says, making air quotes. "My father is always fussing about it." She adds a deep drawl to her voice and says, imitating her father's voice, "'Ernie, good Lawd, you got our house lookin' like a confessional—all this traffic!'" Switching to an imitation of the honey voice I remembered, she now imitates Ernie: "'Now, Armand, ya know I'm just doing the Lawd's work … now get outta here.'" Mahaley cracks herself up.

"Well, okay, who do I have next?"

"You're free for the next two hours. You had a couple of cancellations. Your last appointment is a new person—anxiety about a new relationship," she says and then closes her laptop.

Great. The last thing I want to talk about is a relationship.

"Your mother is amazing," I add. "What was she doing here?"

"Oh, my parents came to have lunch with me. It was a late lunch. They hung out for a while, critiquing my new boyfriend. You remember the one I told you about—or asked you about, I think?" she asks. I can tell by the lost look on her face that she is revisiting that moment in the car.

"Yes, you asked me. Well, nonetheless your mom is great. So, when are we having tea?" I smile warmly. I actually look forward to this, so I must really need it.

Pulling up the calendar, she says, "Let's see: Thursday, eight thirty in the morning. In a couple of days, prepare to be Ernestized." Mahaley cracks up at her own wit.

"Very funny, Mahaley. By the way, how did you schedule a time without asking me first?"

"You might be my boss, Dr. Rivers," she says in an extremely measured way as she puts her head down and looks up, leaning forward, "but Earnestine Ophelia Banks is my *mother*."

"Point taken," I say with a smile. "Okay, I am going to grab a bite. I will be right back." I begin to turn around.

"Oh, wait! Um, yeah, they left you a note!" Mahaley says while reaching her hand out with a piece of a paper.

"Who?" I inquire.

I am a bit frightened. Maybe they are angry because of how I left the session.

"The Riley-Buttons," she says in a you-should've-known kind of sarcastic way.

I take a deep breath and slowly unfold the note.

Dear Dr. Meadows,

We so appreciate the time you took with us today. It was so powerful—painful but powerful. You leaving the session was very creative! You knew we would talk and connect with one another. We set up another appointment, but we needed to share right away how amazing this was for both of us. It was awesome.

Belle and Joe

This actually makes me laugh out loud. At first I snicker, but soon I start to bellow and cannot stand up. What a day.

"My God," I say while laughing out loud. "They think that was an intervention! Oh, God." I just cannot stop laughing and shaking my head.

Mahaley looks amused. "That must've been a funny letter."

"No, not really," I say, still laughing and wiping away my tears. "So, what's the name of the next client?" I take deep breaths, trying to bring myself to normal.

"I don't know. I mean, I cannot pronounce the name. It's weird." She pulls up the schedule.

"Let me see," I say.

Mahaley turns the laptop to me. In horror and elation, I see a familiar name.

At seven o'clock this evening, I'll be seeing someone named Anxiety Eoghan McGhee.

A barely audible "What?" manages to leave my mouth. My body grows limp. I lose my grip on the note, and it falls from my hand like a lone snowflake.

"Dr. Meadows?"

I can barely hear Mahaley. I cannot even respond to her. My mind is racing. What is he doing here? I mean, why is he coming here? I am petrified and excited at the same time. My thoughts are racing. He is not here for help; I know it. A new relationship? Me? He is here to see me—about me? Or could it be about Belle? Oh my God. This has been the worse day ever.

"Dr. Meadows?"

I abruptly turn my head. Mahaley is a little stunned by the sudden movement.

"Are you okay? You look like you have seen a ghost!" she says.

"I'm good. Yes, I am okay. Ghost? No. Just a long, long day," I say.

Seen a ghost? Man—if she only knew.

Every fiber of my body wants to call him and ask why or tell him to stay home.

Even though Belle is not here, for some reason this feels like *her* territory, even though it is *my* practice. I must remember I am the only one who truly knows we are triangulated.

I thank Mahaley and tell her that I look forward to meeting with her mother. I then go to my office. The day's events have been so emotional that I need to rest.

Setting my phone alarm for thirty minutes prior to Eoghan's arrival, I begin to meditate. Deep breathing helps bring me back to a state of calm.

I ask God to help me figure this out. I am lost, and worse, I feel lost in this whole triangulated love affair.

I can feel the grip of consciousness slipping from me as my body takes over, bearing the gift of oblivion.

21

BLACK SATINS

I cannot believe my mother spent the entire visit fussing at me. Like I really have time for this! How in the Sam hell do you get on my damn back about how I should have been there for him, but he wasn't even there? Jude's thoughts consume him as he prepares the daily sales reports.

His thoughts move back and forth from River to Jezzy.

I cannot keep living like this. We all deserve better. Why am I trying to hold on to either of them?

"Hey, man, you got a minute?" a voice asked with a brief knock at the door.

"Come in, Max." Jude's sees him from the window and beckons him in.

"Maximilian James, my top seller. What can I do you for?" Jude asks.

"Got time for a few tonight? I gotta work some stuff out."

"Hmm, sure. Six thirty? Black Satins? You know where it is?"

"Yep, I do. Cool."

Jude returns to his thoughts and reports. *What does Max want to talk to me about? That's weird. We really ain't cool like that. It must be serious if he came to me. Well, I got two hours until I find out. He needs to talk to my wife. She's the therapist of the family.*

Family. Hmm. Riv seems rather distant lately—more than usual. His thoughts float to her hands running through his hair as they acknowledged the separateness in their union.

He stops for a minute and stares at the picture of River on his desk.

She really does not deserve this, he thinks to himself.

Shaking the thought off, he returns to his report. *I can drown the guilt at Black Satins in a couple of hours*, he thinks and chuckles to himself.

Black Satins is crowded for a Tuesday night.

Max waves Jude over. He already has a couple of beers at the table. Looks like there are a couple of empty ones too.

"Hey, man, I gotcha a couple. Those yours," he points.

"Thanks, man. What's up?" Jude asks.

"Just sit."

This must be serious. What the hell does he want?

"How are you and Riv?"

"Hmm, okay, I guess. Why? What's this about, Max?"

Max can barely contain himself. Tears are welling in his eyes. Jude looks around to see who is watching.

"Man, what the hell is wrong with you?" Jude asks as he leans forward, trying to yell a whisper.

"My wife," he manages to get out.

"Dude, that ain't worth a special meeting with me. What's up?"

"Cancer. It is back, and it's bad."

Jude sits back in his chair. He had heard about Max's wife over the years. He knew she was in remission and had lost her breasts, but the couple had overcame the trauma of her illness.

"Man, I'm sorry." Jude is still confused about why Max has come to him. He never has done so before. "Whatever you need—you need time off?"

"Yeah, but that is not why I asked you here," Max states.

"Okay, then what's up?" *Damn, this is the third time I've asked him*, he thinks to himself.

"She's dying. You 'member that chick six months ago? The one that like to touch everybody? I sold her that used Pontiac?"

"No, Max. You know how many women come into the dealership? You're asking me to remember one? And one from six months ago?" Jude's voice begins to show impatience.

"Sure, you do. She came in a little overdressed for car shopping. Had on a little black dress."

"Oh … yeah. I do remember her." The image of long legs that ended in red stilettos enters Jude's consciousness. A smile crosses his face. Momentarily lost in her sexiness, Jude forgets he is here with Max and shakes his head.

"Wait, why are we talking 'bout her? What the hell does that have to do with everything going on with your wife?"

Max pauses.

He slowly begins to speak.

"I cheated on Elizabeth with her, and I want to tell her. I want to be clean of this."

Jude's eyes widen. *Why is he coming to me about this?* he thinks to himself.

"Why are you telling me? 'Cause my wife's a counselor?"

"Yeah, but that is not it. I see y'all pictures, and over the years I've seen her come up to the dealership."

"So?"

"Y'all look like y'all good. Me and Lizzy been having a hard time for years. We only got better in the last year or so."

Jude's impatience escapes him. "Again, so you've seen pictures, and my wife comes to the dealership?" his voice begs for connections.

"Y'all look happy. I've always wanted what you and River have. I came to you because I thought you could tell me if I should tell Liz about that girl. I want to be clean of this, and I cannot stand holding it in."

Jude sits back and lifts his eyes to the ceiling. "And that's why you came to me. You figure my marriage is strong and we are happy, so I can tell you if it's the right thing to do?"

"Yes. So?"

Jude looks down at the beer in his hand as he digests the irony of the moment.

"Get the waitress to bring a Hennessy Max, we are going to need it."

Max waves the waitress over and order drinks.

The two engage in awkward small talk and a safe discussion about children, sports, idiots at work, and watches. The air thickens with unfinished business in between the small talk. Max feebly attempts to draw the discussion back to the origin of their meeting. A skillful manipulator, Jude averts the topic like a trained truth assassin. After a few avoidances, he realizes he must find something meaningful to say.

Taking a deep breath, Jude mulls over lying to Max or being honest. He conjures up a fantastical lie to tell Max, but his thoughts run to Max's dying wife. He vaguely remembers her company events, talking to his wife, getting punch, and laughing at one of his inappropriate jokes. He remembers the cards and donations that were created in her honor during the years she had fallen ill. Not realizing he was holding his breath, he exhales.

"Man, where you go? I've been calling your name—beer got you?" Max says with a smile.

Max, not realizing that Joe unconsciously left the room, shakes his head back into reality.

The waitress arrives with the liquid designed to make hard things easy. They toast to the health of his wife.

"If I was a bettin' man, I'd say you was avoiding the question, Jude."

Looking down at his drink, Jude says, "Naw … just thinkin'. This is heavy, Max."

"I know." The two sit in silence for a while.

Finally, Jude breaks out: "Okay, um, look, are you telling her for you or for her? I mean, why hurt her if you don't have to?"

"I know … I thought of that. But, something is telling me I should. I mean it gets stronger … it's becoming all I think about." Max sits back and looks hard at Jude. "Honestly, something today told me I should ask you."

Jude laughs nervously. Looking around the bar, guilt begins to simmer in his heart; knowing he is a fraud makes him feel rotten.

"Look, if you feel like you must tell her, then tell her. I mean, she may be upset. You think she'll leave?" Jude asks.

"I don't know, but she has always been good to me. She deserves to be treated right, you know? She is the best thing that ever happened to me, and I messed up."

"Yeah, 'bout that ... why did you do it?" Jude asks.

"I know, it was weakness. I was wrapped up in all of this and couldn't cope. It was an easy distraction from it all."

"Easy distraction from it all," Jude repeats just loud enough for Max to hear.

"Yeah, easy. I mean, you know how it is sometimes. You just don't wanna see it." Max continues to talk, but Jude is lost in the words "easy distraction from it all." They hit him like a ton of bricks.

He realizes that he has been distracting himself all of these years, but from what? A door has appeared in his heart, and he is searching his mind for the key. *Why am I doing this?* He thinks to himself. *And Riv, my God. She does not deserve this.* Jude winces at the years of dishonesty and begins to feel the weight of his own lifeless marriage.

"Man, I wanna thank you for helping me figure this out. I just gotta figure out when and where," Max says feeling accomplished.

"No problem," Jude responds, somewhat confused. *I really did not do anything*, he thinks to himself. *Shit, he sure opened the pits of hell for me.* Grabbing his jacket, he says, "Let's go."

Often the purpose of our encounters isn't obvious. We may initially believe we are being there for others, when in fact we are the ones in need. We are nourished in our own lives through others' revelations and encounters. Our hearts also have the answers to many of our complex questions. We only need to speak our questions aloud to another spirit to hear our truth and confirm what we already know. The truth is never hard to figure out. Living with the consequences of the truth? Well, that's a different story.

22

RIVER'S CHRYSALIS

"Hey, beautiful." The words pour from Eoghan's lips like the morning sun.

I smile. This is such a wonderful dream. Eoghan's kiss lands softly on my cheek. I smile, welcoming another and another and wait. I open my eyes. Good God! I am not dreaming! I stumble over myself, almost falling off the couch. Eoghan's warm laughter eases the embarrassment.

I gather myself, straightening my clothes and hair.

"You look fine—actually, more than fine." He draws me to him with one arm around my waist. I haven't found my words yet. Staring at him, I just love the space we are sharing. His presence makes everything make sense, even in this chaos.

He kisses me, slightly tugging at my bottom lip. My head exsanguinates, making me feel dizzy.

"Why—why are you here? How did you get back here?" I manage to muster a logical sequence of words.

He laughs. "Riv, love, a mere secretary cannot keep me from you. I wanted to see you. I needed to see you."

"Are you going to sit, Mr. Anxiety, or hold me the whole time?" I ask. Smiling, I offer him a seat.

"I am not here really as a client. I refuse to let your 'oaths' keep us apart. It's bad enough that your 'vows' are doing it." He laughs, amused at his own wit. "Anyhow, is that really a question? I can stand here and hold you all night. I just wanted to see all of you. I want to be in all of your world, so I started with your work."

I grab his hands, and standing, we hold each other's hands. Our lips are almost touching. It is such a vulnerable place to stand so close to a person. I love the tension in the moment. Our breathing becomes heavier and in sync.

I break first. Laughing, I pull back. "Come on, let's sit down."

"Which is your chair?" he asks. I point to the wingback.

"I'm going to sit in your chair for a moment. Do you mind?"

"No, feel free. I have been sitting in it all day."

I sit on the couch where Belle usually sits. A twinge of guilt wrenches my stomach. I push the inclination to allow the experience to simmer down. I want to enjoy this moment with Eoghan.

"So, I'm gonna ask you some questions." Eoghan deepens his voice. Grabbing my notebook and pen, he cocks his head to the side.

"You in full therapist mode, huh?" I ask with a laugh. It's not a normal laugh. It is the laugh of a child. It surprises me. I haven't heard that joy in a long time.

Eoghan is not moved by my laugh. He is taking this role-play seriously. "So, River, your mother. How old is she?"

"Sixty-four," I answer. I then sit up and fold my hands on my lap, taking note of Eoghan's serious cue.

"Interesting," he smiles crookedly.

"No, it's not. And we don't say that for *everything*." I shoo him.

"Okay, okay … another question. What is your relationship with your mother?" he asks.

"We have a good relationship. I love her dearly. We try to go out to dinner at least once a week."

I envision my mother sitting across the dinner table. She asks the usual questions: "How was work? How's Jude? How are you?"

I play the usual script in my head, not once mentioning Eoghan. She did notice at our last dinner that something was different. She said I had an "extra sparkle" about me. I just smiled and redirected the topic.

"Really, once a week? So, what is she like?" Eoghan asks.

"Is this session about me or my mother? I might be getting a little jealous!" I ask curiously.

"No need. I just want to know where you come from." He is serious.

Sitting back and looking up, I think of my mother. "Okay, well she is a powerful woman. She is a woman who not only knows her own worth but helps others know theirs as well. She is a survivor like no other. You ever see the first *Terminator* movie?" I ask.

"Yes" he says.

"She is the original Sarah Conner. She is a warrior among warriors. She is prepared for any fight for those she call her own. She is the second coming of Harriet Tubman, freeing those around her from self-imposed mental and emotional slavery. She wears the essence of First Lady Michelle Obama. Her strength is quiet but apparent. She is Cleopatra; her beauty draws you, but her intelligence keeps you. That, my friend, is my mother."

Eoghan leans forward, intrigued. "That is the cloth from which you are cut?"

"Yes," I state flatly. "I know this to be true."

"Let's see what you have to say about your father."

"Well, they divorced when I was young. But I still have his blood running through my veins. He died when I was in high school."

"What do you know about him?" Eoghan asks.

"Interesting that you would ask. I feel the presence and the absence of my father all the time. The presence of my father was his ability to stand up for himself. He was abused when he was young. He had enough confidence in his ability to care for himself, so he ran away from home. He bore the spirit of John Cousteau. He was an adventurer who failed to acknowledge fear and human-made boundaries. He was a power that only needed direction. That is the blood that runs through these veins. That is his presence that I feel daily," I answer.

Eoghan pauses for a moment, allowing the weight of my father's presence to fill the room.

"Okay, how do you feel about his absence?" he asks.

"I see my father's face every time I see a reflection of myself. I have a daily reminder that he is here with me. I am always aware of the stamp he put on the world, and he left with my image of him. The father/daughter relationship is a special relationship. He was my introduction to man," she says with a brief pause.

Then she continues. "Even in his absence, he remains my introduction to man. I cannot talk to my father and seek his counsel in real life. I cannot hear his laugh, a laugh that was maniacal like my own. I cannot see the world as he saw it. He was not one for traditional employment, if you know what I mean, but he was brilliant—just misguided. Sometimes, I feel that I have inherited that part of him." I am beginning to feel the pain of this discussion. "So, that's it. I want to sit on the porch swing and drink coffee with my father while he says inappropriate stuff that I am slightly embarrassed by."

My face is growing warm, as the wound is emitting grief to my heart.

Eoghan looks around for tissue, and I laugh. He doesn't know my philosophy.
"It's okay. Let me have this," I say.
"Are you able to continue?" he asks, looking worried.

"Yes."

"He died while you were in high school?" he asks.

"Yes."

"What was your relationship like up until then? Did you have one?"
Here we go. This is going to be painful. Why am I allowing him to take me here?

"It was kind of touch and go. There was so much bad blood, I think from my mom and dad, that I kind of got caught up in it all. What I do know is that as a little girl, I was the apple of his eye, as they say," I say and smile. "One day my uncle told me that I was always under my dad's foot and that we were inseparable. It is nice to know that he really loved me, though I have no memory of him telling me so. So, I have this yearning"—I pause and close my eyes as the moment begins to consume me—"for him." Opening my eyes, I continue. "It is hard for me to explain. I spent time with him when I was older, but my dad was chasing something or, better yet, someone. He did not intend to neglect us; he just never saw the blind spots."

I refocus my attention on Eoghan. I realize that this whole time, I have not really been looking at Eoghan. I have been lost in the space, much like my clients.

Eoghan is studying me through his questions and watching how I tell the story.

"Chasing," Eoghan repeats.

"Yes, chasing himself, I suspect. He was chasing an idea of who he was supposed to be, you know? I was told he never was a nine-to-five kind of guy. He was always thinking of some kind of scheme to get ahead. He always saw the destination but could not respect the journey, I suppose."

We often fail to respect the process of living and being human. We fail to understand the importance of the journey. We believe that we can outwit evolution. We cannot seem to grasp the importance of the chrysalis. A caterpillar cannot be a butterfly just because it wants to. It has to go through a four-stage process. If it fails to go through that process, it cannot be a butterfly. The caterpillar or, better put, butterfly larva, initially must eat an enormous amount of food in order to prepare for the process.

We need to do the same: we need to feed emotionally, psychologically, and spiritually. Now, the outside of a caterpillar does not grow. It must molt or shed its skin, as it can no longer fit its body. Humans need to do the same kind of shedding. We need to shed old beliefs, habits, and ways that no longer serve our best interests. As we are fed proper nutrition for our emotional, psychological, and spiritual domains, we must also shed maladaptive thoughts, emotions, and behaviors. Next, the caterpillar must do something pretty remarkable: it must form a pupa, or chrysalis.

Now, here is where the mystery happens. At this stage, it is neither a caterpillar nor a butterfly. Is that not amazing? A radical metamorphosis occurs during this stage, while the creature is in isolation. It does not rush this stage, as it must go through it in order to be. If we allow it, we too go through this stage in life. We can feel alone, confused, unsure, and frightened during this period, but it is a necessary phase for our mental and physical growth.

This stage can be painful, as life unfolds with all her elements to strengthen or break us. If we have chosen to feed ourselves the proper nutrition, we will bear fruit. Being a butterfly begins with being a caterpillar. You must be humble enough to respect *and* embrace the entire process.

"How about you, River? Do you respect the journey?" Eoghan asks.

I sit for a moment, and I allow the question to sit with my spirit. Do I respect the journey?

"Journey of life … yes, yes I do. I always see it in my clients."

"What about love? The journey to love?" He rests his chin in his hand, leaning forward.

Laughing, I respond, "Well, love is always a journey. There is never a destination with love."

"Not true," Eoghan responds.

"How so?"

"Well, as you stated, there is a journey to all things. While love itself is a journey, there is a separate process to get to love. I mean, typically you do not meet someone and just fall in love with him or her. You might love the person in a we-are-all-human kind of way, but that is not love of the heart," he explains.

Eoghan continues explaining by giving examples, but I stop listening after he says "typically." What does that mean?

"How is this, Riv? You being on this end of things—sitting in that chair as opposed to this one?" Rubbing the arm of the wingback, he raises an eyebrow and smiles.

"It feels naked. Extremely vulnerable. Exposed," I admit.

"Good," he declares.

"Good? I feel uncomfortable, off kilter, and vulnerable, and that is good? You wanted me here?" I ask, muffling a laugh.

Eoghan grows serious. "Yes, it is fertile ground for my final question."

I open my arms in total surrender and declare, "Okay, okay … let me have it. How more naked can this feel?"

"It's a simple question."
"Well, I have a simple answer," I say with sheer confidence.
"Do you love me?"
It feels as though something rips through my chest and snatches my heart out while it continues to beat. My lungs deflate. My legs and arms become limp. All the saliva dries and leaves my mouth like a desert. This is utterly frightening. Until today, I was living in limbo, a bit of a fantasy. This is real now or, better put, I am acknowledging the reality. I know the moment I answer the truth everything will need to change.
"A simple answer, River," he almost demands.
"Yes," I manage to squeak, biting my bottom lip.

It is silent for what seems like hours.
He stands, grabs my hands, and lifts me to my feet.
Holding me close, he kisses my lips. I am so dizzy right now. I want to faint. I can feel my heart beating hard, fast, and somewhat irregularly. A heart attack maybe?
"Quiet your spirit, River. I can feel the anxiety emitting from you. Remember, that is why I made the appointment!" he laughs.
I laugh nervously. "Yeah … looks like the joke is on me. I am the one with anxiety."
"No, you are not the only one. I am anxious too," he says, his voice beginning to shake.
"Why?" I ask.
Eoghan pulls me a little closer, a little tighter. There is barely a division between us.
"Because I love you too, River. My God. I love you."
The breath of his words draws me to his lips.
As beautiful as this moment is, what is to come is not. It is time for me to make a decision. Suitcases of pain and guilt are prepared for the trip I booked the moment I told this man I loved him.

23

A JONES FOR LOVE

"Belle, are you going to be outside long? The movie is starting soon," Joe yells from the foyer.

"We'll be in shortly," Belle yells back. Jasmine rests her head on her mom's lap.

"This swing is so relaxing," Belle says to herself. Her thoughts then turn toward Eoghan. *I wonder how he is doing. I miss him so much.* Looking down at Jasmine, she runs her hand through her hair. *With everything going on with Jazzy, I have been distracted.* "I am so sorry that I ... we hurt you, Jazzy."

"I know, Mommy. I love you." Jasmine says as she looks up to her mother.

Belle's thoughts drift back to Eoghan. *Does he miss me? It has been a few weeks, and I just need to know what happened. I can't even tell if I'm reinvested in my marriage. There is something happening, but I am not sure what.*

Sensing her mother's depressed mood, Jasmine asks, "Mommy, we just need a little faith, and everything will be okay."

"Oh, Jazzy. You are my miracle worker. You are right. I need faith that God will work all things out for the good of our little family, baby girl."

"Pray with me, Mommy."

Jasmine sits upright and holds Belle's hands. Belle smiles at Jasmine, and together they bow their heads.

"I'll lead, Mom," Jasmine says. "Dear God, I pray that you will heal our family. I pray that we are able to work together and get along. I pray that my mom and dad love one another. In Jesus's name. Amen."

Belle squeezes Jasmine's hand. "You have no idea what you mean to me," Belle says. Jasmine lays her head back in her mother's lap, collapsing into the safeness of her warmth.

Belle looks down at the coils of her daughter's hair. Gently pulling, she begins to pray to herself. *Dear Heavenly Father, please help me understand what I am supposed to do. Please forgive me for my sins. Please help me move through this, as I am not sure that I am willing to walk away from Eoghan. I know you are not pleased with me, but I am hurting. Please touch and heal my heart.*

"Come on, baby. Let's go inside. Dad and I are getting ready to go."

"You ready, babe?" Joe asks.

"Yeah, I'm ready. Let's go. What are we going to see?" Belle asks.

Smiling, Joe says, "You don't remember? We are going to the old school theater. We are seeing *Love Jones*."

The ride to the theater is quiet. Both Joe and Belle are lost in convoluted emotional swamps.

Joe grabs Belle's hand while walking into the dark theater. *Maybe this will remind us of who we were*, he thinks.

This movie is going to do nothing but remind me of what I am losing, Belle thinks.

Grabbing his phone, Joe glances at the screen: missed call from Randy. A mix of emotions stirs inside of Joe.

Joe's attention is divided as he listens to the opening song: "They say I'm hopeless, like a penny with a hole in it."

He smiles, as he is able to connect with a feeling of hopelessness. *I want my marriage, but I feel the need to hold on to this—to her. Why do I hold on to the "possibility of this thing," when I have the real thing right here?*

Looking over at Belle, Joe watches her being deeply engrossed in the movie. Smiling, he looks as if this is the first time he ever saw her. A stranger—her heart wrapped in the poetry, a language she speaks no more.

He can see the deep connection the film is making to the awakenings of her spirit as she remembers her original self.

He smiles at the persistence of the character Darius. He keeps pushing for the chance to share time and space with the woman he wants, Nina.

I need to be that persistent. I need to be able to draw this woman back. I need her to want to be drawn to me. I have to take the time and put in the time," he thinks to himself.

Grabbing her hand, he feels her warmth. He laughs at the emotional game being played by the characters in the film. Rubbing her hand, his heart saddens as he understands that he has caught a glimpse of the light she used to carry. He realizes he has been living with just a shadow of her inner spirit for many years.

The beautiful thing about love is that before hostility and apathy settle in, there are many opportunities to repair the damage. With time and work, the heart can heal to become stronger. Unfortunately, in the name of love, people play so many emotional games. These games prohibit us from entering the true sanctuary of love. The games people play imprison both people in individual cells, which is a sad state of affairs. The possibility of giving and receiving true love is forever thwarted by our cardinal sins. It really doesn't matter what your religious background is; these behaviors can birth destruction in your personal life, especially in relationships. Hubristic pride, greed, lust, malicious envy, gluttony, inordinate anger, and sloth are excessive qualities. We all possess them and employ them during times of weakness. However, there are times when we let the sensation of sin *become* who we are.

Instead, we should not allow sin to define our essence; instead, we should capture it and change it back to purity. There is a saying that humans have overlooked for centuries: take every thought captive. This action could very well change the climate of any sin.

The authenticity of people in their relationships with others is like a light that can be dimmed, causing it to exist in a state of perpetual imbalance. The games played in relationships end without winners on either side, and the union becomes the biggest loser.

24

EARNESTINE'S GIFT AND EOGHAN'S BETRAYAL

As I await my meeting with Earnestine, I am so excited—but a little nervous too.

"Mahaley, any pointers for meeting with your mom?" I ask, sipping coffee.

Mahaley closes her laptop and looks up at the ceiling. "I would just say, just be yourself and *don't lie!*"

I laugh, spitting out some of my coffee. "Why do you say it like that?"

Mahaley looks up, seemingly searching for an adequate answer.

"'Cause, it is like she is all-knowing. She doesn't look at you; she looks through you. I have never been able to lie to my mother. I cannot even put on a happy face when I am really upset; she sees right through it."

Smiling and using my most highbrow voice, I say, "Mahaley, I'm a therapist. I am the master of disguise. I am well trained in maneuvering. She won't get to or at me if I do not want her to."

Mahaley chuckles. "Okay *Doctor* Meadows. Don't say I didn't warn you. I cannot wait to see your face tomorrow after you meet with her. Just kidding. She's harmless, really. She gives life. Have fun."

Grabbing my purse, I am unknowingly on my way to the first of a series of conversations that will change the direction of my life.

The drive to Earnestine's is quiet. I want to get my game face on. As I pull up to the house, I notice how much it instantly makes me comfortable.

The house is welcoming from the outside. I chuckle to myself as I think of Hansel and Gretel. Her house lures one in with promises of comfort. The circular brick driveway begs you to remember the spell of an era when one visits for a while and leaves a changed person. The perimeter of the driveway is enchanted with a lush variety of spring flowers—green hydrangeas, pink roses, white narcissuses, pink hyacinths, and pink wax flowers.

I am instantly charmed. The stone house is small and distinct. Sitting among the cloned colonials, it challenges progression. Its size is of no factor, as it forces one to turn from the ordinary hustle and bustle of daily living to embrace curiosity. Ivy sprawls the stone, further indicating its many years of existence: the earth reaches up to embrace the home. The substantial flat stone roof commands respect as well as demonstrates preservation and strength. Wow, I cannot wait to see the inside. I am in awe of the house, and I haven't even seen the entire property. "Do I need bread crumbs to leave?" I ask with a chuckle to myself.

Why am I sitting in the car? Maybe I am a bit intimidated by the seemingly innocent gentleness that can result in a vulnerable volcano on my end. I chuckle again at the thought while unbuckling my seatbelt. Walking toward the door, I feel an eerie sense of trepidation. The door is lavender, and its contrast against the dark stone begs me to come inside.

There is not a doorbell, so do I just knock?

"Let yourself in, River. I've been expecting you."

I open the door to a sea of reds, oranges, and mahoganies. She is obviously a fan of wood, as there is natural wood everywhere. Her home is a magnificent sunset, which you can share, almost like being wrapped up in an afghan with your lover to connect your souls. I am pleased. What an odd feeling to be "pleased."

She waves me over to a large red sofa. A number of multicolor pillows with gold thread dot its surface. I grab a purple one with gold threading, hold it against my chest, and lean back.

She is sitting diagonally from me in a large golden accent chair. "I've taken the liberty to make a couple of different types of tea. Please forgive me, as I did not ask you first. I kind of like to play around with tea and people's personalities," Earnestine exclaims in her honey voice.

She points over to the large cherry wood coffee table. I expected her house to be full of dollies and old dolls, but it is not. My eyes slowly scan the place. I notice it is actually quite traditional; however, her life experiences are all over the place.

Earnestine notices my mental whereabouts. "Yes, I have lived here for over fifty years. Many families have come and gone. My husband Armand is out back in the garden. He is too old to do any real work; he just likes being out there." She pauses to laugh. "Now the tea. We have two choices. I have King Osmanthus oolong and Tieguanyin tea." A smile that already has the answer spreads across her face. "Now, which would you like to have?"

I can feel the threads of connection throughout the room. The aroma of the tea and the mystery of my visit ensnare me.

Under normal circumstances, many individuals like to get right to the point. I appreciate the ceremony, in this case, and I want to travel down this road with her.

"Choose … hmm … I would like to try both. However, I suspect there is a story with each. I also suspect there is a reason why you felt they are right for me to choose one or maybe both." I offer a sly smile and feel smugly smart. Little do I know my world will be ripped open after this ceremony is done.

"Very clever of you, River. Yes, there is a story to each tea, because each tea offers a different flavor.

"Starting with the King Osmanthus tea, before I go into the flavor, it is important that you understand the history, or better stated, the myth. The osmanthus flower is tied to the moon in Chinese custom. There was a beautiful Chinese princess who was the wife of a great archer by the name of Houyi. This great warrior possessed the elixir of immortality. When Houyi, the great warrior, was not home, his apprentice attempted to break in and take the elixir. Chang'e, the princess, refused to give it to him and drank it herself, and she immediately went to the moon. Houyi was grief-stricken. He processed this loss by making her favorite pastries. Now during every harvest, the Chinese recount her story of love lost while eating moon pies. Chang'e is the Chinese goddess of the moon, and the osmanthus flower is connected to love."

Her voice is heavy but sweet. It is somewhat hypnotizing, as the smell of the teas consumes me. I do not speak, only nod and consume.

"Try it, she says. "Close your eyes, and allow for the taste to saturate your palate."

She hands me a small iron cup full of the tea. It is warm to touch. Closing my eyes, I sip. I am enveloped in light apricots, but there is something heavier, almost woody.

"Very good, yes?" she asks.

"Yes, it is complex," I respond.

"Absolutely, River. It is complex. It has the essence of flowers, fruit, and honey, yet the undertone of the forest. Good insight." She smiles and sips.

Sitting up, Earnestine turns her head, facing what I can only assume to be the kitchen. "Armand! Are you in the house? Can you bring us some ginger sugar?"

"Why don't you get all that you need when you are having company?" he asks. "Every time, I have to come out to bring you something. Don't make no damn sense." His husky voice, with a slight hoarseness, makes its way into the warm room.

"Here I come. Lawd," he says, his irritation, seemingly routine, continuing.

"Armand, this is River. You know, Mahaley's boss."

Mahaley's father is about six feet tall. His moderate build suggests a formerly muscular body. His skin is the color of perfect peanuts. His rich brown eyes penetrate, suggesting a lack of tolerance.

"Um, nice to meet you, Mr. Banks." I stand and offer my hand. Smiling, he takes my hand in both of his and shakes it vigorously.

"Well, nice to meet you, finally, River. I hear so much about you. Mahaley cannot seem to stop talking about you. *Dr. Meadows this, Dr. Meadows that,*" he says, his voice becoming shrill.

"Your daughter is a wonderful person. I am lucky to have her."

I stand and look at both of them for a moment. Earnestine is a beautiful woman. She is quite short and stocky. Her hair is white, glossy, and contrasted by her dark eyebrows. Her cocoa face has been carefully made up. Her eyes are striking. They are hazel, demanding truth at all times. She and Armand—they fit together.

"Why, thank you. She is lucky to have you too," he responds.

Armand drops the ginger sugar rocks on the table and walks back into the kitchen.

"Now, for the Tieguanyin tea taste," she states.

I finish the King Osmanthus tea and reach my iron cup out for the Tieguanyin tea.

"I am pleasantly surprised by the delicate orchid aroma that embraces me. It is intoxicating."

"Very good again, River. You connect very well. Tieguanyin has an interesting story as well. *Tie* means iron and *guanyin* is the goddess of mercy. She (or he) is the lord of compassion and love. *Guanyin* means 'the one who perceives the sounds of the world,'" she explains.

"Okay … I see you have quite the niche for tea. Why did you choose these options for me?" I ask.

"They are not options, River. They are adaptations of you. Let's begin with King Osmanthus tea. The history is of love; the flower as I explained is connected to love in Chinese custom. You, I suspect, are losing love but also finding it. The tea itself has delicate notes of honey, apricots, and flowers. Yet it is also has a distinctly woodsy, leathery undertone. That is also you. You are delicate and sweet, but make no mistake about it: you have a strength that cannot be ignored. It fills the room.

"Now, the Tieguayin tea is a bit different, and a little more complex. As I stated, *tie* means iron and *guanyin* is the lord of compassion and love. You embody that, River. You do what you do because of who you are, not because of some degree you acquired. You are not only compassionate, but you also have an acute ability to understand the unspoken. That is what makes you good at what you do. You are one who understands the sounds of the world. You understand the sounds of human beings … specifically the humans who are in pain. You tune into their vibrations, even in the slightest sense, and bring them to the surface.

"These are vibrations that even the people themselves cannot feel, because years of suppression have drowned them deep within their souls. You take those vibrations, which are loud, messy, and useless noises, and turn them into music. You rearrange the notes. This is what and who you are, River: a human composer. That is the gift God has given you. Now it is your vibrations *I* can hear, and I can sense they need to be rearranged." She leans back and returns to sipping her tea.

I am paralyzed by her words. I cannot believe she impaled me with her thoughts. I drop my teacup on the floor as tears begin to fall freely down my face. She says nothing but continues to sip her tea.

****

Thoughts of Belle cross my mind while shaving.

Okay, I have to call Belle and let her know. I have already fallen for Riv, but I just can't ignore Belle. I do not want to hurt her, but I know she is hurting already. She was there for me during the darkest days of my life. I owe her that much. Damn, I feel like I betrayed her. Maybe I can meet her for lunch. Maybe I can ease this guilt, so it won't hurt her so much. I can speak to her about the need for her to work on her marriage, but I cannot tell her that I fell for someone else. I remember when I first met her. She came to a city council meeting full of life. She was fighting for more police support in her mother's ward. She had noticed that crime had increased in the area and was sincerely concerned for her aging mother's safety.

I chuckle and then nick my face.

Yeah, I remember smiling at her because I could feel her passion. She was on fire, and I have mad respect for that. She also interrupted me every chance she got. She came with stats after stats, story after story. She forced us to respect her. It was her fire that drew me into her—the fire that needed to protect others. I remember my assistant, Bob, leaning over and whispering, "Damn man, put a muzzle on her already."

"Ma'am ... ma'am, what is your name?" I asked her.

"Belle. Belle Riley-Button," she said emphatically with her arms crossed, as if to indicate it was none of my business.

Riley-Button, that name still makes me laugh.

"Okay, Miss Riley-Button ..."

"Mrs. ... Mrs. Riley-Button," she corrected me.

I remember thinking, *Look lady, I'm just trying to help. I am not trying to approach you with your jacked-up name.*

"*Mrs.* Riley-Button, the council has heard you and has taken note of your concerns. We will consider them when we discuss the change in police presence in that ward," I said, hoping the emphasis on *Mrs.* would settle her down.

"This is not just about police presence. I am not just looking for protection for my mom and punishment for others. I want to bring back the recreation centers. At least three of them have been shut down within the past five years. If you follow the data, petty crime has increased steadily during this time. My complaint is that you have taken the community away from the community. These kids and young adults need activities and things to do. They need to be inspired to greatness. I hope that you will 'take note' of my concerns. More importantly, I hope you feel responsible and accountable for the change of heart in our community. You accepted the responsibility to be a positive influence on people. You agreed to protect the heartbeat of that community. And just so you know, I will not be pacified."

I loved the fight in her. It inspired me to fight for her and all that she spoke of. In a world that seems focused on acquisition, she was a breath of fresh air. She reminded me of why I went into this business to begin with.

I remember meeting her at the door. She looked my way, somewhat frazzled. "Let me help you with your briefcase," I offered. I then added, "Mrs. Riley-Button, please, if you will let me help you to your car."

The woman turned to me and said, "I am quite capable, thank you very much."

I can tell the spirit of the women's suffrage movement was wrapped in that statement. It was probably shaking its head at another man who keeps women down. I remember how I felt at the moment; it is discouraging when a person assumes your intent without asking. Sighing, I said to her, "Woman, it is clear you are quite capable. You have demonstrated that beautifully today. My goal in helping you is not to demonstrate your inability to help yourself. Please allow me to make my parents proud and treat you like the royalty you are."

Her look softened. The defenses she had up came down. I was glad she was able to see that I was not her enemy.

As she handed me her bag, I added, "We are on the same side. Where is your car?"

Walking to her car, we laughed at the craziness that went on in that day's meeting. She was a light and refreshing spirit able to let me forget darkness, if only for a moment.

Getting her to the car, I knew I wanted to spend more time with her, even if just to pick her brain about her concept of community work. At least, that is the lie I sold myself.

"Mrs. Riley-Button," I began.

Touching my arm, she said, "Belle. Please call me Belle."

"Okay, Belle. Would you and your husband be interested in going to lunch with me? I'd like to pick your brain more on community matters. You have a fire I respect, and it just needs to be channeled in the right direction."

"Sure, we'd be delighted. Name the date, place, and time. We would love to be a part of real change in the community," she added.

"Okay … how about a little cafe on Spring Street? It is not far from Rice Park in the vicinity where all the apartments and town homes are located. How about next Tuesday? Six o'clock?" I ask.

"I do not have my calendar with me, but that sounds good. I look forward to working with you Mr. Councilman," she said with a smile and extended hand.

"Eoghan McGhee, ma'am. E-O-G-H-A-N, but pronounced Yo-when," I said with a laugh. I closed the door to her car, and she was gone.

My memory of Belle fades to black. I remember I have things to do. I am almost ready to get out of here. I have got to get to work. I still have to figure out how to tell her what's going on with me.

I like the idea of going back to the place where it all started. Sipping my coffee, my mind drifts back to that first meeting again. For some reason, I was a bit anxious about the Riley-Buttons coming to meet with me. I am not sure why exactly, but I was. I looked at the door, and there she was. She had on a beautiful red dress that not only displayed her feminine prowess but the fire within. I waved to her and beckoned for her to join me.

Sitting down, I remember asking her, while looking around, "Where's your husband?"

"Oh, Joe?" she replied. "He cannot make it. He had something to do," she says, putting her briefcase on the table.

This overwhelming feeling of utter joy presented itself within my body. Wow. *This is exactly what I was I hoping for*, I remember thinking.

The rest, they say, is history.

As I enter the car, a text comes through: "Please call." It's from Belle. Interesting timing.

"Belle, hey, I wanna go to that cafe where we met—remember? I know we have a lot to talk about. Let's meet up next Tuesday. 6 p.m.?"

Deep breath. Hit send.

It takes a minute for Belle to respond.

"Okay. See you then. I miss you," her text reads.

"See you then. Enjoy the rest of your day, Belle," I respond.

Okay. Here we go.

I spend the rest of the day in a fog of work, struggling to extract myself from Belle. I go over various discussions and approaches, none which seem worthy or effective.

****

I strive to collect myself, and I feel as though I have just been exposed by Earnestine. How can someone who doesn't know you completely break you down to a cellular level? It is fascinating when energy instantly emits from your body, and you have no idea how or why.

Earnestine looks relaxed and pleased with herself. I look up to see her looking down toward her lap; she then sips her tea and slightly chuckles. I am not amused.

Quietly and slowly, I say to her, "Is this funny, Ms. Earnestine?"

"Well, yes and no," she says, making direct eye contact. "My sweet. You will be fine. See, Armand and I have fifty years together. We have weathered many storms in the many lives we have lived together. You are a child in my eyes. Please do not take that as an insult. It is a privilege for me to share this gift. God has woven Armand and I so strongly. We are two people but truly have become one. Not everyone gets this gift. Sure, many people get married, but not many people *are* married. I am a gift to my husband, and he is a gift to me … although he likes to complain," she says with a laugh." What I would like to share with you is this gift."

"What gift?" I ask.

A hearty laugh bellows from Earnestine. "My child, the gift of love. The gift of knowing you are worthy. The gift of understanding. The gift of sacrifice. The gifts God has already given you that you have failed to recognize. Our marriage is a beacon, and this was revealed to us a long time ago—a story I'll share with you later. When I saw you in the bathroom, I knew what it was about. I may not know the particulars, but I know the tears that erupt from a woman because of the pain of a man. I was planning to mind my own business, but then I was led to turn around and comfort you. As I walked back to Mahaley, I knew I had to see you again. You, my dear, are trapped—or better put, you feel trapped. But never mind all that. Tell me about him."

"My husband?" I ask.

"Armand, can you bring some of that tea cake in here?" Earnestine yells, turning her head toward the kitchen again.

"Woman, I am in here reading the paper. You knew full well you were having guests. I'm a-coming." The sound of an angrily folding newspaper makes me laugh.

She turns to me. "No, dear. Not your husband. Him. The one who has your heart."

I feel ashamed. I trace the top of my iron cup with my finger, trying to find the right words. I mean, this woman has been in a successful marriage for fifty years. Now she wants me to tell her about my inability to successfully follow my vows, when she knows that I want to follow my heart.

I begin. "You made a statement: 'Many may get married but are not married.' You have no idea how much this resonates with me."

When I begin to tell her this story, I just do it. My own mother does not even know all of it. I tell her everything I can recollect. More importantly, I tell her that I feel like I am now just surviving and not thriving. She listens intently and with great interest as I explain the "real love" I am experiencing. I express my confusion regarding my instant connection with him. I fuddle through my embarrassment about how he is connected with one of my clients. As I explain the immense guilt and how much I am ashamed of myself, she abruptly stops me.

"Sweetie, guilt I understand. There are people involved other than you who will be hurt. I would be careful with shame. Shame is twofold. Shame can help us refrain from doing things we should not do, or shame can allow for us to descend into an abyss of great darkness. This darkness is not from God. Your circumstance is not something that was happenstance. There were symptoms that you and your husband ignored. You ignored them from the very beginning. The wedding is not the marriage. More importantly, there were roads that each of you, and by that, I mean all parties in this, needed to take," the honey voice offers in solace.

"So, you are saying this should have happened?" I ask incredulously.

"Well, hmm … I should clarify more. This was *going* to happen. There were conditions for the perfect storm. Now, I am going to say something that may be hard to hear," she states.

Earnestine pauses momentarily. "More tea?"

Smiling but confused I say yes.

She pours the Tinguanyin tea.

"It may not be so hard for you to hear, now that I think about it. You are the one who perceives sound. Therefore, you will understand that vibrations of the soul, especially negative ones, can be passed on to others. These ancestral ghosts haunt our present and our future. They are the perfect storm."

She looks up at me and sips.

"The perfect storm. Can you say more?" I ask.

"My dear, how much do you know about your family history? Does your family ever talk about the darkness that occurred in your line?" Earnestine does not wait for a response and continues.

"Probably not, as families do not do this. Families hoard secrets, as you know. Families allow for traumatic or what they may consider to be shameful experiences to chart the course through their lineage. As you know, when we do not acknowledge and face our demons, they manifest in us and in our children. The idea of generational curses is not new. Rapes, murders, deaths, molestations, drugs, and a host of other experiences can trickle their way down to our descendants, infecting them. This infection can chart the course for how a person will live his or her life."

"I understand. So you are saying that ancestral sins or traumas can be included in my own narrative? It's amazing that we are talking about this, because I have had discussions such as these before," I say.

"Very good, River. I knew you would understand. You see the comprehensive story, so it is hard to see the elements of your story and the map of where it all came from." Earnestine sits back and smiles the kind of smile you have when you know you are right. I chuckle to myself, as I can tell she is so proud of herself.

"This doesn't mean that one gets a 'pass,'" Earnestine says with air quotes.

"What do you mean?" I ask, knowing exactly what she means. I want her to say it.

"It means that you are still responsible. It means that you must become aware of the choices in your life and how they impact you and others around you. It means that you cannot operate in limbo while situations fester. You must seek to understand where you came from to better understand where you are going. Most of the time our parents and grandparents put on the face that they want us to see. I understand this much as a parent myself."

She looks over at an old photograph hanging on the wall and continues.

"However, we can unknowingly pass down misinformation about our love of the self and of others. Once I understood that for myself, my marriage was not good … it was remarkable. Armand was already prepared and had done some work on himself. He was ready to submit to the union of one. I, on the other hand? Not so much, and the worst part is that I did not even know it. But that's a story for another day. For you, child, I encourage you to seek your past in order to understand your present so you can make the choice for your future."

"Miss Ginger Rocks in there, be ready soon," Armand yells from the kitchen. I can hear the amusement in his voice. I sense the cue and begin to gather my things. She gestures for me to slow down and offers her hands to me. I am not quite sure what to do. She shakes them again, and I place my hands in hers. They are warm and soft. The years do not seem to have touched them. She grips softly, and love and care seem to emit from them.

"My dear, before you go racing out of here, know this: a design greater than yourself is at work. Believe me!" She says this with an air that pertains more to herself than to me.

Armand walks in with a light jacket and a sweater for Earnestine.

I stand and say, "Thank you, Mr. Banks, for allowing me into your home to spend time with your wife." I look directly at her and add, "She is something special."

Armand laughs and touches my shoulder. "I knew that the moment I met her. She had a light brighter than anyone's in the room. She just didn't know it ... then." There was a slightly darker tone when he added "then."

"Now, now, Armand. I am ready. Ms. River has some business to attend to, and you are holding her up!"

I am standing but not quite prepared to leave.

"Where are you guys off to?" I ask.

"The park," they answer in unison. "We like to sit at the park and just be ... us old folk," Armand responds, smiling and looking at Earnestine with adoration.

"Let's meet next week: same time, same tea," she adds.

I nod in agreement.

"Where are you off to now, River?" Earnestine asks.

I pick up my purse and take a deep breath laced in despondency.

"Too see my mother."

Earnestine smiles, knowing exactly why I am going.

We hug, and they walk me to the door. We all leave together.

I offer them a ride, and they decline. They say they like to walk to the park.

I watch them from the rearview mirror. He puts her sweater on her and slides his hand in hers. They are adorable. I am smiling as I admire them. I wonder what Armand meant by 'then'? I suppose I'll find out next time we meet.

As I turn the corner, my thoughts change to the upcoming visit with my mother. My mother. Will she be okay with sharing her life and her mother's life with me?

I hope so. I am a bit fearful, but I am unsure of why.

25

SESSION 11: BELLE SEES A GHOST

"Belle, uh, hurry up," Joe yells. "Dr. Meadows is waiting on us, and we are late."

"Okay, okay," Belle yells back. She scrambles from the Jeep and then tosses her hair up in a bun at the crown of her head.

I watch from the window. My thoughts are all over the place. I am still reeling from the discussion with Earnestine and later with my mother. My thoughts run to Eoghan and our first kiss. I become excited again. As I reminiscence, guilt begins to simmer. How odd is it that one can experience such a duality of experience, joy and guilt?

I remember that I was not quite able to breathe. I wanted, I mean I really wanted to hold my breath. His ability to barely touch me but touch me everywhere is just making me crazy. My guilt about Belle—I mean, does he belong to her? My guilt about my own husband—two wrongs don't make a right. Right?

What is this emotion? I cannot reconcile it with the emotions I am used to. Is it immense joy laced with despair? Please explain, God. What am I supposed to do here?

I must get my head together. I must. They will remember me leaving before, and I have to kind of play that off too.

"Get your head in the game, River. They are walking in the door," I say out loud to push myself. Let me tell Mahaley to ask them to wait a couple of minutes.

"Mr. and Mrs. Riley-Buttons! It is so nice to see you guys! Dr. Meadows will be right out to see you. I saw you guys pull up, so I told her you were here. She'll be right out," Mahaley informs them.

"Thank you, Mahaley. Sorry we are late," Joe says, turning toward Belle. "Can we go ahead and schedule the next appointment?"

"Sure, Dr. Meadows has an opening Thursday the eighth at six o'clock in the evening. How's that?" Mahaley asks.

Belle looks confused and pulls out her phone. "I do not think that Thursday is the eighth."

"Sure it is," Mahaley says, a little annoyed.

"No. No it's not," Belle says, smiling.

"Look." Mahaley swivels the screen so that the Riley-Buttons can see the dates.

As quickly as she turns it toward them, she turns it back around.

"Sorry, I was in the wrong week. It has been such a crazy past couple of weeks."

"That's okay, Mahaley. We have all been there," Joe reassures.

Belle is unable to hear any of the dialogue regarding the calendar mishap and the newly scheduled appointment. She thinks she saw something that her mind will not allow her to believe. *There is no way I saw that. I must be going crazy*, Belle thinks to herself.

She saw typed on the screen, "Eoghan—Anxiety, 7 p.m."

Like a zombie, Belle walks to the lobby and sits with Joe.

"You okay, Belle? Goodness girl, you look like you have seen a ghost," Joe says, tapping her leg. Belle grunts with an edge of sarcastic laughter. He has no idea how right he is on this one.

I just cannot believe I saw that. I did not see that. I have to be sick with what has been going on; I am seeing things, Belle thinks to herself.

"Riley-Buttons?" River calls, beckoning them back.

This time both sit on the same loveseat. *Such good progress*, River thinks to herself.

"So, it has been a bit since we last met. How are things?" River asks, tilting her head to the side.

Grabbing Belle's hand, Joe responds first. "I think we are slowly improving. I think we are sealing some of the cracks in our foundation."

"What did you mean by that, Joe?" River asks.

"I mean that I think we had to have this happen. Things had to come to a head, you know? Even everything with Jazzy. We had to see what was and, more importantly, who was important."

"Okay, that is a good thing. What about you, Belle?"

Belle looks up at River. "I am sorry. What did you ask me? I'm a little distracted."

"What is your take on how things are going so far?" River repeats. "Are you okay?"

"Um, yes. Just … anyway, we have made some strides, I suppose. He, Joe, did enroll in school. He said he realized that he cannot always be dependent on this job that will eventually be too hard for him to do. Also …"

Belle unknowingly pauses as "Eoghan—Anxiety, 7 p.m." flashes in her mind.

"Belle? Are you okay? Were you still talking?" River sits up, concerned, and begins an internal panicked dialogue with herself: *Oh my God. I wonder if she knows. I am so paranoid. Her eyes are so glassy. I bet she knows about us. What am I going to do? What am I going to say to her?*

Joe begins to look concerned. "Belle?"

"Sorry, I was thinking about something at work—something I forgot to do. Anyhow, that is really it. There are some new beginnings. I guess that is all you can ask for at this point."

"Okay, I am glad you are okay, Belle. This next question is going to be hard. However, it is imperative that you both answer honestly."

River deeply inhales. She knows she wants to know the answer to the next question for both therapeutic and personal reasons. She cannot seem to untangle the two.

"Have you both discontinued communicating with or seeing the people you were seeing outside your marriage?" River asks, trying to hide the desperation in her voice.

Belle's head seems to unnaturally swivel hard in River's direction. It is as if she is defensive or protective. They are both unusually quiet, and River is not sure if it means they both are still engaging in their affairs or they are waiting on each other to respond. River suspects the latter and is holding her breath.

Joe responds first. "Well, I haven't. I mean, I've talked to her to explain why I cannot see her and that I am working on my marriage." There is a tinge of irritation in his voice.

River wonders, *Is it because Belle hasn't responded or that he wants to see the woman? Not sure. That will unfold eventually.*

He squeezes Belle's hand, signaling that it is her turn.

"Oh, um, no, I haven't *talked* to him."

River thinks it's interesting that Belle placed a stronger emphasis on *talked*. She wonders, *Does she mean that she has not talked to him to end it? Does she mean she has not talked to him period? Does she mean she has not "talked," but she damn sure has done other things?* River is suddenly incensed.

She continues to talk to herself in her head: *Whoa, whoa. River, come back. I am making myself crazy over here.*

"Okay, Belle, so does he not know that you guys are working on your marriage?" River is so nervous and again starts thinking to herself while waiting for Belle's response: *This is stupid. Living in this duality is for the birds. On the one hand, I really do clinically want to know what is going on, so I can help them become one. On the other hand, I am fighting to not try to serve myself.*

"No," her voice is cracking, and she is shaking her head as if to shake away the tears. "We haven't been communicating either." Despite the small smile she provides, there is pain in her voice.

That painful sound of loss was familiar to River. She recognized it in her mother when she went to her house after visiting with Earnestine.

"Okay, this is painful, I know. You both are taking a risk at trying to trust each other's love again. I can imagine how difficult and scary that must be."

The three of them go over some adaptive and maladaptive stress responses, and River provides some homework for them to have coffee with one another and people watch. She tells them to go to the airport and evaluate couples and families as they arrive or depart from each other. They are to create stories around them. River explains to them that she cannot tell them why until they return for their next session and describe their experience. They both seem to hate the idea but agree to do it.

"Well, guys, it looks like you are pointed in a forward direction. You may not be moving fast, but that is okay. You will get there. Did you already schedule your next time?

"Eoghan—Anxiety, 7 p.m." flashes in Belle's mind.

"Uh, yes. We did," Belle responds. "Come on, Joe. I'm having coffee with friends this evening at six. I need to get home and shower and relax first."

"Okay, babe," Joe responds, smiling with victory of the possible.

River closes the door and grabs her keys. *I need a glass of wine, music, and my private sanctuary*, she thinks to herself.

26

MAX'S CONFESSION INCREASES JUDE'S GUILT

"Jezzy, can I call you later? Yeah, yeah. I know we haven't seen each other in a couple of days. Woman, look … okay, okay … I have to pick *my wife* up, and we have to go to my mother's. Yes … yes … I wish it were you too. Damn, Jezzy, I do not know when, so don't pressure me like this. I said okay. I gotta go; someone is coming in the office." Jude hangs up the phone.

"This broad," he says out loud. He had to lie to get her off the phone. Picking up a picture of River, he examines her face. *She has so much light,* he thinks to himself. *What happened? I happened. I happen all the time. I keep happening. I just keep happening. Max damn near killed me with the story of his wife. He chose me to talk to? Hell, I would not have chosen me.*

Max dips his head in Jude's office door unexpectedly. "What's up, big man?"

Leaning back, Jude puts his hands behind his head.

"Max! My man, what's good? You have a deal that you want to run through?

"Yeah."

"Come in. I am good, not too busy."

Max brings in the paperwork and begins to discuss the application.

Looking at the paperwork, Jude hesitates to ask questions about Max's wife but does so anyway. Stammering, he says, "Hmm, Max, um, how is she?"

"She who? My wife?"

"Yes."

"Oh, she is not so good. The will to live has left her mind altogether now. Better put, I think she has made peace with it. It does not refer to her succumbing to the cancer: it refers to her making peace with the fight. She now wants to make sure she spends her"—Max pauses, unable to say the words. His body becomes overwhelmed with pain, and he struggles to hold in.

Jude senses his pain and puts his hand on his shoulder. He finishes for Max: " ... remaining time."

"Uh, yes, yeah ... with family and friends. So, yeah ... that is where we are."

"Max, why do you come to work every day? Why don't you take some time off? This stuff doesn't matter. It'll always be here. Your job will be here," Jude assures him.

"I appreciate that, Jude, but I need to do this. I need to see other people and not be the guy whose wife is dying of cancer. I need for people to not look at me all the time with pity. The look is almost as if we both are dying and I am feeling it, Jude. I am dying. Being with people who do not know allows me to feel alive. I get to watch them argue over stupid things like the color of the car, Bluetooth, leather over cloth. I need the mundane right now. 'Cause what I got at home ... the despair that waits for me when I open the door and everything is sucked away is real depressing."

"Okay, I get it, and I am so sorry. Did you ever tell her? I mean, did you decide?" Jude asks.

"Oh, the girl? Man, women are something else. You know, I went to create this elaborate speech to tell her. I was going to explain to her that I had something very difficult to say, and before anything happened to her I wanted to be clean about our life and marriage. I was going to explain how I needed her forgiveness for all the mistakes I have made in our marriage and friendship and that she had to understand I would not have it any other way. So, here I am, sitting at the dining room table, and she is lying on the couch. She casually turns her head to me and says, 'Oh, the girl? I know about that, and I know you are not seeing her anymore. I know it was that one time. I already forgave you, and I understand.'"

Jude's face falls flat on the floor. "You cannot be serious, Max. Hell no, man. She said that?"

"Hell yes! I just sat there, not knowing what to say, because I did not write that in my speech," Max says, laughing.

Jude sits up. "So, what … man, what the hell did you do?"

"At first I wanted to ask her how she found out, but I almost did not want to know. So I began to ask her what she knew. She interrupted me and asked me to walk over to her by the couch. I go over and kneel beside her, right?"

Jude nods his head, enthralled.

"She turns her head to me and tells me the story of how we met. She reminds me of our childhood. We were childhood friends. I know, you didn't know that. Anyhow, man, she recounts stories of when I would be mean to her as a kid and how I acted when I regretted what I did. This one time, we were playing kickball, and I was mad because she did not pick me to be on her team; she had picked someone else. When I was in position to get her 'out,' I threw the ball extra hard. It didn't hurt her, but she knew I was tripping 'cause she looked at me with this *why did you do that* face. Anyhow, after the game I would not even look at her. I was ashamed. For days, I would not walk down her street to pick her up so we could play. I would see her with her mom and just wave. It took about a week—which, for a kid, is almost five years—but I got over it. I could not look at her directly for long periods of time. I was overly nice to her for about a week too, because I felt guilty. You should've seen me: I was trying to catch the ice cream man to buy her a Bomb Pop. I can see why she did not choose me to be on her team that day; I was slow. I would look for little trinkets at the local flea market to buy whatever two dollars could buy. The funny part is that she let that go on for about a week and then told me, "You do not have to feel bad about hitting me with the ball anymore. I forgive you.'"

Jude stares at Max, trying to figure out what the story has to do with what they are going through today.

Max continues. "I asked her why she was telling me these stories. She looked at me with, and I can barely describe it, but it was almost a look of pity, but more like genuine love. She is an amazing woman. So, she finally says, 'Max, you did the same exact thing as an adult. You thought you were hiding your secret affair from me. But when you came back around

185

to being Max again, you were being just a little too nice to me. I knew you had done something, and I knew it was bad. I did not have to go far to look for it, either. It came looking for you, actually. She called, I picked up the phone, and she tried to help you, Max. She really did. I honor her for that, but the fear in her voice told me she was someone she should not be. So, I asked her if she was having an affair with my husband. I told her I was sick, and I would appreciate it if she would not lie to me. She told me everything. She also told me that you told her you could not ever see her again, that you were weak in your pain. Max, I love you, and I know you are hurting. You did not do this to hurt me; you did this to relieve your hurt. I forgive you.'"

Jude, no lie, that had me really fucked up!" Max exclaimed.

"Jesus, man," Jude responds incredulously.

"Exactly," Max says.

"Can you give me a second, Max? I have to make a quick call," Jude asks, picking up his cell.

"Sure man. Let me know about the paperwork, because that couple will be back tomorrow, and I want to seal the deal. Thank you for listening. It means a lot to me."

"No problem. Anytime." Jude stands to shake his hand, but Max pulls him in and they embrace.

"No, really, thank you," Max says.

Sitting alone in his office, Jude picks up the picture of River, and tears flow down his face. *What am I doing?* he asks himself. *I need to talk to her and find out where her head is.*

Grabbing his keys and jacket, he walks out of the office, gets in his car, and heads home.

27

RIVER'S HAMON

I love sitting in my sanctuary alone, glass of wine in my hand, enjoying the quiet. The quiet room helps me sort out my inner madness and confusion and get answers I need for perplexing situations like this one. I grab my playlist. Jazz works. What type of Jazz? Nina Simone. That sounds good. I go through the titles and decide to listen to each song relevant to my life.

Nina Simone's "Who Am I" makes sense, because I am totally confused as to who this person is right now. Yes, let's start with this.

Laying the playlist out, I follow it with "I Want Some Sugar in My Bowl." Laughing out loud to myself, I say, "Oh my, lawd, yes, I need that sugar daddy."

Next is "Since I Fell For You." Come on and speak to me, Ms. Nina. His love brings such misery and pain …

"Do I Move You?" Give it to me, Nina. His touch and my quiver …

"In the Dark." Move me, Nina. His fingertips on my hips …

"My Man's Gone Now." Take me with you, Nina, to that promised land.

"Damn," I say out loud as I pour another glass.

My thoughts turn from him to my mother.

"Oh Child." Encourage me, Nina. Things are going to brighten. We'll walk together in the beautiful sun.

Thinking back on my discussion with my mother and her relationship with my father is interesting. I was surprised by the information my mother shared with me about her love for my father.

It was kind of funny to sit there, listening to her talk, because it took her by surprise that I wanted to know about their love.

"What's this for, dear?" she asked.

"Just curious, Mom. I would like to know more about my origins."

I never had really asked her how they met or how strong their love was for each other. It was amazing to find out that they were friends—good friends, in fact.

"Yeah, we worked together in a factory. I was eighteen years old at the time," she said.

So young.

"You ever know when someone is supposed to be in your life. I knew we were intertwined, that we were supposed to meet and be with one another, you know?"

Boy, did I absolutely know. I watched her go back in time. Her eyes looked up and to the right, slightly squinting in search of a time long passed. Then she laughed and said, "Fishing: your father loved to fish. We would go and just sit in the quiet at the lake and be still. There is something soothing about the water, something that brings you back to earth. We forgot all about life's stresses. We allowed the rock of the soothing water to take us away, out into God's beautiful sunset."

I closed my eyes when she told this story, trying to envision their connection. I remembered that water does take us back to the womb of Mother Earth. A gentle rocking boat splashing its waves coupled with the strength of a massive expansion into the unknown is comforting. It makes you know there is a greater spirit at work within this thing we call life.

"So, you felt a connection when you guys first met?" I asked.

"Yes, dear. I mean, when we spoke it was like we were the only persons in the room. You kids got it hard today. There are so many distractions taking you away from each other. There are sometimes other people involved in your life who should not be there. Back in my time, it was you and him against the world. If you struggled, you struggled together, because you were dedicated to one another. More importantly, you were dedicated to the union, you know?" she responded, and then she smiled, obviously in thought.

"What is it, Mom? What are you thinking of?" I asked. I could tell this discussion brought back a lot of memories she had not been prompted to recall in a long time.

"We used to frequent secondhand stores, those thrift shops. It was not all like the rage it is today to make a buck by repurposing and selling. It was like we were going treasure hunting," she said, laughing.

I let her sit in her lost-in-space zone for a while. I wanted her to enjoy it, because I knew the story did not end well.

Her voice grew quiet. "Treasure hunting. We could tell the story about each item we bought. We all have a story, Riv. However, *we* have to decide if we are going to have a hand in writing our story or just let life happen."

"Is that what went wrong with you guys? Life happened?" It sounded so discouraging.

"In a way dear, yes. We forgot us. We became individuals again, forgetting the union we had together. Our behaviors were no longer conducive to the union. My father died when I was a young child. I realized that I was searching for something he was never going to be able to give me—a father. He was searching for something I was never going to be able to give him—a mother. We walked into our union unaware of the strength of our needs and the deficiencies in our individual lives."

"Do you think you could have overcome them if you knew what each person needed from the beginning of the relationship?" I almost pleaded.

"Yes. But we were not aware at the time. We needed counsel; we were not rooted in each other. If we submitted to the union ordained by God, we might have been okay, you know?" she added, trying to maintain a pain-free disposition.

I wanted her to go back to a place more pleasant. "Tell me more about how you guys spent time."

She bounced right back, eyes lit up as history of a brighter time circled her heart. It was as if I was not even in the room. This was fascinating to see.

"He had this old Studebaker. I mean, it was an old car. He was so proud of that car. We would go on picnics and hang out, oh my!" She placed her hand on her cheek, looking down and smiling at the love she had.

Suddenly she looked up directly in my eyes and gave me a hard look, as if I'd invaded some private space.

"What's this all about, Riv? I know you and Jude are not doing so well. It is very obvious."

What? My mind was blowing up. How did she know? I thought I was pretty good at keeping my stuff under wraps.

"It is? How so, Mom?"

"The energy you guys give or, better put, fail to give when you are together tells me you are not one. I can tell that much. There is a significant rift present when I am with you two." She was quiet for a moment and beckoned me to follow her. "You know what? Come with me. This is appropriate, *and* it is time."

My mother took my hand and brought me to the attic. We traveled through all the clutter that years of acquisition can bring. I saw old hula-hoops, stuffed animals, and metal skates that had seen better days. We went toward the back of the room, and I began to grow increasingly anxious. I remembered being told as a kid that I could never go back in this room if I knew what was good for me.

"I know I told you guys to never go back here, but I want you to come with me now. There is something special I want you to see."

The corridor seemed to last forever. I guess when you are a kid and something forbidden is in your midst, time and space seem to change.

She opened the door and ushered me in. She stayed right outside the door, allowing me to take it in. My God, it was a beautiful white space with a small cheery oblong table on the floor. A fluffy white shag rug graced the matte cherry wood. Thick white European satin pillows lay in front of the table. The wall opposite the pillows was lined with framed letters and black and white photos. The wall to the right of the pillows held three long white shelves, which were covered with white candles of all different sizes and two vases with bouquets of beautifully colorful flowers. There was also a window that peered out over the backyard, which was also a picturesque setting to behold. Her own *sanctuary*! Hers was more beautiful than mine.

Although I had never seen this room, it had not surprised me to see it decorated so artistically. My mother appreciates the energy of a space. However, what was surprising was the wall behind the pillow. On the wall hung a katana, and its sheath hung beneath it.

I could not speak for a moment, because I was taking it all in. *What does this mean?* I thought to myself. I walked over to the wall where the photographs hung. There were photos of all of us, including my father. Looking at the photos, you could tell we were unaware that they were being taken. The wall also had framed letters hanging, apparently prayers. She had prayers for herself, the kids, my father, her mother, and her siblings, and they all were hanging on the walls. I was speechless, and my stomach began to ache as I read the letters about my marriage on the wall.

My fingers touched the edge of a photo when I was a child. I was skating out of the driveway. My hair was in two plaits down my back. I smiled at the innocence of the photograph.

I walked over toward the back of the room to touch the oddest thing in that space: the katana. My mother walked in just as I was about to touch it.

"Let me. I need to explain this to you."

She took the katana off of its mount. "This is a Koto Nihonto, or as most would call it, a katana. During one of our secondhand store dates, your father and I came across this very special sword. It is special because of its age and how it was forged," she said, looking at the katana as if it were a precious jewel.

"This sword was made in 1574."

My eyes popped, and my mouth ran dry. What a precious jewel.

"Yes, I know," she said, answering my expression. "See, a collector died, and his descendants had no idea of its value. After the estate sale, the katana ended up buried among boxes at the thrift shop. Your father was rummaging through them and came across the sheath. He said it had a special type of energy. The storekeeper did not know the value of the sword, and neither did we. He told us to give him a few bucks for it and we could have it. We offered him twenty dollars, and he took it. The clerk walked away mumbling something about it not being American anyway. Later on, I did some reading on the subject of this type of sword. I had to look high and low for someone to help us understand what we had in our possession. Your father and I ended up going to a university, and the Japanese Culture Society was able to help us understand the history of the sword."

All I could say was, "Wow."

"See, for many the value of the piece is in its age, and quite frankly, it should be. However, please don't get me wrong, but more important is in how the sword was made. Have a seat on the pillow, baby." Mom pointed to one of the fluffy white pillows on the floor. I felt compelled to remove my shoes, relax, sit, and listen.

She walked over to me with the sword in her hands and said, "Now, touch the base and hold it tight, Riv. This is also known as the scabbard. Can you feel the weight of it?" she said as she let go. "Isn't it both lethal and beautiful?"

"Yes. Yes." I felt as if I was ten years old again and Mom was teaching me a special lesson, as she used to do. I could barely manage holding the sword, not because of the weight but because I could sense the years and secrets it held in its reflective metal.

"Now, listen to how it is forged. This is something. You will see why it is important soon." Mom was captivated by the sword's history and the information she wanted to share with me. I patiently sat, listened, and took in every word she spoke. This sword is really fascinating piece of history.

"A bar of iron is heated and repeatedly folded about one hundred times. The shape is forged, and then its edges are hardened with black clay. The remainder, which is still flexible, is red clay. This is amazing, Riv. The way the different clays are applied will create what is called the *hamon*. The sword will stay hidden until the polisher polishes it. I do not want to get too far ahead of myself, so let me back up. The sword is heated and cooled with water, transforming the steel. The black and red clay cool at different rates and form a delicate pattern as the hamon is applied. Shoot! Again I am ahead of myself," she said, shaking her head.

"It is imperative to understand how delicate and meticulous this process is. The idea of heating and cooling allows for the sword's strength to be developed. The more this occurs, the stronger the sword develops. In life, you are consistently blazed with tribulations. If you permit it, these tribulations will temper and transform you, forging a strength inside of you that is so beautiful." Her eyes filled with adoration.

"Okay, now for the amazing part." Her face lit up.

"Amazing, Mom? This is all amazing."

"No, listen. Remember the hamon?" she asked.

"Yes, it's made with the red and black clay covering the sword while it is heated and quickly cooled?" I felt proud that I remembered.

"Yes, that is correct. The hamon will display a beautiful design once the polisher polishes it. That is an intricate process in itself. It is still traumatic to the sword, but to varying degrees of trauma. Each level of polishing requires a special grindstone, and each one becomes finer and finer. It can take many hours just to polish a sword. There are several levels of polishing, and a master polisher, a *togishi* polisher, will take the tedious and respectful process of putting his soul into his work. He respects the sword's strength and embraces its inherent beauty. After the sword is processed through several levels of grinding, an intricate design emerges—the hamon."

She should have added "ta-dah," because her explanation ended like a magic trick.

"What are you saying, Mom? I think that is amazing from an historical point of view, but what are you saying to me?" I asked. She sat and snuggled up close beside me on the pillow. Then she looked over at me with that "you are my baby girl" look.

"My dear sweet River. The hamon in you is being brought out by God. He is your polisher. He is the Master Polisher. Where you see trauma, pain, and fear, He sees beauty. The different tribulations in your life are meant to polish you, to bring out your own hamon. This is God's glory, my sweet—if you allow it to do its work. My prayers across the wall are for the hamons hidden in everyone I love. I pray that each of my loved ones be tempered and polished with the love of God. That each of you become the new, distinct creature He has designed you to be." Her face softened as she looked deeper into my face.

I looked at her face too. I could see and feel her energy and the love that poured from her into me. I rested my head in my mother's bosom and cried. "I love you, Mom," was all I could keep saying.

The sound of footsteps takes me out of my memory of the meeting with my mother and back into my private sanctuary. Nina has long since stop singing, and Billie Holiday has taken over.

I hear a familiar voice, further helping remove me mentally from my sanctuary. "River! You up there?" Jude calls.

"Yes."

There is no way to hide the dismay in my voice.

28

JASMINE CLOSES BELLE'S CHAPTER

"Jazzy, can you come out here and sit with me?" I call into the house. I could sure use the company. I specifically *need* her company. Funny how sometimes the ones we need to help cope with something are the ones we are responsible for pouring our souls into. They remind us of what it means to find "renewal" in our lives. They remind us that there is a new day, and Lord knows I need a new day today. I need to remember everything has a purpose in our lives and that wonderful things end, because they were never meant to last forever.

"Coming, Mom. Would you like some coffee? I put a pot on. I'll be out there as soon as the coffee is ready," Jaz yells from the house.

"Sure, my precious little one," Belle responds.

I have to try to get past this numb feeling. I cannot believe Eoghan told me at the coffee shop that he fell for someone else. I was numb. During our time together I was so sure he was mine. How could that be? I was never his. He is right about that.

While I wait for Jazzy, I mentally travel back to our coffee-shop meeting. I sat at that table where Jazzy had found us, tracing the mosaic design of the table with my fingers while he explained his distance and separation from me. I felt like I was being disconnected from a life-support system. He told me that he was wrong for ever being with me. He said he had taken advantage of my pain because he'd been covered in his own. He grabbed my hand and told me that our relationship had been numbing the pain in his life. That hurt me to my core, and the lump in my throat grew tremendously. I slowly pulled my hand back. I looked down at the table as a distraction, and I tried to hide the hurt by eating a croissant with apricot jam. I never realized that we were never going to be one.

"Some chapters in our lives need to be closed, even if they are good chapters, because there are greater chapters being written," he told me.

Are you fucking serious? I remember thinking. I wanted to be mad as hell, but I could not bring myself to do it. I felt like cursing him out in public, yelling and screaming at the top of my lungs and calling him all kinds of nasty names. He was not wrong for taking me and having me in his own way. I needed to take responsibility for my own actions because I took him too, and I am a married woman. However, I just was not prepared to let those feelings of passion and lust go down the drain forever. We will be gone forever. Now, what should I do?

"Here, Mommy, I got your coffee just like you like it." Jazzy hands me a mug.

"Thank you, sweetie. Have a seat here with me so you can lay your head in my lap. I want to play in your hair, baby."

Jaz looks up to her Mom, smiling. "Sure, Ma. What you gotta work out?" she asks.

"Stop being so smart, little girl," Belle states while laughing. "Just be here with me."

Jasmine lays her head in the lap of her mother. Belle, as promised, begins running her fingers through her hair, looking at the huge willow trees surrounding the front and backyard. There is a nice breeze orchestrating the sounds of the front porch swing and swaying trees in the yard into a simple melody and dance routine. I am lost in my silence and nature's song.

"Mommy, remember when Granny passed away?" Jaz asks.

"Yes, I do, sweetie. Why are you asking that?" I look down and gently rub Jasmine's face.

"I was just thinking about how she was so sick. And you could tell she was scared. She was always such a strong person. I never knew her to be sick before. What was she, ninety-two?" Jasmine looks up at her mother.

"Yeah, Jaz." I wonder where she is going with this. I am already in enough pain thinking about Eoghan. I am hoping the tone of my voice can hint to her to let this go for right now.

"I 'member seeing her in that hospital, Mommy. She did not look the same. It was as if all of that care took something from her. It was keeping her alive, but it was not allowing her to live."

I close my eyes and allow my head to lean back against the couch. I cannot do this right now. Tears well up in my eyes.

"Jaz, why are you bringing this up?" I manage to get out. Does the pain ever end?

"No, Mommy, I do not mean to make you sad. I was just thinking how free Granny is now. She is free, like truly free. She was able to transform from that sick person who could not live and now she is a soul that could be free again. She did not leave us, Mommy. She left her body."

Did she really need to do this now? Tears are falls from my eyes. I cannot hold it in anymore.

"Mommy, we all have to leave things that are keeping us sick."

I sit straight up, almost knocking Jasmine out of my lap.

Was staying with Eoghan keeping me sick? I mean, it actually helped me to see what was wrong with my home. But once I realized that, did it keep me stuck? Is it actually adding a disease to an already ailing marriage? My head begins to spin again.

Gathering his wallet, keys, and phone, Joe races out the door. It is his usual routine of being late for work. "I have to stop this shit," he says aloud, also part of Joe's usual morning script. Jumping into the car, he feels his phone buzz. "Randy" crosses the screen. "What does she want?" Joe says, looking directly at the phone. Not sure if he should answer, he swipes left.

"Hello?"

"Hey, Joe, how're you? I haven't seen you in a while, and I've missed you." The familiar silky voice of Delilah pours through the line.

"Hey. Yeah, well, I told you we were going to try to work things out, and you know what that means," Joe says, trying to sound confident.

"I know what you think it should mean, but why did you pick up the phone then?" Delilah asks.

"Look, I just needed to know you were okay. And ..."

"So, you care about me?" Delilah cuts him off.

"Sure, I care about you, Dee, but it is more than that. I care about my wife and marriage too. Most importantly, I care about it more," Joe says, his confidence strengthening.

"You sure weren't saying that when you were with me now, were you? Where was your wife then? What? I can't hear you, Joe. You sure weren't calling her name were you? I know you care about me!" Delilah's seething voice crackles under the change in Joe's demeanor.

"You right, Dee. You right. I wasn't. My wife wasn't there. Neither was I, if I am being honest. I am my best version of myself when I am with her. I just would not hold up my end. I do not know if I am going to get this right with Belle, but I damn sure ain't going to get it wrong by keeping this up. Dee, you are a beautiful, deserving woman. Find a man who will give you all you deserve, not what's leftover. 'Cause that's all you ever really got from me." Joe disconnects the line.

Damn, that felt good, Joe thinks to himself. *Real good.*

"Let me call my wife," Joe says out loud to himself.

"Hello?"

"Yeah, hey, babe. I have go to that supervisor-training program after work today. I am going to pick up dinner and drop it off before I go, so you do not have to handle it. I know you got a lot on your plate. Oh, I also looked into refinancing the house. I made some calls on it. I think we may qualify for a better rate. I'll give you the details later," Joe states, almost as if proving himself.

"That's great, Joe. I am—what can I say?—a little surprised. It is nice to see you take the lead and handle stuff. I love that," Belle responds.

"And I love you. Look, we have to meet with Dr. River soon, and I want us to lay out a two-year and a five-year plan. I mean, we don't need her approval, but I want us to go in the right direction. More importantly, I want us both seeking the same direction. We also have to tell her about the airport," Joe declares.

"Um, wow … okay. I agree. We already got an appointment set up, I believe. I like it. I'll start working on the plan."

Joe cuts Belle off. "No, that is not what I wanted. I want us both to work on the plan together. I have some ideas too. If you are not too tired when I get home, we'll lay some things out together."

Belle responds extremely surprised. "Well, damn. Okay. See you later. Have a good day at work and the training."

I sit the phone down and lean against the wall. Well, who the hell was that? Was that my husband? This has been one crazy week. Jasmine had me really jacked up about my mother. It is funny to see how one story can actually make another story make sense. God has a funny way of teaching you lessons sometimes.

Maybe I don't need Eoghan anymore. Maybe he was just something or someone I needed to ease the pain of what I was experiencing in my own life. I don't know anymore, but I do know one thing: that call was an absolute turn on. I feel myself smile, I pick up my keys, and I call to Jasmine.

"Jasmine, let's go. I have to go to work. You can't keep being late to school."

29

COFFEE WITH ARMAND

"Mahaley, your mother is absolutely amazing, and your father is super cool too. I just spent most of my time with your mother," I say, offering her a bottled water.

"I know. They are amazing folks. Sometimes they make it hard to be me," Mahaley adds.

"How so?"

"Well, think about your experience. You left there probably with more questions than answers, and your life is changed. Yes?" Mahaley looks intense.

"Well …" I pause, rubbing my hand through my hair. "Um, yes."

"Exactly. You had a moment with them. I had a lifetime. This is not good for my self-esteem, because I do not feel as though I could ever live up to them. It is like living with Yoda from *Star Wars*." She laughs. We both laugh.

"I can see that. It can feel like pressure. But Mahaley, they have had a lifetime of experiences. You cannot be them. You should not be them. You have to be okay with where you are right now—this space, this moment, this version of you. If you allow it, you will shed and continue to become a better version of you. You will never catch up or win a race against someone who's had a lifetime's head start. More importantly, when you understand it is not a race, you have already won. You understand?" I ask.

"I do. You are so much like my parents. I guess that is why I was drawn to you." Mahaley smiles.

"That is such a compliment. But I have a long way to go, sister. I have to meet someone for lunch today." Eoghan's face crosses my mind. "What are you doing for lunch?"

"Oh, my father is coming up. He is taking me out to lunch," Mahaley responds.

"That's cool. Let me know when he arrives. I'd like to at least say hi. Wait, where you guys going?"

"I don't know. He said something about a Lebanese restaurant around here. Why? You want to go? I actually was going to cancel. Remember that guy I told you about a while back?"

I nod.

"Well, he is leaving town for work, and I wanted to see him off. I did not have the heart to cancel with my dad, so I was just going to call him later. Do you mind having lunch with my dad?"

"Lunch with Mr. Banks?" I ask, almost to myself. How did this happen? I was just curious on where they were going. Mr. Banks seems to be a person of few words. I look at Mahaley, her large brown eyes full of hope that I would accept this request. Good grief, she even has a pleading look on her face. I have to learn to say no.

"Okay, I can move my lunch, Mahaley. Is he coming here, or are you meeting him?"

"You are the best, Dr. Meadows!" Her voice is three octaves higher. She begins to rummage through her purse. "I am supposed to meet him there. I am getting the address out of my phone," she says with glee.

I take down the address and look at her. "You owe me one, Mahaley. You owe me. I hope he is worth your ditching your father," I say with a laugh.

"No problem. I am sure he will love you. And don't say that! I am not ditching my dad. I am only postponing our date. I really just want to see my friend off. I can have dinner with my dad later. I'll call him and let him know you are coming. Now, you only have two sessions until lunchtime," she says with a song.

Those sessions seem to fly by. I am curious about what my alone time with Mr. Banks will be like.

Mahaley gives me a hug before she jumps in her car. Off she goes to the airport. I look at the address of the Lebanese restaurant and plug it into my GPS. Karam is only ten minutes away. Cool. I do not have to drive too far. I hope Mahaley is back by three o'clock, as she has to reopen the office.

I spend time thinking about Eoghan. He was disappointed about moving our lunch date but agreed to see me a bit later, after work. It is sometimes so hard to keep wearing this mask all day. My husband absolutely flipped on me while I was in my sanctuary. I just stopped short of being honest and telling him about Eoghan.

"Here it is," I say out loud.

This is an interesting restaurant. Its decor is arabesque. Kufic script dots the entrance and exit. Geometric Kufic tiles demand seeing the culture on its own terms. It is beautiful and endearing. I skim the room, looking for Mr. Banks. He is patiently turning the page of a newspaper, sipping what I can only assume to be coffee or tea. I inform the host that I am meeting someone for lunch and ask if I can just walk to him.

She waves me on. I stand in front of Mr. Banks, waiting on him to look up.

"You're late, Mahaley," he says without even glancing up.

Um, Mahaley was supposed to let him know I was coming.

Oh, Mahaley.

"Well, I am sorry, Mr. Banks. I just found out I was coming a couple of hours ago." I say with a smile, knowing he will be surprised.

Mr. Banks quickly looks up and sets down his cup.

"Dr. Meadows."

"River," I correct.

"River, to what do I owe the pleasure?" Mr. Banks leans his shoulder against the wall and looks up at me.

"Well, Mahaley had an obligation to take care of."

"You mean a man?" he interrupts.

I smile. "Well, I would love to have lunch with you, Mr. Banks, if you will have me." I curtsy to lighten the mood.

He smiles and chuckles. "Have a seat, River. I'd love to."

Our waitress arrives to take our orders. Armand points to me, signaling that I should order first. "I'll have the tabouli and falafel."

"I am ravenous, River, so I will have the tabouli, falafel, and beef shawarma."

What are you, drinking, Mr. Banks? Looks like tea," I say while looking at his cup.

Armand nods to the waitress, asking her to bring me a cup of what he is having.

"Not tea, my friend. It is coffee. Arabic coffee. *Al-qahwa*. Not quite what your American Westernized palette is used to for a morning beverage. You smell the spices? Saffron, cinnamon, and cloves?" He hands me his cup.

"Yes, I do." I look up at him. I wonder if this is going to be another lesson on tea and how it is connected to my life.

He must have read my mind because he immediately laughs and states, "No worries, River. The tea thing is Earnestine. I just like the taste." He waves his hand to summon the aroma and laughs.

I laugh in return. "Yes, Ms. Earnestine can definitely go there."

"Was she wrong?" he asks.

"No. I would say she was right on point. She was right on point with a lot of things," I respond.

"She usually is. She was not always like that, Riv. Ernie has had to go through her process too."

Ernie. How adorable.

"How so? I mean, if I may ask," I say. This coffee is good.

"Why, of course. When I met Ernie, she was in a very dark place. She had no idea where she was going. She was lost. I mean, she did not know what her direction in life was. She had just ended a relationship with a fellow, and it tore her to pieces. I mean, she really had no idea who she was. She lost the relationship because he wanted to get married and she did not. She wanted to 'find herself.' She really did not have to find herself. She only had to realize who she was."

"Find herself?" I repeat.

"Yes. Do you want to know what I think?" Armand asks, circling his middle finger around the coffee cup. He does not wait for a response. "I think she and that young man did not create a spark together and were not friends. See, she worked in a hospital at the time as a receptionist, and she was trying to go to school for nursing. I worked there as well. I was studying radiology but was working as a janitor. I would see her at lunch. She would be peering over her lunch, watching all the nurses congregate. I knew she wanted to be one of them and *of* them, if that makes sense."

I nod to indicate understanding.

"So, we were two of five African Americans in that hospital who were not lying in the basement's morgue. Those were some tough times for us then. We all stuck together. I knew the moment I caught a whiff of her fragrance that she would be the woman in and of my life forever."

Armand has drifted back in time, and I can almost picture the scene with him and a younger Ernie.

"Wow," I say to myself, not realizing it is loud enough to hear.

"Yes, *wow* was I all could think too, River. We were acquaintances, but I wanted more. I made sure I carried her bag whenever I would walk her to the bus stop. Of course, I did not do all of those things in the name of chivalry. I had an agenda." He busts out laughing. "I needed her to remember me. Those blazing hazel eyes unnerved me every time they commanded my attention. There was a fire in her that she did not see, but I did. See, it was not any ordinary fire. It was almost mythological. As I got to know her through our walks to the bus stop and while waiting with her, I realized she was like a phoenix. She became my inspiration as I fell in love with her death and rebirth. Nothing could ever keep her down, and I needed her energy to continue my studies. As time went on, our friendship became something indescribable. That is still key for relationships. You must be friends. Lust is temporary, passion is elusive, and love can fade, but friendships that are true friendships are the foundation God builds marriage on."

The waitress brings over our food, and it is delicious. I start to speak, but Armand closes his eyes and states, "Just eat and enjoy." We eat in silence, something that is unusual for me. However, I am able to savor the flavors in a way I have never been able to. I am able to embrace the texture of the food and connect with the sustenance granted to me.

We finish, and I am satisfied. We proceed to coffee.

"Did you enjoy you meal?" he asks.

"Yes, I did. That was wonderful. I did not realize how much distraction and conversation take away from the experience of your meal," I say with a smile.

"No one does. It drives Mahaley crazy." We both laugh.

"So, as I was saying, she has this fire and this ability to recover and renew in a way I had never known, and I needed that. I could tell her how frustrated I was that school was taking a long time. Even though I was doing the right thing, she said I was always trying to control God. I told her, chuckling, that God should give us more insight into how things are going to work out. I also added that if I had it my way, I would do things a bit differently."

He begins to sound far away, as if he is in that place where he shared time with her.

"We all want to have the grand plan, Mr. Banks. I suppose that takes the fun out it," I add, thinking I am making a profound statement.

"But of course, Riv. You know what Ernie said? She turned to me as we sat at that bus stop. I can remember it as if it was today. It was in the fall, which is her favorite time of year. She played with the red, yellow, and orange leaves underneath her feet. The colors of the leaves against her eyes belonged together. It was like looking at siblings and knowing they are related just by how familiar they look to one another. Anyhow, this woman, with all the fire in her, incinerated me. She said, 'Armand. Armand Banks. You are the clay, and you have the audacity to tell the Master Potter how to do His job. You have the mindset of the clay, and yet you have an opinion to offer the Master Potter? How arrogant of you. Maybe you should trust the Master Potter, as He has molded you from his clay and breathed his spirit into you. You may be of his image, but you damn sure are not his equal!'"

I stay quiet for a moment. The Master Potter. Am I telling the Master Potter how to do His job? Do I trust the Master Potter? Why would I not trust the Master Potter? I notice my silence gets the attention of Armand. I will need to process this more later. To fill the space I add, "She got you together, huh? That sure shut you down."

"Of course it did. I fell in love with her unique ability to see the world.

I traveled the world through her mind, and she traveled the world through mine. We went everywhere and nowhere at the same time."

Armand can sense my confusion. Smiling, he says, "You young folks are missing out. All the technology you have to bring you together, and yet you are still disconnected. Technology takes away a lot of quiet nothingness; you miss out on sharing vibrations with a person instead of with blue light emitting from soulless glowing rectangular pieces of steel that are battery-and-chip-powered. The energy coming from the person you love is interrupted or disrupted by the trance lost in answering technology's demand for attention. You lose connection or, better put, you lose the human signal. When you have the one and can just sit in the company of each other's energy, then you have become one before you even realize you have become one."

Who are these people?

"Mr. Banks, you and Ms. Earnestine really know how to bring light into the world. You both have a way of seeing the world that I really need to see. You are so right. Will you excuse me for a moment?"

"But, of course."

I stand and he stands, pulling my chair. I shuffle to the bathroom and text Eoghan.

"Hey," I send.

"Love," he responds.

I bring my phone to my chest. Oh my God. I really love this man.

"I really want to see you this evening. Do you think I can come by?" I send.

I bite my lip. I have never been at his home.

There is a pause.

Far too long a pause.

Still no response?

My anxiety is peaking. I am just about to send a text to change my mind when his response comes through.

"Yes."

I am screaming in my head. I rush back to the table where Mr. Banks continues talking. This time, we talk about Mahaley. My mind is on fire.

All I can think of is Eoghan. I want the sweet nothingness that I know Eoghan and I have. I need it. I thank Mr. Banks for such an amazing lunch, and of course, he ends it with a message.

"River, my dear. Whatever you are seeking, you already have. You only need to realize and accept it. It may be scary, because it is risky, but if it is real, it is worth it." I hug and kiss him on the cheek and run back to the office to see my last two clients.

I get back to the office and am happy to discover that my last two clients have canceled. Great. I can talk to Mahaley about her father. It is my hope that she takes the time to truly understand what she has in her parents. They are not just taking care of her; they are literally helping her grow like a delicate flower. They water, fertilize, and prune her when needed. They even erect stalks in order to provide the extra support she needs to help her be the best human she can be. What a gift she has in them.

Individuals are sometimes infused with each other to teach one another what they each need at a particular moment. We must take heed to listen for these signs of water, fertilization, pruning, or support. Even if we are in the position of the helper, we are simultaneously the ones being helped. We have to recognize that all relationships are bidirectional and require sharing energy. We discard old skin and transform as we encounter our teachers, who are also our students. The one who realizes this symbiotic relationship of the master/student dynamic truly actualizes freedom.

Eoghan texts me his address. The ride is about forty-five minutes. It gives me time to calm down and think. I call Jude to tell him that I am going to be late. Before I can even begin, he asks, "Can we talk about the letter?"

"Oh, yeah. I have been thinking about it. Let's go out this weekend, have dinner, and go over it," I say flatly. "By the way, I am going to be later than usual this evening." I try to disguise my joyful anticipation.

He responds with his usual "That's fine; I'm working anyway" line. This time, however, it is laced with regret.

I am sure that the regret is because of our last encounter, when he came upstairs to my sanctuary. Somehow my mind wanders back to it. I truly want to listen to my love playlist now, but the regret in Jude's voice forces me to remember his letter.

30

THE LETTER

"Riv, babe, you busy?" he calls up. Of course I am.

"No, I am just sitting here debriefing," I answer.

"Can I come up?" he asks with a hopeful tone.

No. Stay downstairs. Damn. Don't you have your own space?

"Sure. Come up," I say instead.

Do I have any backbone or boundaries?

"There is something you need to know. I am not sure what to do about us anymore. I am sure that you can tell that we are just buying time," he says as he walks up the stairs.

"Come on up. Yes, I know. We've already discussed this," I say as I drink more Riesling.

He sits right next to me. "Do you have another glass?" he asks.

"Of course not. You know this. Why would I bring a second glass?" I am annoyed now.

"Yeah, yeah, you're right. Can I have a sip of yours?"

I cannot believe this.

I hand him the glass.

"What is it, Jude? Spit it out. You are stalling."

He pauses. Staring at the glass, he asks, "Do you love me?"

"Honest answer?" I ask, sitting back against the wall.

"Honesty, Riv … Honesty." Jude sips, not looking at me at all.

"Jude, I used to love you. I do not feel the same anymore. There has been so much destruction in our relationship that I no longer am connected the way I was when we first met. I *know* what you have been doing. I have known for a long time. The years of lying and sneaking around, the years of watching you switch out your gym clothes for other clothes in the trunk of your car. I mean, I have always known. I just stopped caring. I learned to occupy myself with work and the lives of others. It kept me from seeing the deep gouging that is taking place in my own heart. I am being sanguine. When the life left, I did not try to put it back. If I am being honest, this is where I am right now."

I close my eyes, not quite willing to see the damage I've caused.

"I understand," he says.

He gets up, kisses me on the cheek, and informs me that there is a letter downstairs waiting for me. He leaves me lingering with the sounds of Miles Davis.

A letter?

I am a bit fearful, but I do not know why. What is in the letter? Is he leaving? Does he know? What is going on? I want to act as if I do not want to run downstairs and read the letter—you know, play it cool—but I'll be damned if I did not run down those stairs.

The letter rests on the chaise and is sealed in an envelope. I bite my lip nervously. It is as if I anticipate *Eoghan Eoghan Eoghan* to be written all over it.

I unseal the envelope.

I suddenly feel sick.

This is dumb. Take the damn letter out, River.

I begin to pull it, the letter, from the envelope. As I open it, I shuffle over to the window to see if Jude is still here.

Good! His car is gone. I can be nervous and sick all by myself.

River,

I knew I was going to talk to you after a meeting I had with a coworker today. He reminded me of how precious the gift of a good woman is. See, he is about to lose his woman to cancer. He has to force himself to cram a lifetime into a few remaining months of her life.

He talked about a mistake he had made and how he now struggled over whether or not to tell her. River, she already knew. She knew he'd had an affair. She also knew why. She understood the pain he was suffering, but he'd tried to cover it up. She also knew the pain he was suffering while harboring his guilt. However, she freed him from that guilt by telling him what she already knew and that she was okay with it.

After we spoke, I could only think of the years of turmoil I have caused you. The years of turmoil I have caused us. I suspect that you already know too. What I cannot figure out is why you stayed. See, I knew when I met you there was a diamond there. You just kept growing and becoming, and I just watched you become. I think that I do not deserve you most of time, and I wonder if that is why I keep the company of other women. I know that they are blind to who I am. I know that they are deaf to the insecurity hiding beneath my surface. They are ignorant to the games I play in order to maintain this masquerade. You have said, time and time again, that my parents have had a significant impact on my life. I have only rejected your interpretation in the past. I was insulted by being exposed by the woman who could see past my bullshit and could see who I really am. I now want to expose myself.

I want you to know that I am willing to work on the things I need to work on in order to be a better man. I know that I may have lost you. However, I am willing to take that risk. I cannot no longer maintain the person I am at this point or the person I portray myself to be. It is taking too much of my energy to continue to live like this, because it is not who I want to be or who I long to be.

Something tells me that you are distracted. I can tell that you are happier. *Happy* is not the word. You are daydreaming again. I love the lost look that you get when you are actually present with me. Now, the look I see when you are with me is a dark, soulless glaze. I do not want to be the grim reaper of your heart, Riv. I just wanted to share with you in order to come clean. My hands and heart have been dirty long enough. I am sorry. I do not know if you will ever forgive me or even if you should forgive me. I just know that I must reach deep into my soul in order to save myself. I love you. I always will love you. I love you enough to not hurt you anymore.

Love forever,
Jude

31

THE WOMAN IN THE PHOTO

I arrive at Eoghan's condo. It is ultramodern, with sleek lines and minimal landscaping. The grounds Zen-like. The setting is energizing. Beige sand, rocks, and minimal hedges seem to have the distinct purpose of stimulating and soothing the soul. They intentionally create an aura of calmness within.

It is just beautiful.

There is a small wooden porch with various Bonsai trees in the corners. I take time to embrace this moment. I haven't even put the car in park yet. I look down at my dress. Am I too professional looking? I'm wearing a black swing wrap dress with my hair up in a high curly ponytail. Should I take my hair down? I check myself in the mirror. Let's see: a little more Ruby Woo red lipstick should dress it up a little. I hate being so nervous. I am a grown-ass woman. I have no business feeling like a little kid starting a new school on the first day. I wonder what is going on inside his house now. What is he thinking? II must know in order to surrender to the tidal waves my blood is enduring. It is truly like being reunited with oneself.

Why is she sitting out there like that? Eoghan thinks to himself as he peers out through the bamboo blinds. *Is she changing her mind? Should I have said no? Why does she not want to come over here? Does she no longer want to see or talk to me? She's coming over my house to tell me she is working things out with her husband? I should've withdrawn myself when I knew I was falling in love with her. I knew it was too good to be true. Damn! Looks like I'll be back at A Prima Vista's bar again to hang out with Conrado. Shit! She turned the lights out! Okay, let me get myself together. I've been broken before and lived. I am sure this death will be temporary too. I can withstand it.*

"Is that my phone?" Eoghan says out loud, jogging to the couch.

"Hey, I'm outside your door." A text from "Home."

"Well, come inside our door," Eoghan texts back.

Damn that was a risk, Eoghan thinks to himself. *Why do I not have any self-control with this woman? What the hell did she do to me? My dudes would laugh at me if they saw how hooked I am. Is she going to text back or just come to the door? Just come to the damn door so I don't have to be going crazy in my own damn head.*

Eoghan hears the door open and calls out, "In here. Come on back. I was just waking up from a nap. There's a bottle of wine and a glass on the banister to your left. Pour yourself a glass if you want; you can set your stuff there. I'm changing my shirt. The living room is to your right. Make yourself at home."

"Okay! Will do!" River yells.

That was utter bullshit. Eoghan thinks to himself and laughs. *I have been up tripping about her visit ever since she texted me. Changing my shirt? I have changed shirts at least three times already. Business look? Relaxed-at-home look? No-big-deal-cleaning-the-garage look? I stuck with relaxed at home.*

That was an interesting word he used: *our.* I love the sound of it. I kept saying it as I walked up to the door. It was "ours" the moment I heard the song of his voice.

His house is clean—very clean, in fact. He likes the minimal look. It is warm and inviting, but it is not as warm as my house, I would say. His house reminds me of a vacation home—lots of neutral colors. It is calming though. I suspect that is the point. After a day of dealing with politics, I suppose he needs to distance himself from the chaos. The only real colors I see are brown and green—colors of the earth, I suppose. I will ask him about it when he comes out. I savor the Riesling. He must have remembered.

"River," he calls with that song again. The melody of his voice is hypnotizing.

"Eoghan, thank you for having me." I stand to hug him. I can barely handle the electricity between the crevasse.

"No, I am glad you are here. You get to see more of me." Eoghan grabs my hands, wrapping them around him, still holding them.

I suspect he is going to kiss me, but he doesn't. I am so damn disappointed. Instead he places his face on the meeting place of my neck and collarbone and gently places three kisses there. This is too much; I shudder under them.

"I could do this all day," Eoghan says. "But, I suspect that is not why you came here."

"Well," I respond.

He interrupts my response. "Have a seat, take your ponytail down, and relax with me." Eoghan pours himself a glass of wine.

We talk about the events of our day. I tell him about the lunch I had with Mr. Banks and the meeting with Earnestine. He is truly a good listener. I guess he showed that when he was playing the role of being my therapist! I tell him what they mean to me and how I feel my life is entering a chasm and that I must not be afraid of what is on the other side of it.

He listens attentively, offering anecdotal responses, but he mostly listens. He plays in my hair, twirling each curl between his fingers. I don't really see him watching me, because I am lost in my own conversation. The narrative is something I really wanted to share with him, because I believe he cares.

My head rests on his shoulder, and I struggle to find a way to bring up Belle. I do not know how to do it and stay legal by not giving away her identity. I push the thought away.

"I want to read something to you," I say as I pull Jude's letter out. I read the letter. Eoghan watches me intensely. I wonder why. After I finish, he sits back and takes a deep breath, closing his eyes.

"What are you saying to me, Riv, by reading that letter?" he asks.

"That I know what I want. I know who I want. That I know what I have to do to get what I want."

"So that is why you are here. So you can do what you need to do?" his voice is agitated by uncertainty.

"Yes, what's wrong? Why do you sound like that?"

"Really? Are you serious? You texted me to come over, read your husband's letter that he wrote to you … I gather you are working things out with him? You needed to just tell me. You needed to tell me that we were through! Damn, River. That's fine. I get it. He finally figured out what he had, and you want to give him a chance. If that is want you want, River, I only want you to be happy. If you are happy with him, then be with him," Eoghan says with a voice of surrender.

I can barely conceal my laughter. He truly misread my intentions. I grab his hand, and he attempts to pull it back. I grab it and pull it toward me.

"Eoghan. I came here to tell you I love you. I came here to tell you that I will not be working things out with my husband, and I will be divorcing him. I was long gone before you arrived in my life. You were the new life that I have longed for all my life. So, all that spill you gave me laced in assumption is untrue."

A small smile creeps onto Eoghan face. "Will you excuse me for a minute?"

I manage to only chuckle a little. "Sure."

Eoghan walks to the bathroom and looks into the mirror.

"My dearest Summer," he says to himself. "I will always have a place for you in my heart. When I lost you, I thought I could never have another love in my life. I never thought that I could give someone all my love, heart, and soul again. I know as you watch over me that you want me to be happy. She….River, makes me happy Summer. More important than happy, she makes me feel like I am home again. I am telling you this, because I want you to know I will never forget you. That I will always love you. I am going to marry River, and I want to give her the forever I promised to you."

He sure is taking a long time in there. I get up from the couch to take in the beauty of the room. He has pictures on the mantel. These must be pictures of his parents, maybe a picture of a graduation from college. He looks just like his mother. She is a heavyset woman, with eyes that have seen the setting of a thousand suns. Her face is round, but her cheekbones are prominent. Her smile is full and lures me into her seemingly warm and inviting nature. The dress she is wearing is full with black and white polka dots, which gives her a retro look. Eoghan's father has his hand on Eoghan's shoulder. His head is tilted up, making a statement: "This is my boy. My boy has made it." There is a look of pride on his face along with a slight smile. He looks almost military, there is a certain order about him.

Finally, there is a picture of a woman. She is outside, lying on the grass on a blanket. There is a shadow of a man over her. She has her hand out as if to tell the photographer not to take the picture, although she is laughing. It's not just any laugh; it's a laugh of pure joy. What a beautiful soul. Her brown eyes crease under the pressure of joy. I can feel the moment, and I pick up the simple wood frame and bring it to my face for closer inspection. Her tresses are long, brown, and wavy, with highlights circling around her heart-shaped face. She is the color of a dark peach. Her red undertones also catch my attention. Her eyes are full of light, taking in her love for the photographer. I know who this is. This must be her.

His wife.

I walk back into the living room and see River holding the frame. My stomach drops as I watch my love look at my love. I quietly walk backwards so I will not be seen as I observe her. What is she thinking? She is a smart woman. I know she's figured out who is in that photograph. I watch her trace the outline of the picture with her finger and sigh. She places the picture with utter care back on the mantel. She stands there for a moment—not moving, not talking. Her hands clasp the back of her neck as she looks up to the sky as if to beg for understanding.

I've made my peace with Summer.

River will have to understand that she is not in competition with Summer. River will have to know that the love I have for her includes the love I had for Summer. Summer holds a special place in my heart, but River holds my heart.

After a big sigh, I put the picture down and walk back to the couch. Flipping through the magazines, I just cannot get my thoughts away from the pain that must singe his heart. I want his wounds to be my wounds. We will heal together. I could stare at the back of her stately neck forever. I want her.

I continue to observe her. She has no idea that I am just taking her in, consuming the fragrance of lilac that emits from her body.

I really want to touch her.

I walk up, lift her hair, and gently place three long kisses down her neck.

My eyes close, and I allow my head to collapse under the shocking softness of his touch.

He wraps my hair around his hand, gently turning my head. His kisses the outline of my jawline down to my collarbone, causing me to shiver as if I've lost fifty degrees of body heat.

The magazine falls to the floor.

"Eoghan," I say. My voice is all air.

"River, not now. Don't worry. Just be in this moment with me," he says as he covers my neck in kisses that linger longer with each encounter.

He walks around the couch in front of me and sits on the table.

"I am sorry I jumped to conclusions. I thought I was going to lose you. I want you in my life. Just you. No one else. I do not want any other man in your life. I need to wake to your touch daily."

After all of those kisses, I can barely take in what he is saying. I want something entirely different now. My focus is not on what he is talking about.

He stands me up and kisses my lips and mouth. Finally! I drown in him. I cannot get enough of it. We consume each other. He grabs my hand and walks me toward what I can only assume to be his bedroom, and then he stops short.

"What's wrong?" I ask.

He turns, and his eyes burn with desire. "No, not until you truly belong to me."

"What?"

"No," he repeats, "not until you truly belong to me. I want to know what that is like. I want to be one with you when you can truly be one with me."

"You've got to be…..kidding!" I attempt to cool myself down. Hell, I am a little mad as we walk back to the couch. I understand though. I need to handle the world on the other side of the chasm. He sits and I lie down, allowing him full access to my hair. We sit and talk for what seems like hours. He explains his Zen garden to me and what made him develop it in his space. I just want to hear his voice. The song he sings to me when he speaks, the energy he emits, is the music and the connection we have together. This is our musical arrangement. This is living.

I notice the time and explain that I have to get going. We end the evening with him asking me for a timeline. I am taken aback, because I did not even think of one. "You cannot live in both worlds, River. You must choose one. You cannot fully enjoy either world when you only visit."

"I know. I know." He kisses my lip, gently biting it.

I don't want to go back home.

"I love you, River Meadows. I know you love me. That is the beginning. Build a life with me."

I grab my keys. Barely able to breathe or concentrate, I tell him to come see me next week at the practice.

"I love you, Eoghan," I say as I turn and walk out the door.

Starting the car, I sit back and breathe in deeply.

"Jude," I say exhaling. Damn, this is going to be hard.

32

TO BE VULNERABLE IS TO BE LOVED

It has been quite a few days since I have been over Eoghan's or have even seen him. We have talked a few times, and we have texted a lot. I guess I feel nervous about the feat before me. I almost would rather Jude walk away. Instead, I have to make the decision and implement it. I cannot fathom how to do this or even anticipate how Jude will react. I have been in a fog for more than a week as I adjust myself to anticipating my new normal. I'm struggling to maintain my clinical interest in clients, but I make do.

I know that tomorrow I will be seeing the Riley-Buttons. I am curious about how they are doing. They seem to be making progress. I am also pleased that Mahaley has been so fantastic at noticing that I need extra help. On that note, I am excited that I will get to see Earnestine today. I wonder if she will have a special tea for me!

The day seems to drag on as I wait to pull up to the cottage where the Banks reside. Finally, I arrive. The flowers emit such a mesmerizing scent. Taking a deep breath in, I slowly exhale.

The house has the same warm feeling as before, and it almost hugs me to come closer. It's the kind of hug that allows me to release any protective defenses I may otherwise try to cling to. This place is a safe haven for the brokenhearted, like me. My heart gets to expose itself, and its unwanted elements are released, enabling my soul to love again. It has been a long-awaited catharsis for me, and that is what the Banks have helped me do: release, especially Ms. Earnestine. My spirit is free again!

Ms. Earnestine is dressed in sagely appropriate clothing. I laugh to myself. She has on a long poncho and several necklaces. She offers me tea as before and says, "I am so glad to see you, River. The tea is the same as before," she says with a laugh. "You will have only Tieguanyin tea today. I think that it is appropriate for what lays before you, my sweet.

"You will need to tune into the vibration and strike a compassionate note. You will need to rearrange the notes, changing the music, specifically your music." Earnestine looks up at me with intensity, I can feel her burrowing into my heart. "See, my sweet, you and your husband share notes, but you do not share the same song. When you rearrange the notes, you will inadvertently change his music. However, you must have mercy and compassion for yourself. Listen to the sounds, remember?"

I am having trouble responding to her. I know she is right. I have to play the song according to the notes I am supposed to have. This music I have with Eoghan is what I understand and what speaks to my soul.

"I understand. I must reconcile and change what is painful without hurting anyone," I add.

"Yes. Yes, you do, and yes, it is. See, not only will it hurt him, but it will also hurt you. You will grieve this too, my child. You will grieve the loss of your marriage even if it is a bad one. It is still a loss in your life. Many people fail to understand that losses do not keep record of who was right or who was wrong. They only know that loss has been summoned and that all parties will taste the bitter juice of its fruit. You are supposed to survive it all. As a therapist, you know this, River. Pain is a teacher. Avoiding pain is avoiding life," she responds while sipping her tea.

"Are you telling me to leave my marriage?" I ask, somewhat incredulous.

"No, no. I am really telling you to execute the decision you already have arrived at."

She doesn't miss a beat. I exhale, and my body collapses into the truth.

"Let me tell you something, my love. Armand and I have had a long life together. He recognized me before I recognized him. What I mean by that is that he *saw* me and my essence before I could even see that essence in myself. I was not in a good place, as you know," she says with a wink.

Lunch. She is referring to the lunch I had with Mr. Banks.

I smile.

"So, anyway, on a daily basis, this man," she says as she looks up to the right to access the memory, "this unassuming man had the strength and tenacity of a quiet lion. He would walk me to the bus stop, carry my things, merge himself with me. After a while, I could not imagine a day without that walk. We were walking together in sync, and my walk was a stumble without him." Furrowing her eyebrows and biting her lip she seems to re-experience the mental stress of that solitary walk.

I want to reach out to her to bring her back to the moment. I think better of it. I allow it to be. I need to see this unfold and to watch her process her memories to gain a better understanding of my own.

There is no need to reach out to her, because she returns to our conversation on her own.

"See, our fifty years of marriage have not been without conflict. However, you must understand how to handle the conflict. I have learned how to adjust my paddle to the ebbs and flows of marriage. People make the mistake of believing marriage always flows in an upward motion. It waxes and wanes, ebbs and flows. There are times when we both have had to go back and regenerate after an initial confrontation and reflect. We always go back to our friendship. There is a partnership in conflict, my friend. More importantly we always go back to our core. The core is what allows us to continually reconcile."

"What's the core?" I interrupt.

"God," she responds in amusement, as if I should have already have known the answer.

"The God. Armand saw in me before I knew it was there and the God I realized in him. Our walk together was difficult at first. He wanted to *prove he was the man*," she says sarcastically. "It took a while for him to realize I already knew that. He had nothing to prove to me anyway. When he finally woke up to the fact that this was not important to me, he finally allowed me to partner with him without losing who he was or is.

"Ego is the kind of thing that can kill a marriage. It is when the players in a marriage think they are on competing teams. This competition will only destroy the marriage.

"You have to be careful and not allow the pressures of our ever-changing world to destroy what you have built together. Your strength as a woman fully complements the strength of your man. His strength as a man fully complements your strength as his woman. You are both valuable pieces of the marriage puzzle. The pieces you each bring into the marriage will determine the picture that you, your children, and the world sees," she says. She reaches over to gently squeeze my hand.

"Together we have seen the world change, and it is not over for us yet. It is not supposed to be. What we had to recognize is that we had to steady the boat together, River. Our paddles had to work together and not against each other. We would have been floating in circles and not going anywhere if we hadn't start paddling in the same direction. We would have lost everything, including our union."

Earnestine sits quietly for a moment, seemingly to gather the right words.

Marriage requires that we are constantly dying to each other. By this I mean that we allow ourselves to relinquish what we believe we need individually and hold onto each other to stay safe. In marriage we are supposed to always be safe but vulnerable to each other. The world asks that we put up walls and never share our perceived weaknesses. Only the strong can be vulnerable. The lack of vulnerability is death to marriage. You understand?" she asks.

"Of course. Jude and I are not even in the same boat," I say with a laugh.

"Well, my sweet. Have compassion. You both are struggling. Do you think you are just reacting to his transgressions, or do you think this love you describe is independent of him?" she asks.

"What do you mean?"

"Well, sometimes these affairs could not survive on their own. The commonality only exists in the pain that each party is suffering from. Basically, your relationship with this man requires the pain from Jude to survive," Earnestine responds.

Turning her head, she yells to the kitchen. "Armand, can you bring us some tea cake?"

She looks back at me, smiling.

I smile back, knowing some grudging will occur.

"Woman, you insist on doing this. You know I am in here reading the paper. I know you just want to see all of this sexiness!" he says with a laugh.

We laugh right along with him.

He sets the teacakes down. She grabs his hand and squeezes it as he turns to walk back in the kitchen. He never even looks at her but squeezes right back. No words are spoken—not even a look in the eye. All the love they have for each other fills the room loud enough to destroy any set of good eardrums. I realize that I've just heard their song. That moment—that moment, my God. That was an awesome display of one life, not two lives striving to maintain independence. They are two lives that have come together to create a new thing.

I think I am about to die. The love in that moment is something words cannot fully describe. No word is deserving of such an honor. I can feel tears welling up in my eyes. I want that. I want mine every day. I want my Eoghan.

"Actually, he is right," Earnestine says. "He is whom I truly want, and I want to see him and hear his voice every single day and moment of my life. I know full well I do not have his everything when I have someone over. I just want his presence. He's my love, River. I know you understand that."

"I … um, I do." I respond. I need to change the subject momentarily. "Earnestine, did you have people speak into your marriage? Did you have support?"

Sensing the discomfort, Earnestine smiles. "Yes and no. See, you have to be extremely careful who you allow to speak into your marriage. Not everyone has good intentions. There are those who may have good intentions but bad information."

Earnestine cocks her head to the side.

"You have to ensure that you have the right ear—you know what I mean? Think about it. Let's say you have a diamond ring that is a family heirloom, and it needs some work. Would you take it to just anyone? Hell no! You would research this company. You would check out their reputation. You would get references. You would probably check to see if they have had any complaints, right?"

"Right," I state emphatically.

"Exactly. You do this because it is something you cherish. You know that you have something that is one of a kind. Knowing this, you would not just give the ring's care over to anyone. That would be foolish, yes?" she asks.

"Yes," I respond.

Placing her tea on the tray, she holds her hand out to me.

I place my hands in hers.

"So, you are here, my sweet. You are learning how to navigate some treacherous waters in your life right now. You do not need help making a decision. You only need to execute the decision you have already made. When you make that decision, *you give it your all.*"

Her statement is laced with desperation. She continues: "River, hold nothing back. It is a risk. The fall is hard, my love. But the experience is something only God, the glory of love, created. Do not lose out on the creation of God because of fear.

"So many people stay in relationships that are safe for them. They are accustomed to the prison they have jailed themselves in. They are familiar with the level of pain it offers, and they are quite used to it. It becomes the limp in their hearts. So, they live in quiet despair. These people are not fully alive."

A heaviness begins to coat Earnestine's voice. Is it the sound of regret, maybe?

"Why do you sound so sad, Ms. Earnestine?" I am curious.

"I guess because I could have missed out. Armand saw something before I did, as I explained before. I was not willing to let go of all of me. I was not ready to be exposed. He was showing his true self and was fully vulnerable, and I was not ready to do that. I was hurting from a past relationship. That could have ruined this ... this I have with him. He saw the connection. I could not see it because my filter was tainted from past hurt. You are a therapist, River, so you know this already. He took my pain and made it his."

I look up and can see from afar that Armand is watching from the kitchen. He stands at the doorframe. He can sense her pain. Wow, he is caring for her just by standing there.

He walks up to her and places his hand on her shoulder. She reaches and touches it. Smiling, she has clearly been centered by his touch.

The moment grows silent. I allow it. I need to absorb its energy.

I think this is a good time for me to leave. I start to gather my things.

"Don't run, River. You can stay. We just need a moment. Be in it with us," Armand says.

"I know. But there are some things I need to take care of. I know what you have is something special. I mean, it is truly something special. I am honored to say it is something that I have witnessed. To be in the presence of true love! To experience it and watch it unfold right before my eyes is why my God guided me here. I am honored to have witnessed true love, that special love that I have hoped for all my life. Thank you for sharing your love for one another with me," I say, almost in tears.

"You and Ms. Earnestine are a gift. I hope you know that. Your mentorship is something that I want to continue."

"Absolutely, River," Earnestine responds. "Do not forget the gift you are to others. See, we are all on different planes, but we are also on the same life continuum. You are responsible for those behind you. Use the gift that God has given you. You have been built for it."

My mind moves to my mother and the katana—the polisher and my hamon.

I tell the Banks about my mother and our visit. They are enthralled with the part about the prayer room with the katana. I am happy, and I feel like I have something to offer them.

"You see, River, there is guidance all around you. God always looks after His people. This is about more than a man you love. This is about you and who you are as a woman. You have the chance to light the world more brightly now as the grinding stone becomes even finer. You cannot allow your light to be dimmed by being safe." Earnestine says squeezing Armand's hand.

"Yes, ma'am. Thank you both so much."

I hug them both, and Armand kisses me on the cheek.

As I pull out of the driveway, my thoughts turn to Eoghan and Jude. Then something new emerges: my thoughts turn to myself.

Who are you, River? What is the purpose of this new light, this uncovering, this unveiling of yourself?

33

TWO DUFFLE BAGS ON THE SIDE OF THE COUCH

I arrive home pretty late from the Banks' house. I find myself driving around with no destination. I drive all over the city, through areas I am familiar and unfamiliar with. I want to turn on the music, but something in me needs silence. I need to be in my head and touch my heart. The moments to come will be pivotal for me, and I know it. I do not think I am just avoiding by meandering. It is more that I am integrating my thoughts and feelings.

I allow my mind to intensely focus on what I am doing and where I am within myself. The window is open slightly, and a small whistle of air forces its way in. It creates a slight chill that I want to experience right now. I can hear the sound of the drive, the happy chatter of those in the car next to me as we sit at the light, and the awkward silence. I see the blue glow that emits from the rectangular plastic of headlights. While I am driving, there are all types of natural music in the air to support or change the mood around me. Streetlights are whizzing by—some dimmed, some out altogether. The night is unusually quiet.

There are not a lot of people around. The night appears to belong to those who are of the night. People who become invisible to day walkers, such as the homeless, prostitutes, addicts, and their suppliers, dot the streets. They remind us of society's social sickness, which we refuse to heal even in our collective consciousness.

When I finally pull up in the driveway, I can see that Jude is home. Every light in the house is on. This is odd. For some reason, I feel a sense of dread, heavy like a winter coat. I begin to breathe deeply, fully conscious of the life source entering my lungs. Then I slowly exhale and clutch, figuratively speaking, my make-believe coat so the fear will be removed. As before, the click of the key and turning of the lock seem extra loud, or maybe my senses are just acute at the moment.

Why am I holding my breath? Breathe, River, breathe. *Execute the decision you have already made.* I carefully place my keys in the key bowl on the bench. *Why am I trying to be so quiet?* I am not sneaking into my own house. *Is this guilt I am experiencing? Why do I feel guilty? Am I guil*ty? I can feel myself approaching panic; the train to anxiety has taken off, and I have purchased a first-class ticket.

I can see the back of Jude's head. He does not even turn around as I walk into the living room. For the first time in a long time, I really look at the room. Whereas Earnestine's living room has rich colors that create an atmosphere of time well spent, an atmosphere of warmth and love, I can see that my living room is a bit different. It is coastal, full of light colors. It feels more like a cottage in Maine. Its ambience is more of a "forget what is going on in reality" look. A "relax and breathe" feeling is what it offers. Whereas Earnestine's home reminds me of the earth, my home reminds me of the water. It is designed with neutral colors, such as white and beige with dots of blue, which take me in. It helps me take off the coat of worry and the shoes of fear and forces me to sit down the purse of past hurts. I allow the room to take me in, and the heaviness begins to dissipate. I can now focus.

"Evening, River," Jude says, not looking at me. His back and head are fixated toward the fireplace.

"Hey, Jude. I want to talk," I respond.

"I'm sure you do. I have been sitting here for a few hours, trying to figure out what to say."

He turns his head to the right. I can see his eye, but he is still not looking at me. I walk around and sit on the white sofa opposite him. It has light blue and beige pillows dotting it. Picking up one of the pillows, I hold it close. I must need the security right now. The action of hugging something is comforting.

Jude is still not quite looking at me. That is interesting. He seems to be evading eye contact.

"What is it you would like to say?" I ask.

"Well, I know you have read my letter. I meant that. I know …" He pauses for a moment. "I know you know of some of my escapades. I tell you, you know Max? The salesman at work? He really opened my eyes to what I have been doing to you … to us. He came to me today. He was off the last couple of days. He came into the office today wearing sweatpants and a tee shirt. He looked like he hadn't even bathed yet. He was hung over, I could tell. He was muttering something, and I could not make it out. He was a mess. I finally understood the two words he was saying over and over. *She's gone, she's gone, she's gone.*

"My God, Riv! He told me that she had asked for him to come into the living room and kneel beside her. She told him that the years they spent together were wonderful for her. She told him, practically made him promise, that he would move on and that he deserved to love again.

"She made him promise that he would not die with her. He said her voice was barely audible. She said to put their purpose together behind him, as it was time for her to go home. She was ready, and she needed to go. She said her purpose in life was to prepare him for the next love of his life. He should not allow the devil of guilt to keep him from living and loving again. She explained that she had lived a thousand lives with him and the kids, so losing this one was nothing but formality.

"I was a mess for him, River, but more importantly I was a mess for you. I thought about how I have not allowed you to live. You are not happy here with me, and I know it. I allowed my ego and my need to possess you to keep you from a love you deserve. I have dimmed your light because it was too bright for me. I know that," he says as his voice cracks.

I start to interrupt him, but he puts up his hand, stopping me.

"No, let me finish," he says emphatically.

"I know what you will do, Riv, if I let you talk. You will begin to take care of me and make sure I am okay. You will dilute the truth in order to make sure that I am okay. Your light again, dimmed. I can no longer be the cause of that. This is the gift I want to give you.

"I want to give you something that I haven't given myself. A chance. Does that mean you might take that chance with someone else? Sure it does. Maybe. I cannot and will not control that. That is not what I want. However, I know the version of man I am now will never be enough for us to be whole." Jude's voice struggles as he continues. "I am not ready to be committed. I have some things I must work through first. I have things with my father and mother that have given me some beliefs that have done nothing but cause destruction to you and me. I am ready to work on them."

Jude sits back and takes a deep breath and continues: "But I must work on them alone."

The room is silent. I am not sure what to say. I scan the room, and I can now see two duffle bags packed by the side of the couch.

I stand up and walk over to touch the bags. He watches—for a reaction, I suppose. The stillness of the room is deafening. I need to feel the space and not fill it with words right now. Death is happening—the death of my marriage. I could balance it with the life that is occurring as well for both of us, but I do not want to do that. I need to honor the death in all its fullness.

Sitting back down, I still do not have words. I don't think I want words right now. I search his eyes and can see the pain of growing up. He is choosing the most painful option because it is the right thing to do. For the first time, he is being a husband—by telling me he cannot be one. I have so much love for him right now.

I get up and rest my head on his shoulder. He kisses my forehead and puts his arm around me, leaning his head against mine. I can feel his tears fall as they occasionally strike me. I am overwhelmed, as no one can feel the tears that flow so heavily from my eyes.

"I love you," he says, kissing my hair.

"I can see it now, for the first time in a long time," I respond. "I love you too. I want the best for you."

"I know you do, Riv. I know you do, but now ... I want what is best for you."

I fall asleep on his shoulder. I can feel him quietly placing me on the couch, trying not to disturb my slumber. I am in between the world of the conscious and unconscious but allow him to handle me.

We'll talk more in the morning is my last conscious thought.

The next morning, at half past six, I wake and realize that I have slept with my work clothes on. I am incredibly stiff from sleeping on the couch. I walk past the side of the couch where Jude's bags had been. He must have gone upstairs last night.

I walk toward the kitchen to make us some coffee, and the oddest feeling comes over me.

I run upstairs and look into the bedroom—no Jude.

I run downstairs and look in basement, where the man cave is—no Jude.

I look outside to see if his car is in the driveway—no Jude.

I look to see if he parked in the garage—no Jude.

Jude is gone.

A strange pain wells in the pit of my stomach. River, you are now here. This is what you wanted. Why am I in excruciating pain? I flop to the couch and try to piece together my feelings.

Many people are shocked when they still feel pain over the loss of something that has caused so much pain in their lives. It is not unusual to have such an experience. When death occurs, its finality can be overwhelming.

The death does not just happen to the marriage. It happens to all the components of the marriage: death to familiarity, death to comfort, death to the chosen or reactive identity developed during the course of the marriage, and death to the routine.

However, what is also happening is birth, if you allow it: birth to understanding, birth to a new self, birth to new risks, birth to vulnerability, birth to a new love. We must be prepared to mourn the death of the first to adequately appreciate the new birth of self-love. We must acknowledge the mourning, so it can be our teacher. Pain can be a teacher if used properly.

"Oh my God. I have to go to work today," I say out loud. I try to muddle through the morning. I cannot seem to find anything. I want to call Jude, but something tells me not to. I want to call Eoghan, but something tells me not to. I have to be in this moment. I have to embrace this pain, this process. I go up to my sanctuary with a cup of coffee and text Mahaley.

"Mahaley, good morning. Can you please reschedule my morning session at nine o'clock for eleven o'clock? I know there's an opening."

"Yes, you okay?" Mahaley responds.

"Yes, just tired," I respond.

"My parents get to you again? Put that Yoda spell on you? LOL," she texts back.

"LOL. Right. See you midmorning," I respond, hitting send.

"K, boss. Get rest," she responds.

I turn the phone over, as I do not want to be tempted by the lure of its entertainment. I need to spend some time with my thoughts and myself.

"I can have Eoghan," I say out loud to myself. A smile crosses my face. I can feel my love for him. However, fear is my close companion, reminding me of how hard the fall will be if I lose him.

I sip my coffee and just sit for the moment.

34

A GNAT IN THE GARDEN

We've been doing so much better. I sit on the chaise and commit to watching Belle as she dresses. She has no idea I do this every day. I chuckle, checking my phone.

My thoughts move back to Belle. I really need to make sure I keep this together. She has responded well so far. I can still sense a slight sadness in her, but it is not as strong as it was.

I can tell that it is lifting; the long faraway looks that used to happen daily almost never happen anymore. We have such a long road to go toward our future, and I hope she can see the truth in me again. I owe her that. I can only worry about what I am doing. I know that I can love enough for the both of us. I can love her into loving me again.

Mmhmm … I love those thigh-highs she's putting on. She has such a dance about her. The sway of her hip as she switches legs is just a thing of beauty.

Delilah was—wow—what a waste of time. I was going to allow the distraction of a gnat to destroy the Garden of Eden. I shake my head. I had no idea. Just none. Dudes are forever trying to tell me to get what I can, as life's too short. I ain't getting any younger. Get it while they're willing to give it. They sure would've been right behind me to scoop her up after she left. One thing's for sure, you can't let everyone in your stuff. They will tear your shit up and go home to their own mess.

"You almost ready, babe? I am just waiting on you. Dr. Meadows will be expecting us soon. Don't forget we have to tell her about the airport."

I hear her laughter from the bedroom. "I know! It was crazy! I'm almost ready, Joe. Give me a minute," Belle yells. "Jasmine! Make sure you get your clothes ready to go to Grandma's. Your dad and I are going out to dinner after our appointment."

"Going out the dinner." The sarcastic voice came from Jasmine in the hallway.

"Listen to your mother, Jaz," Joe yells.

"I was! Jasmine exclaims, I am glad you guys are hanging out, having fun."

Joe waits to see if Belle is going to respond. Nothing yet. After a few seconds, Joe says, "Yes, I am too. We are fine, my little sweetie. We will be fine. Do not forget I have that training program next week. I cannot pick you up from school."

"That's right!" Belle exclaims. "You excited?"

"Of course. Anything to make sure my family is okay. I am not willing to say, I am willing to do. That's a promise."

Belle's heart grows warm with hearing the change in Joe. Smiling, she puts her hair high on her head—a messy bun today.

****

Today is less painful than yesterday. I am getting better. Sighing, I begin to think of Eoghan. I am glad the mere thought of him does not make me tailspin into a pit of despair now. It's more like a tropical storm. My thoughts turn to my last intimate moment with him—the moment he would not kiss me. Looking at my lips, I carefully line them. I add a light natural color to highlight my cheekbones. Puckering my lips, I say, "Well, I am kissable," and laugh out loud.

"I see those lips," Joe says.

I swivel to see Joe standing in the doorframe.

Walking toward me, he turns me around, facing the vanity mirror.

"Look at *that* woman. That woman is worth it all. My God, and you are here with me? I have it all. I will never forget it," he says as he kisses the side of my forehead.

I reach my hand around to the back of his neck, pulling him toward me. Looking at his reflection, I speak to it.

"Thank you, Joe. Thank you for having more love and for being willing to recreate what was lost. We still have a ways to go, but I respect you for what you are doing. Thank you for being a husband and waking me out of my world of anesthesia."

"I love you. I love you, Belle. Please believe that."

"I don't need to believe it, Joe. I know it. You are showing me. Come on, let's go."

I smile at Joe—a smile he has not seen in over five years. It's an authentic smile that is full of joy.

I can see the warmth within him grow.

35

SESSION 12: BROWN WING TIPS AND THE CALLA LILLY

Eoghan calls the office looking for an appointment with River. "Hey, Mahaley, Can you squeeze me in? I really need to see her. I can take the last appointment. Oh…. she has an appointment already, but they cancel a lot? Okay, I am going to come early and wait. If they come, they come. If not, I will take the last appointment. Thanks, Mahaley," I say and hang up the phone.

River and I have talked, but we have been distant. I do not like the distance. Am I stalking? Nope. I love her. I just need to see her face. If only for an hour, I just need to see her face. I just need to touch her, to remind me of the woman who awkwardly looked into my eyes and dropped her gaze when she was caught. I need to hold those arms close to me—those arms I caught when she ran from of the restroom and fell into my arms. The electricity that disrupted my being when I first laid eyes on her—I need to feel her electricity running through me. I need a defibrillator, a much needed defibrillator.

I thought Belle was bringing me back. Belle eased the pain that I could no longer tolerate. I did not know that until River came into my life. River does not ease the pain; she creates new space for love.

I want her forever. I do not feel like I have arrived at home until I am in her presence. I am forever orphaned until our next meeting. I really dislike being this vulnerable, but she makes it feel so good.

I am almost at her office.

Okay, let me check in with Mahaley. Then I'll run out and get some flowers after I find out about the appointment canceling *possibly*.

"Just have a seat, Mr. McGhee. I will let you know in a moment if there is a cancelation." Mahaley points toward the lobby.

"No problem. I'll grab a magazine and wait it out in *hope*," I say with a smile. Mahaley offers a wink and a smile.

Rummaging through the magazines, I find one that suits me. I laugh at my quest. You'd think all she sees is women in here by these magazines. The *GQ* magazine is entertaining enough—until a familiar voice sticks my soul a thousand times with the heat of lightening.

I dare not look up. Instead I bury my face deeper in the magazine, hoping this "daymare" is not true.

"I told you we were on time, Joe," Belle yells over to Joe, who begins to check in with Mahaley. As usual, she is hurried. She has a flurry of papers, deciding to work while she waits for Dr. Meadows. She does not initially notice the gentleman sitting across from her. She is too involved with trying to keep her stuff together.

I study her. What is she doing here? They are both here? I glance over to Joe, careful not to bring too much attention to myself. I almost want to get up, but moving might really bring unwanted attention.

Belle drops her purse while trying to get her papers together, and pens, nail files, and lipsticks roll out. She reaches over to pick up the lipstick that rolled over to a pair of very familiar shoes—a burnt brown and walnut pair of wing tips, specifically: Allen Edmonds LGA Warriors.

Belle struggles as she remembers the day Eoghan bought the shoes. They had gone out to eat at the mall during lunch one day. She'd helped him pick them out. They were filled with brown, white, and cream argyle socks. The socks were covered by dark denim. Moments of the affair flash before her: his kisses, his laughter, the intensity in his eyes, his body becoming one with hers. Belle dares not look up further.

Eoghan looks down at her, the top of her head right in front of him. He knows she recognizes the shoes and possibly the socks. He is no longer breathing. They are no longer breathing.

Someone must break the moment.

Oh my God, Belle thinks. *What am I supposed to do?*

She can tell Joe has sat down right next to her, but his words are a mere muffle; she cannot make them out.

I cannot make out the words! What is he saying to me? she thinks. *I am frozen in this moment.*

Eoghan holds his breath. *I know she is frozen. She knows it's me. I do not know how to help her. I know that must be Joe. He is asking her if she is okay and needs help. Why won't she respond? Dammit, please respond! Do not make this any more obvious than it has to be, Belle!*

"Babe, I'll get your stuff. What? Have you had a stroke or something?" he asks. He pulls her up.

Belle works hard to avoid my eyes.

I hand Joe the items by my foot.

"Thanks, man," he says.

I offer a quick, "No prob".

Damn, I'm an asshole. My guilt is overtaking me. I want to get up but am unable to move.

"Eoghan—Anxiety, 7 p.m." crosses Belle's mind, reminding her of the unsolved open wound.

Belle finally gets the courage to look at Eoghan.

Their eyes meet and engage in a silent battle.

Do not jeopardize this, Belle. You will jeopardize the both of us. Do not even acknowledge me! Eoghan's eyes threaten.

What are you doing here? Are you seeing her? Why are you here? You left me! her eyes yell back.

An outside voice interrupts the quiet war between them.

"Mr. McGhee? You are in luck. They canceled. You can come back when the Riley-Buttons have finished. Come back in one hour," Mahaley calls.

Eoghan can barely acknowledge Mahaley. Never taking his eyes off Belle, he slowly gathers his things. The standoff is akin to a standoff between two wolves. Someone must retreat.

"Riley-Buttons?" Mahaley calls. "Dr. Meadows is running a bit behind. She will be with you shortly. There was a crisis with the last session."

Joe thanks Mahaley and looks over at Belle, thinking she is acting like a stroke victim.

Eoghan waits until Joe looks away to grab a magazine.

Softening his look at Belle, Eoghan mouths, "I'm sorry."

He gathers his things and leaves to return in one hour.

Geez, that was a tough session! I have to get Belle and Joe, I am already behind schedule. I will apologize soon as I see them. "Riley-Buttons? Come on in! So sorry for the delay," I declare.

"Belle, you okay?" I ask, looking over at Joe. She looks like a zombie.

Joe nods his head. "She's okay Dr. Meadows. We've just had a long day, right, babe?" he asks her while kissing her cheek.

"Right," Belle manages to get out.

Hmm, something is not right here. Let's see how the session plays out.

"So what's been up? Tell me about the airport homework," I ask.

Joe laughs.

"Yeah, it was crazy. At first, I thought it was a dumb idea. We were just sitting there watching folks. But it was cool," Joe says, nudging Belle.

"Uh, yeah … it was … I mean … I … I mean we … were able to see people either come home or go to their destination. Hmm, can you excuse me for a minute? I am not feeling well. I need to go to the bathroom." Belle jumps up and hurries out of the room.

"Joe, is everything okay? What is going on? She does not look okay. Did something happen?" I ask.

"Um, I do not know, Dr. Meadows. She started acting strangely when we got here. I do not know what it was. She kind of checked out. Can you check on her?" he asks, taking off his cap and scratching his head.

"Sure, um … okay. I am going to check in on her now. Are you okay?" I ask.

"I'm great. She is coming around too, I think. She just has to believe in me again."

"Okay, okay. I'll be right back." I stand up and sit my notebook on the chair.

I stand at the door of the bathroom, and I am not sure what I should do. Is this about Eoghan? My anxiety is going through the roof. It is bad enough I had to can my feelings on Jude. I hope I have enough emotional stability to face this if it is about Eoghan.

Taking a deep breath, I enter. "Belle, you good? What's happening? I can see that you are really not doing well."

Belle slowly opens up the stall door. She stands at the frame, looking at me and not saying a word. There is an ice-cold look in her eyes.

"Why did you not tell me?" she says barely audible, with a hint of a hiss.

"Tell you what, Belle? I do not know what you are talking about. I am a bit taken aback."

Pointing her index finger down, she accents each word.

"He. Was. Here," she says with a hiss again.

Please no, please no. I can feel my heart rate increasing.

"Who Belle? Who was here?" Man, I am good. I think I sound almost normal.

"He. Was. Here," she repeats—same hiss.

"Belle, I need you to help me. Help me understand what you are talking about so I can help you."

Why am I playing this game? I have to. I cannot just say it. I cannot legally do so. Wait; he's not my client. The truth is far worse than that.

"Eoghan! River! Eoghan! You know full well what I am talking about. You know he is your client. How long has he been your client? Did you talk him out of seeing me, because of Joe? I cannot believe you. I trusted you, River! I trusted you!"

My God. What am I going to do? Oh I know. I *know*. I can rely on the ethics of the job.

"Belle, you know the drill; you know how this works. I cannot confirm or deny if someone is a client here. I am not allowed to do that. Would you want someone to know if you were here? This allows me to continue to protect your confidentiality."

Wow, that's a good one. Thank goodness I think fast.

"So are you saying that I cannot even talk to him?" she asks.

My face grows warm. I can feel the anxiety building. This is a pivotal moment. I could lie to her to protect myself. Or I can be honest and accept the natural consequences that will follow. It is time to be a big girl. I have allowed this to continue with no plan of action. But what will occur if we get caught up in this triangle? I wonder if she can sense the deep conflict that I am in. What face am I showing her right now?

I suspect it is shame, because that is what I am experiencing—a deep-rooted trunk of shame. We are here now. We are in this moment. This is the moment to just do the honorable thing and allow the process to unfold.

Exhale deeply.

I mentally collapse into truth. "You can talk to anyone. I am the one who is bound, Belle. Can you return to the session? You guys seem to really have done some great work. I want you to continue to process those moments with him. Take some breaths, Belle, and come back," I add.

Her face softens. Her body begins to relax. There is less rage and hurt emitting from her. Belle, the fire-breathing dragon, has left, returning her to a woman with a conflicted heart.

We walk back to the office in silence. She sees Joe, and he stands to allow her to sit. She hugs him. Actually, it is more like an embrace. I really enjoy seeing that. I can tell it takes him aback a little. He was not expecting it. His eyes grow wide, and he squeezes her tighter. She burrows her head into the nape of his neck and cries.

"I am so sorry we have gone through this, Joe. I have so many conflicts, and I have us and you caught up in them. I still have feelings for him, and I am trying to prioritize. I have to restructure my heart in order to receive your attempt to love me again," she manages to get out.

Joe doesn't say a word. The look on his face cannot adequately be described by language.

It's a look of resolve—the look you have when you've been driving for hours because you are lost, and suddenly a sign appears, indicating your destination. He'd only wanted the opportunity to make it right, and she has cracked the door open. This is all one needs: the birth of a new beginning. And new beginnings are not just for the young.

Momentarily, I can separate from my current crisis. I am enjoying the ember of a new start.

She pulls back, attempting to straighten herself.

He pulls her back to him by the sides of her shirt.

"I love you, Belle, and I know now what that means to you. I am beginning to understand your language." He looks at me for confirmation that he has used the concept accurately.

I nod.

This dude has been reading some books and really listening. He has hit the mark with Belle.

I allow the moment to continue. Wow, I feel like I am at the movies.

"So, can you guys tell me about the airport?" I finally inquire.

They both sit. I notice that Belle has cupped Joe's hand and placed it in her lap. He gently squeezes.

Belle has lightened up, at least for the moment. "Yes, it was fascinating. It felt weird at first, but I was able to see people's love for each other, you know. I was able to see them run toward each other, almost preparing to run through each other. I saw the tears of the hellos and goodbyes, the intimate kisses, the cold pecks, and the one-armed shoulder hugs that almost say, *please* do not touch me. I saw the limp, *I need this to be over* hugs and the distant *I'm on my phone* couples, the ones who do not even look like they are together. Then there were the embraces, the kisses all over the face, the holding hands and walking, the soothing feeling of a hand on a thigh. There were *let me get that hair out of your field of vision* moments. There were smiles and hearty laughter. And there were smirks that indicate another disaster has occurred. There were faraway looks of wishing to be far away. It was really nice and terrible at the same time," Belle explains.

"Excellent. What do you think you got out of it?" I ask.

"Just that there needs to be a true effort and desire to love one another,"

Belle says as her eyes look for Joe's. "That both, and not only one, have got to give it all or nothing. Our hostility toward one another must be talked about and dealt with openly to gain the truth so we can understand each other's needs, wants, and desires. Together we must love each other on each other's terms." She pats Joe's hand indicating his turn.

"I agree. I must be able to love her the way she needs and wants to be loved, and she cannot expect me to read her mind. I need to know when I am not loving according to her definition of 'loving her.' I need to be able to tell her when I am not feeling important with her. I need to feel important. I want to know I am the only one for her. However, I need to make sure *this woman*"—he places hard emphasis on *woman*—"without a doubt knows that I got her front, her back, and her sides, from head to toe. She is safe with me. I must protect her and protect her love."

Joe turns to Belle and says, "You are safe with me, baby."

Belle takes her hand, pulling Joe's chin to her, and gently kisses his lips. It's not a boring, polite kiss either. It is more like a "I'll see you when you get home, as I have something for you" kind of kiss. It is sexy.

I can see fire in his eyes.

Better wrap this up.

We end the session with a plan of action and tools they will continue to use for the next six weeks.

I want to give them an extended amount of time before they see me next. I need this new foundation and not a patch job to solidify their union.

I tell them to make an appointment for six weeks to follow up on their progress.

Belle asks Joe to bring the car up to the door.

Uh oh, she wants to be alone with me.

After he is out of sight, she says, "If Eoghan is here to see me because he is hurt that we are not together anymore, all he has to do is call me. I know you cannot confirm or deny … however you stated it. All he has to do is call me. He has not taken any of my calls or text messages. I think he is seeing someone else. I feel stupid standing here telling you all of this, because you won't tell me why he is here. Regardless, I think he was the medicine I used to deal with what was going on with me and Joe, but I still have feelings for him, you know?" Her face saddens.

I work hard to keep a blank look and not truly respond to her. I offer her one point. "Belle, you said you have begun the process of working out your marriage with Joe. Do you think you still want that?"

"Yes, I do," she says as she nods.

"Then have that, Belle. You defined what Eoghan was for you. You have to decide if you can let him go and why it's important that you do."

My anxiety is growing, because I also need to know why Eoghan is here. I cannot go out there with Belle. I just cannot handle that triangle. The look in my eyes will give it all away.

Belle opens the door to walk out of the office, only to find Eoghan McGhee standing in the frame, preparing to enter.

CPR.

Please, someone give it to me.

My heart stops, and I can swear my soul evaporates from my body. My temperature drops significantly. Please call the time of death.

I cannot bring myself to talk. I just cannot.

Eoghan can see the look in my eyes, and I can swear he reads my mind. He does not say a word.

For what seems like hours, the three of us all stand in the doorway, deciding on what to do next.

Belle notices my face. She must know now. There is no reason that I should have a reaction like this—the reaction of somehow being caught with my hands in the cookie jar.

Belle's eyes shift from me to Eoghan to the flowers he has in his hands.

Flowers? He bought *flowers*? I am having this strange duality of experience where I am in love with flowers but also petrified, because it is clear that this is love, not work.

The pieces seem to be coming together for Belle. I can see her processing the moment.

I really need Eoghan to not look at me right now. His face is more awkward than anything. He seems to be more concerned about me.

This moment seems to go on for hours. Belle breaks the silence.

"Wait, wait … you are not seeing her … you are *seeing* her?" Belle asks.

Belle sharply turns her head toward me, her eyes cutting into my flesh. "How could you? How could you … when you knew? You knew who he was to me?"

There was a plea in her voice. My God, I can feel the geyser of guilt rising.

"Belle," Eoghan begins.

"Don't you dare say shit, Eoghan. You were not breaking up with me in order to save my marriage; you were breaking up with me in order to be with her. That is why you would not kiss me. You could do everything else but refused to kiss me. This is who you were saving that for!" Belle begins to cry.

I can hear the double honk of a horn.

Jesus, Joe is outside.

Wait … what? Could not kiss but could do everything else? What is she talking about? He saw her again? My mind is a swirling mess of confusion, anger, jealousy, embarrassment, and guilt.

I turn to look at Eoghan incredulously. His face tells me the truth.

"Riv, we will talk," he says as he reaches for me. He does not just reach with his hands. I can see him reaching with his eyes. *Just give me a chance to explain*, they say.

"Are you fucking serious? You are fucking my therapist?" Belle yells.

A resounding "NO!" leaves Eoghan. That is the only solace I have. We have not slept with one another. I am so glad that is the one pure thing we have so far.

I cannot afford to process what he did with Belle just yet. I need this to end. I ask Belle if we need to resolve this now or come back another day. I remind her that Joe is sitting outside and how volatile this can and will get.

"No, we can resolve this now. I will talk to Joe and be right back!"

I can hear her mumbling on the way out: "Can't be fucking serious … these assholes here."

Eoghan enters the office and sets the flowers down on the wingback. I pick them up and reflexively smell them.

"What are you doing here, Eoghan?" I ask, managing to keep my voice controlled.

"I made an appointment to see you. I haven't seen you since the day you came over. I missed you. I had no idea you were seeing her!" He points his finger out the door.

I cannot blame him for that. I know he did not know. I cannot hold him accountable for what he did not know.

He continues. "I thought I was doing something nice for you. I wanted to bring you these flowers and have dinner or something. I did not know I was entering this. I know you never knew the name of the woman I was seeing. Oh. Wait, you did. Man, this is just fucked up. I love you though. I need you to know that."

I can hear the fast angry steps of heels clickity-clacking in the hallway. That is the sound of someone who is going to get to the bottom of things. That is the sound of "I'll be damned if …"

I shift my eyes toward the door to signal to Eoghan to stop talking.

He understands and sits back in the chair Joe usually sits in.

Belle returns and leans against the doorframe. She eyes the environment, including the flowers on my lap, and laughs a bit in a kind of maniacal way.

Does she own a gun? My thinking is panicked.

"I told Joe I wanted to thank you personally and talk to you about upcoming appointments." There goes that hiss again. "I asked him to go get some coffee, and I'll be done."

I do not respond. I sit with the multiple thoughts I am having at the moment. Besides, I really do not know what to say. I am wrong but not for the reason she thinks I am. Or am I? I cannot answer that right now.

"So, don't let me run the show. Apparently, I'm in it. I'm the headliner in the stage play *The Fool*." She yells.

That cuts deeply. I deserve that.

Eoghan's head drops and turns away.

"Belle, I'd rather talk to you alone. I think Eoghan being here is only going to agitate you. If you want him to return, I'm good with that. I just need to say something. I think you deserve that."

She nods. Her energy is so angry that it is increasing the temperature of the room.

Eoghan gets up and leaves. "I'll be in the lobby."

No one responds.

"Let me tell you a story, Belle. So at least you understand what happened." I think she deserves that. I mean, it is my business, but I think she deserves it, considering the situation we are in right now.

So, I tell her the story of how we met. I explain the whole thing about Conrado and Thursdays. I explain to her that I had already had feelings for him before I discovered it was the same person she was seeing. I tell her how conflicted I was the day in the bathroom when she was crying out to him. I explain that I feel sorry and never set out to hurt her. I never thought this would come out this way. I explain that I knew she was working on her marriage and that I was ending mine.

Tears are beginning to well up in my eyes. I need to control them.

Belle is eyeing me closely.

"Do you love him?" she asks.

I really do not want to answer this question. I hesitate as I think of all the possible outcomes, but I am compelled to be honest.

"Yes."

I can see the knife of those words pierce her heart. Her eyes close slowly as if she has just let go of life. However, her response surprises me.

"He loves you too," she responds with her eyes closed. "I knew he loved someone when I went to see him. We made love." That statement made me sick to my stomach. "But he would not kiss me. He was resisting me, and I could tell. He was not even really there. I suspected he was with you the whole time."

There is a sense of surrender in her voice.

"River, my issue is I feel betrayed by you. I never 'owned' him. Why did you not tell me when you knew? I know you don't hold confidentiality there?" she asks.

I have no real good answer.

So I give her the truth.

"I was afraid. I hid behind self-disclosure with clients. I could have stopped seeing him, and I did not. This was never intended to hurt you. I did not intend for this to happen. It was an ember that quickly rose into a fire," I respond.

The sound of the double horn again … Joe.

"Do you need Eoghan to come back?" I ask.

"No," she responds.

"Are you coming back in six weeks? I understand if you feel you can no longer work with me," I respond.

"I don't know. I don't know. I have to sort some feelings out. I am not through with this. I just have to get back to the life I am trying to have now with my husband. Maybe this allows me to officially close the chapter on Eoghan. Maybe this is what I needed." She shrugs her shoulders and gathers her things and her purse.

"I'll … I mean, *we'll* let you know."

"Are you going to inform Joe?" I ask. I am not quite sure why I am asking that.

"No. It is not necessary. There is no need to rip that wound open on him," she responds.

I stand, not quite sure what to do next.

She looks at me and then back at the flowers.

"They are beautiful."

She walks out the door. The clickity-clackity sound of her heels sounds less angry now.

I watch her walk down the hall and pass the hallway.

She stops short and looks at Eoghan momentarily.

Her lips part to begin to say something, but it looks like she has thought better of it.

Belle walks out the door and out of Eoghan's life.

I beckon for Eoghan to return to my office. I am prepared to ask him about whatever evening he and Belle shared. I watch him walk toward me. My heart is growing more and more excited. We are free. I want to be angry with him, but my heart will not let me. Besides, what real right do I have to be angry anyway?

My eyes are growing in anticipation. Why is he walking so slowly?

I bite my lip, raising my eyebrows. *Come to me. We are free, Eoghan. We are free!* I keep thinking.

I can see that he has now locked on to my expression. He smiles and quickens his pace.

He stands right before me, sliding my hands into his and wrapping them around his waist. He places his forehead against mine, and we enter each other's souls.

"I want you to be my forever, Riv. I have such a love for the soul you are. I can see you as you were meant to be seen. I know that Jude loves you. I am not here to take you from anyone; only you can make a decision. I know what you told me, but I need to know when. I am not giving you a time table, I just want us to be one."

"What are you saying, Eoghan? Wait, before you continue—I need to be able to tell you: Jude left. I mean he *really* left, Eoghan.

Eoghan looks perplexed but shakes it off for something more desirable.

He gently kisses me, and I gently pull his lip with my teeth. I free my hand from his to shut the office door behind me.

The electricity between us is so sexy. There is nothing sexier than someone who makes love to your mind before even touching or penetrating your body. It has been a constant intertwining with him since the first day at A Prima Vista. This man has made love to my mind every time we have encountered one another. Goodness, I am ready for the next stage.

Kissing my face, his speech is hard to comprehend through the passion. "Baby, I want you, I really do. I will, believe me, I will have you. I just wanted to have you when you could fully have me. My impatience is getting the best of me."

His kisses are not aggressive enough. I bring his mouth toward mine, as I am eager to taste.

I want him now.
He laughs. "A little eager are we, love?"

Eager? I have been fantasizing about this man for the longest! He returns my aggressiveness, running his hands through my hair and exploring my mouth.

I am in heaven. To be kissed by the one who truly holds your heart makes you feel alive.

I am beginning to realize where I am. I am in my office, not at home.

I am so excited by the feeling of freedom and release. I was blind, but now I see. My location is irrelevant—just to be able to celebrate it with Eoghan with a kiss is enough.

"Come on, Riv. He tugs at my hand. We have dinner plans. Let's go."

I suggest he clean up the lipstick from his face. Ruby Woo does not look good on a man. He laughs and heads to the bathroom.

I gather my things, but first the flowers. It is a sea of various shades of purple dotted with fresh greens in a bouquet wrapped in a beautiful red ribbon. I touch the velvet petals of the calla lily. Calla lilies symbolize adoration.

Belle was right.

They are beautiful.

I take them with me to the front office. Mahaley turns around as if she did not hear something that I know she heard. I smile.

"It's okay, Mahaley. I know it was a bit out of control. Let me tell you a couple of things to ease your mind up front. Eoghan is not my client. Never was. Jude and I are no longer together. There's more, and it's a bit crazy, but I will talk to you later. Okay? For now, close up for me."

Her awkward smile turns normal.

"Okay, I just did not know what to do. That was crazy. I am so glad no one else was here. Okay. I cannot wait to hear the rest."

36

THE ROYAL BOX

We arrive at A Prima Vista. Eoghan asks for Conrado, who is so happy to see us. He hugs us like family he has not seen in years.

We sit at the same table where we had our first "date." Conrado beckons for him to come by the bar.

"What is going on?" I ask with a laugh.

"Nothing, sweetie. Give me a moment. I'll be right back."

I watch his and Conrado's exchange. They are looking my way and smiling. Conrado hugs Eoghan—so odd. It is truly as if they have not seen each other in years. Conrado is such a beautiful person. I hope that we can ...*we* ... I love the sound of that ...*we* ... I hope we can spend more personal time with him. He arrives back to the table.

"What was that about?" I ask.

Eoghan sits back, places the tips of his fingers together, and touches his lips. He is lost in thought.

"Riv, my life was in shambles when Summer died. It truly stayed winter in my heart for a long time. I was numbing myself so I did not have to connect to life. I never thought I could find a new space for love or a love of this magnitude and intensity. I know it takes work. It takes so much work. I watched you looking at the picture of her when you were at my place. She, Summer, forever brought life into any place she was in. I

251

was just trying to capture some of it on film. When she left, she took life with her."

I reach my hand out. I *need* to touch him.

He grabs my hand.

"Please give me your wounds, Eoghan. We can heal together."

We sit silent for a while. No food, no drink—just us and a long-stemmed rose in our moment.

Eoghan appears to be studying me.

"What is it?" I ask, breaking the silence.

"What I was trying to say at the office, Riv, is that I want to build with you. When your situation with Jude is at rest, I want to build a life with you. I do not know if you are going to be ready for that so soon after your divorce." Eoghan's head drops. "Wow, I did not mean to say that. I'm sorry. It's just that I want you to make your own decision, to plan your own path." He looks toward me for understanding.

"It's okay". I say..touching his arm. "You've allowed me to be me. I have needed that all my life. I do not have to face life alone. I want to be with you. We will explore the depths together. You are just a catalyst. The decision was made long ago."

Conrado comes over. "Congrats, soon-to-be Mr. and Mrs. McGhee!"

I look to Eoghan, my mouth open.

Smiling with mild embarrassment, he says, "I haven't asked her yet."

Conrado is so embarrassed. "I am so sorry. Let me go back and pour somebody a drink ... namely, me."

I say nothing.

Eoghan pulls a small box from his pocket and sits it on the table.

"Let me keep this simple. River, when you are ready and *able* to wear this in the name of love forever, I'd be honored."

I cannot bring myself to touch the box. It is purple velvet with a gold ring of thread around it. What is inside that box is the rest of my life.

Eoghan allows me to have my moment.

I slowly reach for the box. It seems so far away for some reason.

The box is soft; its velvety fabric has a royal quality.

The box makes a slight popping noise as I open it. I can feel myself ceasing to breathe. I can feel my heart beating rapidly, and I began to tremor.

A single marquise diamond with a band of rose gold sits inside. It is so simple, so elegant. How could a box hold the promise this rings has?

I lift the ring out of the box.

"Don't put it on yet. I want it on a finger that does not legally belong to anyone."

I understand. I place the ring back in the box and close it. I stand up and walk over to his seat and sit on his lap.

"I love you, and I understand. The answer … I want you to hear when I can truly be yours," I respond.

He leans forward and places a soft kiss on my lips.

"We should order," he says.

We both laugh.

The remainder of the evening is like no other evening with Eoghan has been. It always seems like the best one is yet to come. Our ability to connect with each other is so uncanny and unusual. We talk about more of our dreams and disappointments of life.

We finally say goodbye to Conrado, thanking him for being a conduit for us. The drive back to the practice is quiet—a good quiet. Our words are not necessary. With Eoghan's one hand on the wheel and another holding mine, we say all we need to say.

37

SESSION 13: THE HEART—EOGHAN
SCRIBES AND JOE TAKES IT BACK

"Riley-Buttons—2 p.m. Tune up."

I am shocked to see their name on my schedule even though Mahaley called me the moment they scheduled. She remembered how the last session went, and boy was it messy.

"Wow, I am so shocked they are coming, considering …," I say to Mahaley.

"I know, Dr. Meadows, it has been six months. After what happened, I just thought …," Mahaley lets me finish the sentence.

"I know, I know … say no more. Me too. Anything else going on?" I ask.

"Yeah, Eoghan dropped off this gift. It is wrapped so beautifully, I did not want to open it, but I kinda want to. You know how it is. Anyway, he said he wanted you to see it so you can obsess over it for the rest of the day." She starts laughing. "Dr. Meadows, that man sure does pay a lot of attention to you. I know you will make yourself crazy about what's in here." She laughs. handing the box to me.

I turn to walk to my office to ready myself for the Riley-Buttons. It is light and beautifully wrapped in peach, white, and gold ribbons. It is so pretty I do not want to open it at all.

Just keep the gift in the box.

The box is about two feet long, and I cannot gauge what is in it.

I shake it.

No noise.

I look for cracks in the wrapping.

None.

Mahaley yells from the counter. "He said you were going to do that! He said when you do to come here and get this!"

I turn around, laughing.

There on the counter is another gift. Smaller. It has the same wrapping with the same peach, gold, and white ribbons. It is a bit heavier though.

"Open it!" Mahaley squealed. I could not wait until you did all he said you were going to do so I could see what was in it. Come on!" She is clapping her hands in delight.

"He said open this one now and save the next one for when he picks you up for the picnic."

I tear through the wrapping. I bite my lip ... I'm so nervous. What is in it this box?

I lift the lid, and it is a frame. Turning it around, there is a picture of me—a black and white photo.

He must have taken it without my knowledge. I am not looking directly at him. We are on my couch. Actually, it is Conrado and me, except he only has my image in the shot.

We had cooked dinner for Conrado one night, and he was telling us stories of his childhood.

He is downright hilarious—or maybe I just laugh at everything. Yeah, I laugh at everything.

Eoghan had gone into the kitchen to grab the wine. He had been spending a lot of time with me over the past six months. He has absolutely refused to move in with me. He keeps saying, "Not until you are free to be completely mine." Blah, blah, blah. I get it though.

I am laughing in the shot. I am holding me knee with my hands, my eyes closed, and my head is back against the sofa. He caught my profile.

What is this?

"What is this?" Mahaley asks.

"It is a picture of me," I respond.

"No, this," Mahaley says as she hands me a gold envelope.

I'd thought it was the bottom of the box. I take and open the envelope.

A letter from Eoghan.

River,

I spend a lot of time watching you, studying you, observing you. During these past few months, I have really wanted you to know some things. First off, thank you for all the little surprises you leave for me. Thank you for the notes in my gym bag, brief case, and car window and the seductive text messages, where I have to remain calm in the middle of a council meeting.

You have no idea how much I want to leave and go get you.

I am desired by you, and you have no idea what that does to a man. I plan to always do what I can to do right by you. I plan to make you secure with and in me. You will never wonder if you are safe. You are always safe with me. There are battles you will never see because of that. My job as a man is to be just that, the man. Now, I will mess up. I know it may be hard to believe, but I will. I need for you to always be able to talk to me. Tell me what you need and where I missed the mark. I will need to do the same for you, my love. But, let me get back to the point of this letter.

Watching you, I traced my fingers along the picture after I had it developed. I had it in color, but I think it distracted from the impact of the shot. God, you give so much life, Riv. Can you see that? Can you feel the life that leaves you and enters another? You are forever filling the well of another. The life and light you have I fell in love with the moment I met you. I knew when I met you I was home. So, when you look at this picture, know this is how I see you. This is how I know you. This is how I love you.

Forever to be yours,

Eoghan

I hold the frame and the letter close to my chest. I can feel the tears begin to flow.

I walk to the office with both gifts, one that has opened my heart and the other still unopened. I have extreme anticipation about its contents.

"Dr. Meadows, you okay?" Mahaley asks.

I'm exposed.

"Yes, yes … just touched," I turn to walk to my office.

"The Riley-Buttons will be here in ten minutes," she reminds me.

I wave in acknowledgement.

I go back to my office and sit the picture on the table. I stare at the woman in the photo—the woman who was unaware that her essence was being captured. The woman I see is free. How beautiful freedom looks. She has the freedom to fully be who she is from here forward. She has the freedom to spread her wings and take flight in her new life and new self-love. I love who she is right now. I love that she has found her inner-self and inner-spirit, which is the center of true self-love. This gives her a new sense of herself to become who she is destined to be. Will the real River please stand up?!

Far too often we allow people to dim our lights. We become shadows of our former selves because we have taken on the existence of others who come into our lives. We allow ourselves to attach to these people and begin to follow in others' life paths. We become aliens to our own being, and it can be very difficult to detach.

In relationships, the initial "high" couples feel plateaus, as the process of bonding begins. This plateau is a place where couples can strengthen their foundations. However, if they do not build a foundation, the love will lose it's wings. The atrophied wings of love can no longer sustain the weight of resentment that will soon follow. Love cannot and will not soar carrying the cargo of stored pain.

When we accept the limitations imposed on us by others, we are unable to be the spirits God created us to individually be. If the relationships we attach ourselves to are not compatible, we must detach from them at some point in our lives. Our detachment may come in the form of a death, a movement, or another form of separation from these individuals.

However, it is also true that each of us has individuals who are destined to help us realize our capacity and to exercise our ability to soar. These are the people who will help us take flight without fearing the potential to fall, for failure is the biggest risk we take on our journeys toward success in life.

I go out into the lobby and call the Riley-Buttons. I almost did not recognize them! It is great to see they still choose to sit with one another.

This is good! I see Joe is not in his usual work attire. The dirty, grimy clothes with steel-toe boots have been replaced with a nice shirt, tie, and slacks. His head is hatless and showing a fresh haircut. Those eyes that used to be a gray fog are now sharp steel. He looks like an entirely different person.

My anxiety kicks up when I see Belle. I wonder what her feelings are today. Is she still angry? Does she still feel I betrayed her? Does she want Eoghan? Okay, Riv, get out of your damn head and put on your "session face."

Belle is dressed neatly, as usual, but without the mess of papers around her. Maybe they used to allow her to be distracted from the mess she was constantly in. She is sporting a clean suit, and her hair is tied back in a neat bun.

I call them back to the office. They walk together, hand in hand. This is impressive. I wonder what this session is about. The note in the agenda states, "Tune up." Usually this refers to couples that are doing well and want to go over a few principles regarding their relationship.

I'm still nervous. I hope they do not notice. I feel shaky.

They walk in, and I notice Belle scanning the office. It is awesome to see them sit on the same couch.

Yeah, the office is the same as you saw it last. Good God! I forgot about the white roses Eoghan sent a few days ago. I hope she doesn't—never mind. Her eyes shoot right to the vase. She studies them, and I see a small smile cross her face. That's interesting.

Get out of your head, River—out of your head! You can and will do this.

"It is nice to see you two. How are things? What prompted this visit?" I ask.

I work hard not to avoid Belle. I must work through the anxiety.

Joe speaks first. "Well, we are doing well, right, babe?" He leans over to kiss Belle on her cheek. She is receptive, closing her eyes when his lips grace her face. She takes his hand in hers.

Wow! I love it.

The anxiety dissipates. I have no need for it.

"We did not come back in six weeks, as you know. Belle just couldn't do it. I pleaded with her, but she said she needed time. I did not feel like arguing. What I will say is that after that last session with you, she came back a really different person. I mean, I saw that she really wanted to invest in me. I had to take the time to learn how to love her the way she needed to be loved. I had been busy giving her love the way I thought she needed it. Anyhow, I got myself into a training program and graduated. Now I am a supervisor at my job, so I can lead my family in financial stability. I also worked toward learning more about her world, so I can enter it and not be foreigner." Joe sounds so much more assertive. This is great.

"Right," Belle adds. "And I entered his world. We also created our world together and our world as parents of Jaz."

"That is great! Yes, Jasmine ... how is she?" I ask.

"She is doing just wonderfully. Joe spends a lot more time with her. He said he is working on teaching her about the type of man she should want in her life. The important piece is that he is working hard to be that person. I feel safe with Joe now."

Safe. Wow. Eoghan's letter crosses my mind.

Not your time, Riv ... not your time. Focus on the session.

I still am not sure why they are here.

"I think this is wonderful. I am glad that you both have learned how to love each other and, more importantly, how to receive each other's love. This is more than a notion, and it takes so much work. Sometimes things happen in our marriage that we think are meant to break us, but they actually make us stronger, if we allow it," I add.

"Exactly, that is really why we are here. We are doing better. Not 100 percent, but we are getting stronger. I wanted to ensure that we continue on this path. I explained to Belle that if she for some reason needed to go to a different counselor, we could. I do not know why she would, *but* we have to go. I need to make sure my marriage stays on track. The reason is that when we took a break from seeing you, I started seeing my own counselor. I have a mentor at my church who I have been working with. I had my own issues that I am working through. I can see how the lack of my dad and the coldness of my mother impacted me."

I glance over at Belle, who mouths "black widow."

I smile.

"I am still working on this. My mentor at the church makes sure I follow through on what I am supposed to follow through on."

"Wow, Joe. You have been working. You have someone helping you sift through your past. This is wonderful, because it will cease impacting your present and destroying your future."

"Yes, the mentor helps me stay in the present. When I have bouts of selfishness, he reminds me of the flesh and the importance, as he would put it, of 'one flesh.'"

"So the both of you are working to become that one flesh?" I ask.

"Yes," they say in unison.

"Jinx!" Belle yells.

Joe laughs.

She is being playful. This is wonderful to see. Playfulness returning to a relationship is demonstrative of health.

"I," she says, placing her hand on her chest, "have a mentor too, except she is more unofficial—not like Joe's. It is not the same as counseling, though. She has helped me move past some things that I needed to move past. She helped me understand why I needed to go through some of the things I needed to go through. To be honest, you did too."

I work to control my face. How does she mean that?

She can tell I need more understanding.

"What I mean is that I know I shut down on my marriage. I know I was reacting to my environment. During this process with you, I learned that people can operate as walls or ladders."

"What do you mean, Belle?" I believe I understand, but I want her to explain it.

"I mean that people are placed in our lives, and we can view them as barriers or ladders. They can either stop our growth or lift us to a higher place. The funny thing is that a person can be either one of them. We have to decide based on how we view the situation. This process with you was a ladder for me, and I thank you for that." She sits back.

I wonder if she means professionally or personally. Does it even matter? Not as long as it is growth. Growth is growth.

"I see. That is good," I add.

"Right," Joe says, continuing with his new assertiveness, "so I wanted us to return to counseling in order to keep working on stuff together. I explained to Belle that we have to stay ahead of the game. We cannot wait until we fall down in order to reach up for help. We must have a strong network around us so when we do fall, hopefully we do not have far to go. My mentor and counselor help me to understand this. So, that is why we are here."

"Okay. I see: you want to continue working on principles that will continue to strengthen the foundation you are creating?" I ask.

"Absolutely," he state emphatically.

I look over to Belle, and I can see that she admires him now. Wow, what a change to see him take charge and move forward in his marriage.

We spend the remaining time going over what this process will look like. We share what principles are important to them individually and as "one flesh," to use Joe's mentor's phrase.

We agree to schedule quarterly sessions to stay on top of their new communication skills, and if we need to, we can meet monthly if things get tough. Joe shakes my hand and thanks me for working with them.

Belle actually hugs me and, whispering in my ear, says, "Thank you so much. Those flowers are beautiful. He loves you."

I collapse in her hug.

Moments later, Joe returns. "I left my wallet." I walk him over to the sofa, and he grabs it. He turns to me and rocks my world when he states, "He was here that day. I knew it. I knew when she got to the car and looked as if she had seen a ghost. I was going to say something, but instead I decided to put myself in a position where I am the main character in her life and not sitting in the audience. I believe we had that discussion?" He reaches his hand out and says, "Thank you again." Then he leaves.

I cannot believe it. I had no words, not that Joe gave me an opportunity to say anything. I am happy for that though. The moment did not require my input. It only required that I listen and understand. I am in awe of the emotions emitted today.

38

A SONG FOR RIVER AND EOGHAN

I do not have to turn down the volume of my soul for Eoghan; the decibels are not too loud for him. If anything, we have created a song together.

Earnestine and Armand remind me of the melody of our love. They tell me, "Listen for the song you create together. The two of you come with your own music, but you create one song."

It is amazing how much I have learned from them. I love them both.

I prepare myself to leave the office for the day and am excited for the picnic that Eoghan and I have prepared. It is a little warm for fall but really nice out. I really want to know what is in this box! I shake it again—nothing.

I arrive at the park and sit for a moment. I used to come here by myself and think. Now, things have changed. Eoghan sees me and beckons me over.

"Bring the gift," he yells.

Turning around, I grab the gift. I'm so excited! What is in here?

I damn near skip to the lilac blanket that Eoghan has laid out. He has some music playing and food and wine. The whole setup!

"Did you see my letter?" he asks.

"Yes! You tricked me!" I say as I playfully push him.

"No, I did not trick you. I know you, woman," he laughs. "Anyhow, sit and open your gift now."

I am suddenly nervous. I gently remove the gift-wrapping from the box—so gently, in fact, it is as if I am removing a layer of skin from a burn victim. I can get through my nervousness this way. Slow the process down.

Another envelope? A big manila envelope is in the box.

"Open it!" I can hear the impatience in Eoghan's voice.

I open the envelope and can see it is from the courts. I immediately look up to Eoghan. "Is this?"

"Yes, baby. Keep looking."

I open the envelope and read the final papers from the courts.

I am officially divorced. I bite my lip as I sit in this moment. This moment takes the ceiling away from us.

He is watching me.

"Is that all there is in there?" he asks. "Go back to the box."

Taped to the bottom of the box is the marquise diamond with the rose gold band.

"I want you to be all mine, if you will have me. I want to be all yours, River, for as long as God gives us the opportunity of breath. Marry me." He grows silent.

"Will you?" he asks.

I have never wanted anything more: to be married to a man I love, adore, and respect.

Without words, without permission, I straddle Eoghan's lap, gently touching his left earlobe. It's so soft. My fingers study the topography of his face. Like a blind woman, I can read the sculpture of his face. His eyebrows are strong and thick, followed by deeply set eyes. They look like they could cause a burning fire in anything they fixate on. Such strength is in his face. He has a strong jawline. When he smiles, his face gives way to dimples that contrast dominance with play. His lips are full and wrapped in a mustache that dignifies him. I am struggling to not kiss them. Those full lips. My grazing fingers force them to part slightly, bending to my will. The parting allows me a glimpse into his perfect mouth.

Riv, stop yourself. I can feel the heat and energy generating between our minds and souls. I love that he is allowing me to explore in silence.

"Eoghan, is there even an alternative? You never had to ask. Just declare." I'm almost pleading. I can hear the pleading in my voice. He opens his eyes to respond. He picks up the ring and grabs my hand.

"I want to hear the word, River. I *need* it."
I'm working to stifle crying.
"Yes, Eoghan. Yes, of course I will."
I'm beginning to cry. I hold my mouth with one hand, and he places the ring on my finger, shaking eagerly.
He kisses my forehead and then makes his way to softly kiss my lips.

"I promise to love you, River."
"I promise to love you, Eoghan."
I can hear our song. It's beautiful.
I pray to God: "Thank You. Thank You for the people You put in my life to get me to this place."
I lean into Eoghan's arms and close my eyes. I can feel the warmth of the sun across my face. Eoghan is talking about our future. I am not really hearing his words, just the melody of his voice. I can feel his fingers slightly twirling my hair, and I exhale. I am so content lying on the lilac blanket with my head resting on his thigh. I used to come to this park alone—now I come with him. I smile as I remember the road traveled to discover the love of my life. I begin to chuckle; I cannot believe this is real.

Who would have thought that the death of something would allow for the birth of something so wonderful? We are always reborn through the deaths of our experiences, if we allow it.

I take in this moment with my soon-to-be husband, with whom I am happy to spend the duration of my life.
At the moment of conception we take on a contract to engage with life to the fullest. We tackle adversity, which can develop or destroy us.

Our lives should be lived similar to the giant sequoia tree's. It is a massive living thing, the giant sequoia. It is an interdependent and strong organism, nature's skyscraper, standing as high as 275 feet tall. Unlike many trees, the giant sequoia continues to grow and can live over three thousand years. It also bears a lot of fruit. The giant sequoia is no stranger to adversity. It actually thrives on it. Its survival depends on brush fires. The seedlings grow best in burnt soil and ash. The cones have the ability to release seeds as the heat rises from the fire, allowing the cones to dry up and release new life. They are fire resistant, not fire proof, and can heal, with new bark growing over damaged bark.

Giant sequoias feed each other, and they also support their environment. The tree has a relationship with animals and insects that utilize its cones for sustenance while releasing their seeds, ensuring the trees' survival. Finally, the giant sequoias provide for future generations. After the death of a giant sequoia, the tannin acid it releases acts as a natural preservative, which slows the decay process tremendously, resulting in a slow release of nutrients into the earth for literally thousands of years.

Our lives and our souls are a network of connections, much like the giant sequoia. God expects us to support one another and to nourish one another. Adversity should allow us to bear fruit, not crush us.

We should thrive on our ability to overcome. Giant sequoias seek out the light, reaching abnormal heights and ages. We are also called upon to seek out the light within each other and ourselves. We can only recognize light when we allow it in own our lives.

We must also allow others to pour light into us. We are vessels to be poured into and out of as God intended. Death does not conquer us, because we are called to leave a legacy for those we leave behind.

We are immortal. As we share our stories, our traumas, and our triumphs, we live on in the hearts of others.

We are the seedlings that will grow in the heart of the connected soul.

Love is the light we pour.

Pour abundant light into yourself and others. Let it glow like the heavenly sun that blinds us during an early morning sunrise on a new blanket of snow.

Just love. Love deeply, passionately, and truthfully.

ABOUT THE AUTHOR

Billie J. Gilliam is a licensed independent professional clinical counselor and licensed independent chemical dependency counselor in Cleveland, Ohio. She provides clinical services for chemically dependent men and women, individuals with mental health issues, those in need of marital and family counseling, and sufferers from trauma. She also provides mediation, consultation, and education services.

As a clinician, Ms. Gilliam facilitates a process over product ideology in which clients can find the paradigms that disrupt their ability to thrive. We are survivors of all types; however, surviving is not thriving. Her purpose is to help others understand their pain, integrate, and thrive.

We are the essence of stars; our job is to give and receive light. In our relationships, we find ourselves in black holes, either void of light or siphoning the light from others. We must begin to understand that when we grow dark, we must seek others who can provide light.

We must learn to thrive in our rebellion against the dark.

ABOUT THE BOOK

The Session is about the birth, death and resurrection of relationships. Characters find themselves in cycles of destruction, sinking into the darkness of their egos. Dr. River Meadows, a marital therapist, finds herself working with a couple she has an unnerving attraction to. There is a secret that binds them all together while threatening to tear them all apart. While facilitating healing for the Riley-Buttons, she realizes her own marriage is falling apart. She must now decide between the new love of her life and the love of her profession.

You know this story: it is wrought with relationships with others and, most importantly, the relationship with the self. Dr. Meadows encounters others who feed her spirit, helping her become acquainted with her own heart. *The Session* reminds us that no encounter is by accident, love will find a way, and we must seek the light within in order to give it to others.